For Connie,

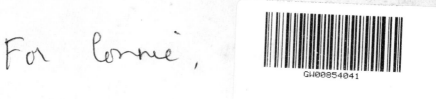

Ralph the Wanderer

Margaret Edwards

Ralph the Wanderer

A Story of Medieval France in four parts

F Margaret Edwards

Illustrated by Elizabeth J West

The Pentland Press Ltd.
Edinburgh · Cambridge · Durham

© F M Edwards 1993

First published in 1993 by
The Pentland Press Ltd
5 Hutton Close
South Church
Durham

ISBN 1 872795 95 1

Typeset by Spire Origination, Norwich
Printed and bound by Antony Rowe Ltd, Chippenham

For

Matthew and William

with thanks to
Margaret James, the former Principal of Kent College,
for the use of her personal library,
and to all our friends who supported us.

Acknowledgements

History Europe; H A L Fisher

Chateaux of the Loire; Arthand

A History of Europe 1198–1378; C W Previté-Orton

Shorter Cambridge Medieval History Vol. II; C W Previté-Orton

The Pageant of England 1216–1272; Thomas B Costain

The Monastic Achievement; George Zarnecki

Monasteries; R J Unstead

Medieval Travellers; Margaret Wade Labarge

Everyman's Book of Saints; C P S Clarke

The Shorter Oxford Dictionary Medieval Europe; Thorndike

The Golden Middle Age; Canon Roger Lloyd

Life in Medieval France; Joan Evans

Wandering Scholars; Helen Waddell

Medieval Latin Lyrics; Helen Waddell

Legacy of the Middle Ages; C G Crump & E F Jacob

Medieval England; ed by H W C Davies

A Short History of the English People; J R Green

Children of History; Eileen Power

Author's Note

I have been asked how I came to write this book. It came about as a result of a visit to Paris, including the Louvre, where the courts of Louis XIII and the young Louis XIV had been held.

Stories of the "Gamins" of the Parisian streets, and the effronteries of the nobles who had harrassed the king with their "Fronde" wars came to mind. I decided to write a novel about the streets of Paris around the life of an apprentice. To widen the scope of the story he was to travel through the Loire Valley. After further research, France of the thirteenth century seemed more peaceful and pleasant than that of the seventeenth. Moreover it was a time of religious growth; Ralph Le Boeuf, a descendant of the Vikings, and a shoe-maker's apprentice, became the central figure in the time of Louis IX.

Contents

RULERS OF

FRANCE   and   ENGLAND

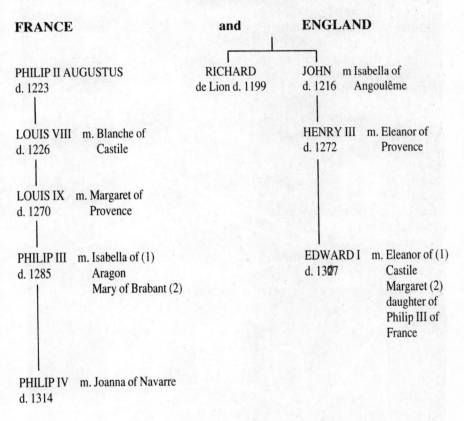

PHILIP II AUGUSTUS
d. 1223

RICHARD
de Lion d. 1199

JOHN   m Isabella of
d. 1216   Angoulême

LOUIS VIII   m. Blanche of
d. 1226   Castile

HENRY III   m. Eleanor of
d. 1272   Provence

LOUIS IX   m. Margaret of
d. 1270   Provence

PHILIP III   m. Isabella of (1)
d. 1285   Aragon
            Mary of Brabant (2)

EDWARD I   m. Eleanor of (1)
d. 1307   Castile
            Margaret (2)
            daughter of
            Philip III of
            France

PHILIP IV   m. Joanna of Navarre
d. 1314

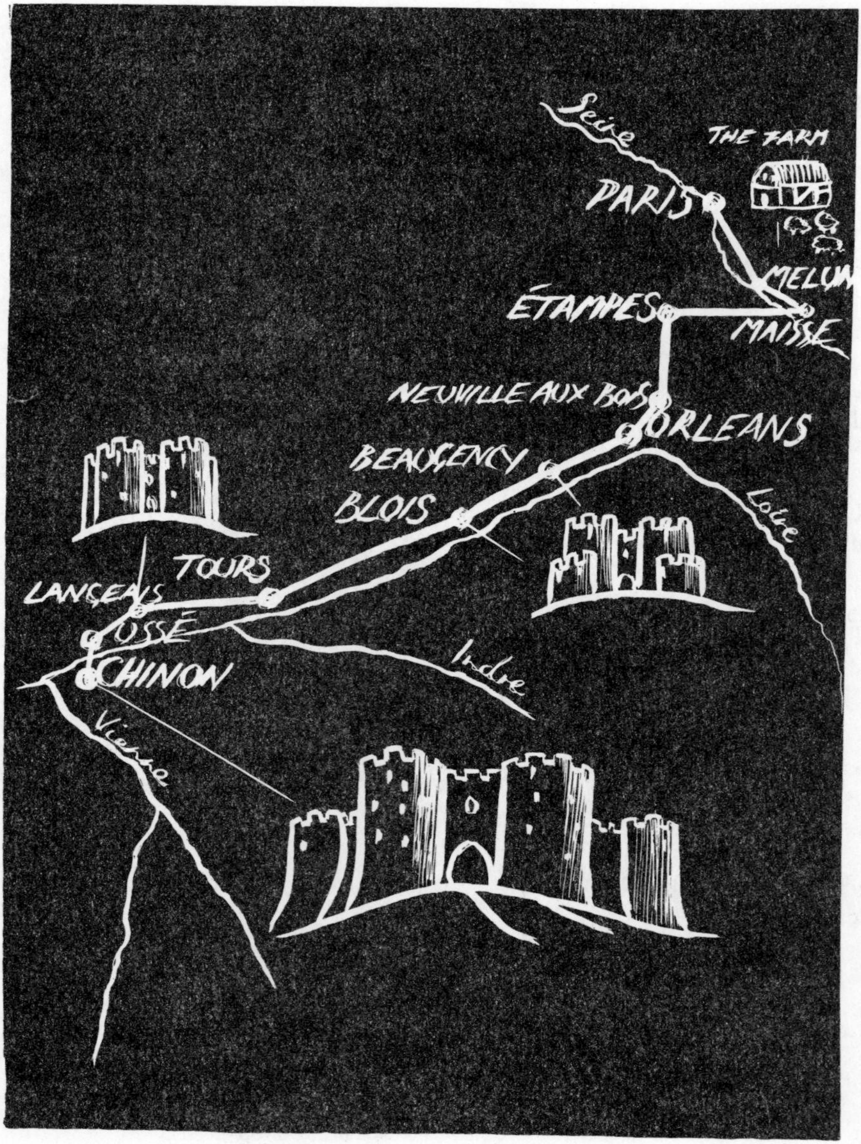
Seine
THE FARM
PARIS
MELUN
ÉTAMPES
MAISSE
NEUVILLE AUX BOIS
ORLEANS
BEAUGENCY
BLOIS
Loire
TOURS
LANGEAIS
USSÉ
CHINON
Indre
Vienne

Part One

Ralph the Wanderer

CHAPTER I

Ralph at Home

Lord Ranulf de Villaincourt walked briskly down a narrow street in the poorer part of Paris. It was cold and growing dark. He had left his servant at the palace, because he wanted to be alone and to feel free to walk where he wished. It was quite safe in Paris in the year 1256. The good King Louis IX had seen to that, with the help of his officers. Lord Ranulf had walked so quickly that he had almost reached the end of the street of the shoemakers before he realised where he was. The shopkeepers had put up their shutters already. A few displayed signs to show that they made boots and shoes; without them he would not have known where he was. Lord Ranulf decided, on the spur of the moment, to buy himself a new pair of boots. Choosing a door at random, he knocked hard on it. The top half opened, and a dishevelled little head looked out, holding a lighted candle.

'Hallo! Can you find a pair of boots to fit me?' asked Lord Ranulf, pointing to his long feet. The little shoemaker gazed with awe at the knight, and noted his handsome face in the candlelight, his long flowing fair hair, his warm cap and short cloak, which showed him to be a person of high rank. A sword hung at his side. The little shoemaker wondered whether he had any boots which were good enough to offer such a fine nobleman.

'Come now, ask me in out of the cold, and let me see what you have,' called out the knight, seeing his hesitation. 'I am Lord Ranulf de Villaincourt.'

'I am Ralph le Boeuf,' replied the shoemaker.

Ranulf stepped inside, and noticed that the little man was about the same age as himself, early twenties. There was a fire in his shop living-room, but the floor was unswept, and contained only the barest wooden furniture. Ralph had been tidying the tools on the working bench, in preparation for the next day, which

3

was a Sunday. Ranulf gave a quick glance over to the shelf, on which a line of oddly-shaped boots and shoes stood. He went to examine them, and began to laugh. 'Surely you did not submit a pair like these to the guild as your Masterpiece?' he said.

The little shoemaker looked very embarrassed. 'I have yet to make my Masterpiece,' he confessed.

'What, at your age? What have you been doing?' asked Ranulf.

'I have always lived and worked here,' replied Ralph, rather sadly, 'but I have not yet managed to cut out a pair which is good enough to set before the guild. I sew quite neatly, but I cannot make the seams fit well. But look at this pair, they are lined with rabbit's fur.'

Lord Ranulf was surprised. 'It is not easy to rear rabbits in these northern parts,' he remarked. 'Where do you keep them?'

'Over there,' replied Ralph, pointing to a hutch in the shadows. His visitor pulled out a stool from under the table, and sat down to try on the shoes. Then he laughed again. 'Oh, do look, one foot is much longer that the other, and the toes turn up and inwards. The courtiers will roar with laughter, but it is a good thing to cheer them up. We do become rather serious. They are long enough to fit me. You see, I have long limbs and feet, like my English mother.' And he tossed his long, fair hair rather arrogantly. Pulling a leather purse from the pocket of his tunic, he tossed a golden livre to Ralph, and left abruptly. One whole livre for one badly-made pair of boots! This was wealth! Ralph was delighted, but also felt a little guilty. He picked up the coin and placed it in the purse on a leather thong round his neck.

He was about to bolt the door again when his next door neighbour's wife, Claude d'Honnête, arrived. She was a pretty, plump lady with tiny, delicate hands, which were partly concealed in the sleeves of her gown. She had been hurrying, and a lock of greying hair escaped from under her white headdress. Her brown homespun gown reached to her feet, and revealed a neatly-shod pair of feet. Her husband, Henri, was a better craftsman than Ralph. She produced a freshly baked loaf from the folds of her gown, and placed it on the table for him.

'I have had a most distinguished visitor!' Ralph exclaimed excitedly. 'Lord Ranulf de Villaincourt. And he bought a pair of boots!'

'I met him on the way,' replied Claude, 'and recognised him. Henri and I have seen him walking about in Paris. He often comes to advise the King.'

'He said he had an English mother,' remarked Ralph. 'How is that?'

'I heard that his father went with our late King, Philip Augustus, to fight in England, when their King John was having trouble with the barons. He must

4

have chosen an English wife then,' replied Claude. 'The present Lord Ranulf inherited his estates on the River Loire, which he looks after, when he is not at Court. He will have to find a wife himself, soon.'

Claude sat on the oak settle by the fire, and stirred the stewpot which hung over it. He asked her about her four children. He wondered how she managed to look after them and her husband, and their little house, and find time to bake bread for him as well. A hen clucked in the background. Startled, Ralph looked round. He kept his hens because he needed their eggs and eventually boiled them in his pot, but he detested them. He got up and opened the back door, letting in an icy blast from the back yard, and shooed the hen into it. Then, feeling rather contrite, he threw a handful of corn after her. 'Don't be late for Mass tomorrow morning,' cautioned Claude, as she rose to leave. 'And allow plenty of time to reach the Church. The streets are very frosty and slippery, especially nearer the centre of the city, where they are paved. This January is exceptionally cold!'

As they opened the door into the street, the sounds of cheerful singing greeted them, and they saw young people leaping round a bonfire. 'They have got a fire going quickly,' remarked Claude. 'It was not lit when I came in. I noticed the pile of dry wood in the gutter.' She smiled and returned to her house and family. Ralph was intrigued by the happy scene and longed to join in, although he felt rather old to do so. But he seized his cloak and cap, and a staff in case the ground was slippery. Pausing only to slam his door shut, he walked up to the crowd on the fringe of the fire. Seeing him approach, a few younger men called out derisively:-

*1'Bonjour, Monsieur le Voyageur.'

*2'Tiens, le voyageur a quitté sa maison.'

He knew they were jeering at him because he came out so rarely. He had his work to do, and anyway, he was not the sort of person to enter into festivities. One lad seized his cap and threw it down. This was a precious garment in the severe cold, and he dived after it. Fortunately, no one wanted to leave the blaze of the fire to chase him, and he escaped safely.

Once inside again, he settled down to eat his supper of stew, which he ladled from the big pot over the fire into his wooden trencher. When he had finished he washed it in a wooden bucket full of water. It was fortunate that his well in the back yard had not frozen.

---

*1Hullo, Mr. Wanderer
*2Look! The wanderer has left his house.

Since his parents had died last year, both of lung disease contracted in the cold weather, he had slept downstairs, in the wooden bed under the counter. This had been made originally for an apprentice and the members of the family had slept upstairs. Although Ralph knew that there was a large feather bed with fine linen sheets in the bedroom, he preferred to tuck into the straw mattress and cover himself with blankets and a sheepskin. It was cosier in the firelight. He enjoyed watching it flicker against the window shutters.

Ralph yawned. He was very sleepy tonight. He threw off his tunic, boots and hose and fell into bed. In his eagerness for sleep he forgot to light the candle clock, which was to tell him when he should get up and go to Mass next morning. Murmuring a hasty pater noster*, he fell asleep.

---

* Our Father

CHAPTER II

The Fire

Ralph overslept and was awakened next morning by Henri, Claude's husband, knocking on the shutters. He had no idea of the time. Henri called, 'If you get up quickly, you will be in time for Mass.' He and his wife and family had just returned from an earlier service.

Ralph got out of bed reluctantly, and poured water from a ewer into a basin. He washed his face and hands hastily and pulled on his clothes. He felt grateful for the long cloak of otterskin, which had been his father's and grandfather's before him. Seizing again his cap and staff, he entered the slippery street. Last night's fire was still smouldering as he hurried in the direction of the towers of the new Cathedral of Nôtre Dame. His own church, where his family had worshipped for generations, was older and lay just beyond it.

The morning sun was rising and shone through the frosty air, showing the two towers of the great Cathedral, with their round rose windows and the pointed arch over the great west door. This was a new style of building. Ralph hurried on to his own little stone church, built in the style of the Normans with rounded windows and a squat, square tower. Here he felt much happier than he would have done in a larger congregation. He knelt on the floor of beaten earth, upright, with the younger people, while their elders leant against the wall during the simple Latin service.

As they left afterwards, the parish priest, Père Jean-Pierre came up to Ralph, and asked, 'How is your Masterpiece coming on?'

Delighted as he was to be singled out for attention, Ralph's spirits dropped a little when he had to reply, 'I have not yet started to make one.'

'You must try,' said the priest, 'because you cannot become a Master unless you do so. Remember that your father was a fine workman and a good Master.

7

Try to be like him. And then you will have a fine business and be able to employ apprentices to help you!'

Ralph left feeling a little low-spirited. Also, he was very hungry. 'If only I had a wife to cook a meal for me,' he thought. 'But who would marry me, when I am twenty three years old, and not yet a Master?' He sighed as he walked through the frosty streets on his way home.

Suddenly his feet slid from under him. A man near him seized him, and pulled him to one side. A sledge raced past them, down the slippery slope of the street. A group of laughing and jeering young men had given it a push, and were now sliding after it, throwing eggs at the figure on it. Fortunately for him most of these fell short.

'What a waste, at a time when eggs are scarce,' remarked Ralph's rescuer.

'They are mostly bad, can't you smell them?' replied another onlooker.

Before the sledge disappeared from view, Ralph noticed the man on it. He was tied securely, and was quite young. Round his neck hung a loaf of bread, which bounded up and down on his chest. He waved defiantly at the crowd. 'Cheat, robber,' they called after him. 'If you do that again we'll expel you from the guild. Greedy brute!'

'What has he done?' Ralph asked his rescuers.

'Given short weight,' was the reply. 'He has a little trap door in his counter, and as he kneads the dough, he slips a little below into a bowl. Soon, he has enough to make an extra loaf. The inspectors of the baker's guild caught him yesterday, gave him a quick trial, and decided on this punishment.'

I'm glad my odd boots have been sold before the shoemaker's inspectors have seen them, thought Ralph, as he walked on. He was thankful that none of the rotten eggs had landed on him.

As he went, he noticed that someone had removed the twiggy brushes which normally hung at the street corners, to be used to fight fires, when needed. Most of the leather buckets still stood there, but the water in them was frozen. He wondered if someone with too much time to spare on a Sunday was having a joke. Then he noticed a cloud of smoke in the air, not too far away. As he came nearer, he saw sparks and then flames. Someone's thatch had caught fire.

This was not unusual, it was nonetheless alarming. It was his own house on fire!

The upper floor had gone, and most of the thatch, although the exertions of the neighbours had saved the roof of Claude and Henri's house. Along the front the water had frozen into icicles as it fell over the chimney. Where the fire had been greatest, the water had not frozen, at least until it had served its purpose.

8

THE FIRE

Mercifully the well-water in Ralph's back yard could be drawn up. His back yard was full of his shoemaker's bench, his tools including his beloved shears and awl, some of the leather, and a few pairs of boots, soiled somewhat from their adventures. Most of the rest had gone, but there had not been much else downstairs except the settle, stool and table.

Ralph stood silent, with his head in his hands. Unable to take in the scene before him. Then he was aware of Philip, who lived opposite, shouting at him, 'Well, everyone else has done their best to save your things, now take a turn yourself!'

Gradually the immensity of his loss came upon him. He had lost his home. Not only that, all the precious possessions of his parents in the upstairs room had gone. To be sure he rarely went up there, but he had felt secure in the knowledge that he possessed a double bed, with a feather mattress, and two pairs of sheets.

There was a hand on his shoulder. It took a long time before he realised that a human being was speaking to him. It was the senior Master, President of the Guild. 'We have saved your tools, Ralph,' he said. 'Later we will talk about the future. For the present you can come to my house for some food.'

CHAPTER III

Ralph's Decision

Charles d'Albert, the most senior Master of the Guild of Bootmakers, lived farther along Ralph's street, in the more prosperous part nearer the centre of Paris. If his wife, Catherine, was surprised to see Ralph with her husband, she gave no sign of it.

'This is Ralph le Boeuf,' said Charles, leading him forward. 'He has been unfortunate enough to lose his house in a fire, and needs help and comfort.'

Catherine knew Ralph, and had seen the fire. 'First things first,' she said. 'Some food.' She ladled out two bowls of broth from the stewpot hanging over the fire. Ralph had forgotten his earlier hunger until now, and was still a little dazed. He drank the broth eagerly, blowing noisily on it first.

'The neighbours managed to put out the fire before it spread to Henri l'Honnête's house next door,' explained Charles, 'but the thatch and the upper floor of Ralph's are badly burned and in need of repair before he can return. I am sure the other members of our guild will help him with this. Although he is not yet a Master, we will stand by him. He has served his apprenticeship, and we hope he will qualify before too long. We must find somewhere for him to sleep during the coming weeks.'

Catherine had been dreading this opening. She looked at Ralph again, so thoroughly dirty and neglected. She pulled herself together. 'He must stay here with us,' she said. 'He can have Thomas' bed downstairs in the shop.' Thomas was their younger son. He had served his apprenticeship and was now spending two years as a journeyman, moving on from one Master to another, in order to earn some money with which to start his own business.

Ralph, who was still suffering from shock, did not know how to refuse Catherine's offer, and he had nowhere to go if he did refuse. He was becoming

11

aware slowly that he had lost his home, his possessions and everything he enjoyed. 'Can I fetch my things?' he said.

'Of course,' replied Charles, 'although I'm afraid you have only a few possessions left. We managed to save your tools, and some leather and a few pairs of the boots you made. You are welcome to bring them here. But your household possessions were lost in the fire.'

So Ralph returned to the smouldering shell of his house, and fetched what he could. 'I really am a wanderer now,' he said to himself. He wanted to weep, but his grief was too great for tears. It cut deep into him, creating a great void inside him.

During the next few days, he lived with Charles and Catherine, eating their food and sleeping in the shop. During the day they tried to encourage him to settle down to work, but he found it hard to concentrate. Catherine's cooking was delicious compared with his own, but he felt awkward at their table, as their habits were more fastidious in every way. She had taken away the clothes he had been wearing under his doublet, and washed them. Meanwhile he was wearing clean ones which had belonged to their younger son. Even in this weather, he was expected to wash his face every day at the pump.

Some members of the Guild had already started to repair his house, and he went along to watch their progress. He found on the first visit that he wasn't expected there, and felt in the way. He began to wonder how much longer this state of affairs could go on and, for the first time in his life, he thought seriously about his future.

As they sat round the fire that evening, he burst out: 'I should like to be a journeyman! Your son Thomas is one, isn't he? Then I could move round the country, and work under different masters, and sell the shoes I have made as I move along from one to another!' Catherine was very surprised. These words revealed a very different side of Ralph from anything she had yet seen. Secretly, she could not help a feeling of relief that his stay might be shortened.

'That is all very well,' remarked Charles, 'but January is not a good month to start out, especially as you are not used to travelling.'

'If I wait,' replied Ralph, 'I shall not go at all. If I do not go, I shall never look upon myself as a real man. I have to prove, to myself and to everybody, what I can do. I must lose my name of being a stay-at-home.'

'Isn't that rather a heavy price to pay for a new reputation? Do not forget that you take yourself with you,' said Charles.

'You must think of your house,' Catherine reminded him. 'Don't you want to be there, when the members of the Guild rebuild it for you?'

'I will watch over that for you, in any case,' promised Charles. 'But I do not think you should be too ambitious. Do not go too far away. One year's absence, rather than two years, as Thomas has undertaken, will be enough for you. Where were you thinking of going?'

As Ralph seemed very lacking in ideas, Charles went on, 'I have a friend who served his apprenticeship with me under the same master, who is now a Master of the Shoemakers' Guild at Chinon. His name is Émile le Juste. The district south of Paris towards Orléans, along the River Loire, is fairly prosperous and peaceful. You could walk through it fairly easily, although it would take you several days to reach Chinon. You could probably stay with Émile for a few months. That would give you a chance to make your masterpiece. I will send a letter of introduction with you.'

'You will also need a map,' suggested Catherine.

'I believe you will go through the city of Orléans and the town of Blois. The area is safer since the English gave up the state of Anjou. Orléans belongs to the King now, and he sees that law and order are maintained there. Blois has had no overlord since the noble family of the town died out recently, but the nobles maintain their estates in the region quite peacefully.'

Although Charles was a Master of the Guild of Shoemakers and could keep accounts, he could only write a little. He explained to Ralph that he would have to ask a priest to write the letter to Émile for him. 'Shall I go to Père Jean-Pierre?' asked Ralph eagerly.

'I would rather take you to one of the Augustinian canons, who live near here,' replied Charles. 'They are like parish priests, and help the members of our Guild especially.'

Ralph agreed. He was very eager to get away, and did not want to raise any objections which might hinder him. The two of them walked along the cold, dry, unswept street to the Canons' house. Ralph was shaking from fear and cold when Brother Ambrose opened the door.

'Come in, come in,' said the Canon, who recognised Charles at once. Putting his arm round Ralph's shoulders, he led him to the fire in the parlour. 'Now, what can I do for you both?' he asked. Ralph stood on the rag rug, by the two wooden, high-backed chairs set out for visitors. At last he began to thaw out in every sense, and listened to what Charles was saying.

'We need a letter for Ralph to take to my friend Émile le Juste, where he will stay, and, I hope, make his Masterpiece.'

'Why do you not stay here to make it?' asked the Canon.

Ralph decided to speak boldly. 'I want to see something of the world before I settle down,' he said. 'Both of Monsieur d'Albert's sons went on journeys.'

'Well said!' exclaimed the Canon. Charles looked very surprised, but kept quiet.

So they waited while Brother Ambrose wrote the letter. As they had expected, he used good rabbit skin instead of vellum, which could have been very expensive. When he had finished, he rolled it up, and addressed the outside. 'No, no, there is nothing to pay,' he said, noticing that Charles was taking out his purse. 'It is a service which I am pleased to give. Go with my blessing,' he said to Ralph, raising his hand. 'And may all the holy angels protect you!'

It was growing dark as they left the Canon's house and made for home.

Ralph was so eager to be on the move that he wanted to pack his bundle that evening, but Catherine persuaded him to wait. 'The best work is never done by candlelight, is it?' she asked. And he knew that this was so. In any case, he could not argue because he was forced to borrow a bag from the d'Alberts. His father's, like so many other pieces of good leather, had been lost in the fire.

As soon as it was light, Catherine helped him to pack, putting in a change of clothing, a comb, knife and spoon, and a pewter mug. Ralph looked a little alarmed at this. 'Suppose I am attacked, and it is stolen?' he asked.

'You must watch and make sure you are not robbed,' she replied.

He put in his favourite tools which had been saved, including his awl, a pair of shears, a few pieces of leather, some thongs, and three pairs of boots which he had finished.

'Those may be useful in exchange for a night or two's lodging,' said Charles. 'Put any coins you have in your purse round your neck and tuck it inside your doublet.' As he did so, Ralph remembered gratefully, but with some shame, the gold livre which Count Ranulf de Villaincourt had paid him for those misshapen boots. Catherine then wrapped enough bread and cheese for two days in a cloth, and placed it within easy reach in the bag. She picked up a strong staff from the corner of the room, and preparations were complete.

Ralph drank the warm milk which Catherine placed before him and ate some of the crusty bread with difficulty. Now that he was ready, it was hard to say goodbye. He knelt before Charles to receive his blessing, put on his capuchon, picked up his pack and staff, and left. They waved as he walked along his own street, past the ruin of his own house, towards the poorer part of the outlying area of Paris, and finally towards the City gate in the walls. After the first time, he did not turn to wave again. What choice had he but to go straight on?

CHAPTER IV

A Journey

A steady stream of people was passing through the gate and heading south, in the same direction as Ralph. Men on horseback, pedlars on foot, noblemen riding, accompanied by a servant or two, also mounted, mingled with farmers driving horses and carts. These were mostly on their way home after selling their wares in the city. Ralph glimpsed an occasional bale of cloth, carefully wrapped, rolling from side to side across the floor of a cart. It might have been possible to ask for a lift, but the drivers did not bother to look at him. He did not give them much opportunity. The sun was coming up, and it felt good to be fit and free, and one's own master. He had spent ten days in restricted conditions, kind as the d'Alberts had been.

Ralph stepped out briskly on the road to Orléans, his old otterskin cloak reaching to his knees and his woollen capuchon protecting his ears. It was Thursday. With good fortune, he should be in Chinon by Sunday week. Charles had plotted his route for him, by way of Orléans and Blois. His first night was to be spent at a Cluniac priory just this side of Melun. The entire distance to Chinon, he had reckoned, was between sixty and seventy leagues. Ralph should manage about seven leagues a day, a little more with luck. He had memorised the names of the main towns and some of the villages on the route, knowing that he would have some difficulty in reading the map which Charles had drawn for him.

His fellow travellers thinned out as they settled down at their individual paces along the road. Ralph outdistanced most of them, swinging his staff in his hand. He was not used to walking with it. The road was good, and surprisingly free from ruts, although hardened by frost. He had left the outlying houses of the city behind him now, and the scrubland lay on either side of the road. He could see the trees of the forest in the distance. It was too cold for birds.

There was a patter of running feet behind him, going in time with gasps for breath. Alarmed, he gripped his staff more firmly and turned to find a youthful, burly figure with tonsured head and clean-shaven chin, clad in the voluminous robe of a Franciscan friar. 'Hello,' panted the newcomer. 'Wait for me! I'm supposed never to be alone, but to mix and talk with people. You look like an excellent travelling companion.' Ralph's heart sank a little. He had so enjoyed his brief freedom. But he realised that company might provide greater safety on the journey, so he said 'I'm making for Orléans, on my way to Chinon.' It sounded impressive.

'Oh, I'm only going as far as the next village,' said the Friar, 'or maybe the one after that. I hope to meet with Brother Anthony somewhere along the route. We generally travel in twos, you know, but I got left behind in Paris to look after a sick man for a day or two. We don't often venture far, just enough in one day to find food, companionship and a bed for the night. You won't reach Orléans for a day or two, will you?'

Ralph explained that he had been advised to ask for shelter at the Priory near Melun for the first night. 'Well, I may just get as far as that,' said the Friar. 'My name is Brother Andrew. I've left my old name behind in the world, of course. What is yours? Tell me about yourself, and why you are going so far?' Ralph did not particularly want to do this, so he simply said he was going to a Master of his Guild in Chinon to work there for a time. Brother Andrew received this happily enough, and went on chattering. They settled down at a steady pace, enjoying the warmth of the winter sun, and its light on the frost. Ralph could not help wondering how the Friar kept his feet warm in those sandals.

A stone hit Ralph's pack, then another. One hit the Friar on the back. 'Look out!' he cried, and ran for the scrub. Ralph was not quick enough, and was surrounded by five youths before he realised what was happening.

They danced round him in a circle, shouting abuse and insults. 'Lâche! Laideron! Laique!' Ralph now both angry and frightened, lashed out with his staff. To his horror, one seized it, with a filthy oath, and threw it away. Then they all came nearer. One put his menacing, bearded face right into Ralph's. Two others seized his pack which the rest undid, throwing about its contents with cruel laughter. Finally, they threw him to the ground, kicked him, rolled him into the heather beside the track, and made off.

Ralph sat up. He was amazed and thankful to find how little hurt he was. There did not seem to be any broken bones, although so much discomfort indicated extensive bruising. His first thought was for the purse round his neck containing his precious coins.

It was still there. He could not have borne the loss of those. To his surprise, a large figure in brown bobbed out of the gorse bushes, and skipped towards him.

'My, I'm badly scratched,' said Brother Andrew.

Ralph was furious. His physical hurt intensified his anger.

'You rogue! You coward!' he shouted. 'You ran for your own safety. Why didn't you stay to protect me?' he said, 'I couldn't have saved you, and I should be even more scarred than I am already. Now, let's see about collecting up your possessions. You are lucky that they were after wanton mischief, and were not petty thieves.' Still angry, Ralph let out a roar of abuse, of words he did not know he had possessed. The 'gamins' of the streets of Paris had had their influence.

Taking no notice whatsoever, the Friar went on collecting Ralph's possessions. First his staff, from the other side of the road, then his pewter mug. His change of clothing and his cap now decorated the gorse bushes, but Andrew picked them up and folded them neatly. Ralph, who now realised the seriousness of the situation, grabbed his packet of bread and cheese. It was still intact. His precious scroll containing the letter to the Master of Chinon was missing. He was forced to calm down and explain its importance to his companion. At this, Andrew did seem alarmed, and they both searched carefully. At last Ralph found it. It had rolled away for some distance at the side of the track. By now, they were both extremely hungry. The precious map was still lost.

'You have some food for your journey, I see,' said the Friar. 'I have to beg for mine. It is one of our rules. I don't imagine you can refuse me now.' Ralph could not, although he looked at the amount of bread and cheese; it seemed very small. The Friar thoughtfully put a little aside for him to pack away, and divided the remainder into two parts. 'You must eat slowly,' he explained. 'Not only will that make the food last longer, but you will become less hungry that way.' Ralph, still upset, and now also ashamed, meekly nodded.

The affair had delayed them considerably, but now they went on their way again. Ralph was now stiff from his fall. 'If they were not robbers, why did they bother to attack me?' he asked.

'Partly because it was their idea of fun,' replied the Friar, 'but also I think because I was walking with you. You see, they thought of me as a clerk in holy orders. There are groups of young men going round who belong to a company called the Pastoureaux. They bear a grudge against the Holy Church, and therefore attack any of its members and its property. They think the church is a wealthy landowner. In some places it may be, but many of us, like the order to which I belong, that of St Francis, have to take a vow of poverty and own nothing. They may have been misled by the sight of some poor people taking a tenth of their corn or sheep, which they can ill afford, to the local monastery. They took advantage of the good King's absence on Crusade to help themselves to the Church's wealth where they could, and to attack anyone belonging to it, or their friends. They probably thought you looked too poor to do any more than molest you.'

True as it may have been, all this was poor comfort to Ralph. Seeing this, the Friar went on to remind him to be thankful that he had recovered his belongings so easily. Ralph's anger began to mount again, but he was forced to keep quiet. They were nearing Melun, and entering part of the great forest of Fontainebleau. The track to the little town led through the trees, partly pines and partly bare oaks, so that the way was almost totally in darkness and hard to find. After stumbling along for a league or so, some lights twinkled from a large stone building on the hillside on their left. These were the oil lamps in the windows of the Priory of Our Lady, placed to guide travellers. Ralph picked out a path to the building, and beckoned Andrew to follow it.

'Not me,' said Andrew. 'Priories and the like are not for me. I'm making for the town of Melun to find my friend,' and he skipped away into the growing darkness.

CHAPTER V

The Priory

Brother Jacques closed the smaller section of the great door of the Priory of Our Lady, sighed, and sat down. At his feet were two wooden bowls, with only a few crumbs of bread and cheese left. The poor were always more hungry in the cold weather. He was relieved that no one had asked for shelter for the night, except that cheeky wandering scholar with the Latin name of Bolognus, which he suspected was invented anyway. Jacques stretched, and sat for a while on the stone bench in the porch. He put off seeing Bolognus again, and the lay brothers in his care, for as long as possible, and even considered finding an excuse for missing Vespers.

The door bell jangled. 'Go away,' called Jacques unkindly, 'I've no more food left.'

A very timid voice replied, 'Please, I'm not hungry, at least not very. I've been told by my Master to put up here for the night.'

'Who the Devil is your Master?' called back Jacques in annoyance, without moving.

'A good man, a Craftsman, Charles d'Albert.' The voice was now getting frantic.

Jacques remembered his calling, and why he was there.

'All right, all right,' he said, getting up to unbolt the little door. A very pathetic figure stood there, with tousled hair showing under his cap, a torn cloak and hose, and swelling eyelids. 'You've been in a fight, my lad,' said Jacques, now more sympathetic. With luck, the youth might give him an excuse to miss Vespers. 'Come in, and leave your companions outside.'

'I'm alone,' said Ralph, still frightened.

'Well, you won't be much longer. There's an amusing lad about your own age here already, and he seems to be able to speak all the civilised languages there are, including Latin.'

As they left the porch, and moved towards the cloisters the sound of Vespers reached them from the chapel. Suddenly Ralph felt very homesick. He longed for his own small church at home and, at the same time, he longed to join the monks in their singing. The familiar chant and words rose and fell:

*'Nunc dimittis servum tuum Domine, secundum verbum tuum cum pace: Quia viderum oculi mei salutem tuam. Quam parasti in oculis omnium populorum. Lumen detegendum Gentibus, et gloria populi tui Israelis.'

Brother Jacques' feelings were quite different. He pointed to the long stone water trough in the cloister, with the communal towel on a stand at the other end. 'You must wash your face and hands now, and your hands again after supper. We are a Cluniac house, and have very strict rules about cleanliness.'

After he had washed, Ralph looked across at the carvings on the stone capitals on the other side of the cloister, which could just be seen in the gloom. They were a frightening sight. Some were clusters of birds of prey with human heads, spitting out food from their mouths. Others were serpents who were spitting out liquid. They were all terrifying. Ralph was used to pictures of the Nativity, and happy scenes of the life of the Saviour, and of the Crucifixion and the Resurrection. He found these carvings unnatural. He did not know that this was the stonemasons' way of giving vent to their feelings in a mainly silent community. He had forgotten the gargoyles of Notre Dame.

He followed Jacques up the stone stairs to the dorter set aside for poor travellers. It was just possible to pick out the dormer windows. The moonlight from them showed two rows of straw mattresses covered with blankets, on a wooden floor. Seated on one, a young red-headed man waved at Ralph and placed his fingers on his mouth with a conspiratorial wink. It was "silence" time, which only a monk could break, and that only in an emergency.

A bell sounded from someway off. This meant supper, so they went down again to the Cloisters. Brother Jacques joined the double line of monks, led by the Prior, and Bolognus motioned Ralph to stand aside and let them pass. As Cluniacs, the brothers wore black robes of the order of St Benedict, with the girdle of three knots at the waist. After them came the novices, similarly clad, then the lay brothers, and finally the workmen, wearing their aprons as a sign of the inferior position. Since the Benedictine Order had accepted the Cluniac

---

* the Nunc Dimittis

reforms, the monks were considered too valuable to the Order to continue to do the manual labour which St Benedict had instituted. They employed six workers at the Priory of Our Lady, consisting of stonemasons, carpenters and shoemakers. The Priory was being extended to include a better house for the Prior, and another for noble guests.

Tonight there were no noble guests to sup at the Prior's table in the refectory. Ralph followed Bolognus to the lower end of the workmen's table. Beyond them were tables for the lay brothers and novices, and at right angles to these, on a dais, was the Prior's table where the senior brothers ate with him. Ralph was impressed by the size and height of the room, with its raftered ceiling of oak supports. It resembled the main hall of a manor house.

It was January the twentieth, the Eve of St Agnes, and her feast began that evening after Vespers.

'Benedictus, benedicat, per Jesus Christum Dominum nostrum,' intoned the Prior. They all sat down. A monk went to the reading desk, and began the story of St Agnes, the young girl who had been martyred by the Romans in 303 AD for refusing to give up her faith and marry. The story was in Latin, which was as familiar to the monks as their own language, no matter from which European country they came. Ralph had been taught the Mass carefully in Latin, but was unable to follow the story. His new friend, the scholar, looked as if he could.

Gorgeous smells of roast venison wafted down from the Prior's table, where they were indulging in large portions, and washing them down with wine. Then the meat was taken round to the novices, then to the lay brothers, and finally to the workmen's table. They were fortunate to find plenty remaining. Ale was served. Ralph found he was ravenously hungry, and seized his portion, chopping off huge pieces with his knife on his wooden platter. He was too hungry to find the silence, broken only the reading, embarrassing. He drank greedily of the ale and was horrified to hear himself giving out an enormous hiccough. To make matters worse the workmen nudged each other, and had difficulty in suppressing their laughter. Bolognus gave him a sympathetic wink.

'Ping!' The Prior had finished his meal, and had rung a little handbell on his table. The reader stopped in the middle of a sentence. Everyone stood up, whether or not they had finished eating. The choirmaster sounded the note.

'Non nobis domine, non nobis, sed nomine tuo da gratias. Non nobis domine,' chanted the monks. It is hard to sing when you have not been given enough time to finish your dinner and are still a little hungry. They led out in twos followed by everyone except the workers. To his relief, Ralph found that they were allowed to stay to finish their meal, which had by now grown cold, unless they wished to say Compline with the monks in the Chapel. Moreover, they could now talk. 'This is because it is the Eve of a Feast Day. Generally, we keep silence,' explained Ralph's neighbour. Ralph discovered that he, too, made boots and shoes, and felt more at home. Soon after, they rose for bed.

Ralph and Bolognus found themselves alone in the large dorter. There was no candle, but the moon shone through the windows. They were expected to take off their boots and outer garments only, and to keep silent. A monk with a lantern looked in to see that all was well. After he had gone, Bolognus began to ask, 'Who are you, my friend, and why are you travelling this way?'

Ralph hesitated. He felt inferior to this confident young man, and did not wish to reply to his questions.

Fortunately, Bolognus did not wait for his answer. 'I'm a wandering scholar,' he said proudly. 'I've just spent a year in Italy, at the University of Bologna. I am on my way to Paris! There, I shall study rhetoric.'

Seeing that Ralph looked very puzzled, he went on, 'That is the art of speaking well, in Latin, of course; it includes arguing, defending one's own point of view and refuting other people's'.

'I'm sure you are very good at it,' said Ralph politely.

Ralph wanted to sleep, but his own private worries, rather than Bolognus' chatter, kept him awake. He was worried about losing the map, and tried to rehearse in his mind the towns he must pass through on the way to Chinon. There was Melun next, quite near, then Étampes, Neuville-aux-Bois, and after that the great city of Orléans. From Orléans, the way lay through Blois, Tours and Ussé. He thought he had the route fixed in his mind. He wished he had not lost his temper with the Friar and thought so unkindly of him. At last he slept.

The bell for Mass awoke them. The monks had already said Matins, Lauds, Prime and Terce. Villagers from the surrounding countryside were welcomed to join the monks at Mass. Today, as it was the Feast of St Agnes, a few had come in. Bolognus showed Ralph the way to the chapel, and explained that they must wash in the cloister again as they passed through. The monks and the other laity were already in their places as they crept in at the back. Mass began. The familiarity of the service made Ralph happy.

No meal was taken at this time, and the monks entered the chapter house when they left Chapel. It was now time for Bolognus and Ralph to say goodbye to the guestmaster, who was also the almoner. 'Here you are,' he said, producing a large hunk of bread and cheese for each of them for the journey. 'God go with you.'

They were travelling in different directions. Bolognus was nearly at the end of his journey, and Ralph had to find his way to Orléans. He had a sudden thought. 'When you reach Paris,' he said, 'go to the street of the Shoemakers and look for Charles and Catherine d'Albert, and tell them I am well.'

'Certainly,' replied Bolognus. 'As they are friends of yours, perhaps they will give me lodgings for a night or two, until I join some other students.'

'I am sure they will. Both their sons are away, and they will enjoy having someone young and cheerful with them,' said Ralph without hesitation.

'Oh, I shan't stay long,' exclaimed Bolognus. 'I want to share a house with a crowd of other students. It's more fun!'

They slithered down the footpath to the main track together, and parted after an affectionate embrace.

CHAPTER VI

To the Farm

Ralph paused on the track to Melun to transfer his dole of bread and cheese from the pocket of his cloak into his pack. He had no cloth to wrap it in, and the remains of the food he had set out with were at the bottom of his possessions. It was too much effort to pack them up together. He was still tired after his first day out, and by the long walk. As he fastened the bag again, he regretted the loss of the map it had contained. But, using his staff, he stepped out bravely towards Melun. This way led him through the forest for about half a league. The bare oaks outnumbered the pines in this area, and let in more of the early sunlight. As the trees grew fewer, he noticed the strips which the peasants farmed on either side of the road. Those on his right were clearly fallow, with sheep huddled in them. Those on the left were probably going to be ploughed for corn, as soon as the frost thawed out. Then some small farm houses came into sight. He found himself walking through the main village street, with smaller houses on either side. One or two displayed the signs of shopowners, such as the baker. Few people were out yet. Two or three peasants gave him a good-natured greeting. The church was closed.

At the end of Melun the track forked, one way leading a little to the east, and the other a little to the west. Ralph hesitated: if only he had the map. He chose the east, towards the sunshine. He hoped to reach Étampes before midday. There was no one to ask.

He went on, past another field of strips on his right. The road was now rising a little and the common land on either side was grazing ground for more sheep. It was the lambing season. No town or village came into view as he walked on. After about an hour, he decided he had made the wrong choice of route, and considered turning back. This seemed a waste of energy, and he sat down to eat the bread and cheese he had brought from the Priory. He considered the situation. This was the first food he had eaten that day, and it helped to restore him. He began to look round for a short cut to the west, to lead him back onto the road he had rejected, to make the third side of a triangle. Eventually he thought he saw a path in the distance, running in that direction, and made across the frozen grass towards it. It petered out into an area of scrub and gorse. He had to admit he was lost. Despair was not very far away, but he had to keep going. It was too cold to stay still.

Fears now assailed him. Suppose he twisted his ankle, broke his leg, or died of starvation and exposure? Through these fears, his simple faith asserted itself, and his panic subsided. On the horizon stood a shepherd's hut. He found the energy to hurry towards it, and pushed open the door. It was empty.

For a long time he lay there, on the heap of straw he had found along one side. There were no shutters on the window, but despite the frosty air, it was warmer than lying in the open. He rummaged through his pack to find the only remaining hunk of bread and cheese, which was now very dry. He ate it and fell asleep.

The rays of the sun through the little window awoke him next morning. He was very cold and stiff. Looking out, he noticed that some sheep had moved over in that direction during the night. This made him hope that he was not completely lost. He picked up his pack and staff, and stood outside wondering which way to turn.

As he was looking round, the figure of a farmer appeared on the horizon. Ralph waited for him to come nearer, 'Hi, lad,' called out the farmer, 'what were you doing in my hut? Are you homeless, a beggar, a pilgrim, or what? Whoever you are, you can't have spent a very good night!'

Ralph hurried towards him, and told him his name and where he was going. 'I'm afraid I lost the way,' he explained. He was speaking with difficulty, because his breath was coming in gasps. He felt very tired and uncomfortable.

'Yes, you need to get back to the road to Étampes,' said the farmer. 'Go through the village of Maisse. I have a farm there, and will show you the way when I have seen if any of my sheep need attention. Stay in the hut while I look at them.'

When he returned, he put his arm round Ralph. 'Won't you come back with me and rest a while at the farm? My wife will give you a meal, and you can go on your way later.'

The path downhill to the farm was a long one. As they went, the farmer pointed out the landmarks, and his farmhouse in the valley. Ralph tried to pay attention, but was acutely aware of the pain in his chest. Every step was an effort. The good farmer tried to cheer him along by telling him about his family. 'My name is Henri and our family name is Fourneau,' he said, 'formerly de Fourneau, but we dropped the "de". We are descended from charcoal burners, but my great-grandfather turned to farming instead. We are tenant farmers, but exceptionally fortunate in our overlord, Count Ranulf de Villaincourt. He treats us as human beings and makes few demands.'

At this Ralph brightened. 'I'm sure that is the name of a nobleman who once came to my shop to buy a pair of boots. He was exceptionally tall, and therefore needed a very long pair. He was most handsome, with long fair curly hair. There was a streak of red in it, and he said that it was because there was a streak of the Norseman in his blood.'

'That's him. How extraordinary,' exclaimed the farmer. 'You told me that you are a shoemaker travelling to work for a Master at Chinon. But what made you decide to leave Paris? Forgive me, but you are no longer very young. You must be almost past the age of most journeymen.'

Ralph, stumbling along beside him, felt ashamed all over again. 'I have not yet managed to make my Masterpiece,' he said, 'and this has caused me so much trouble that I decided to earn some money before trying again. Also, I have been laughed at for my love of staying at home that I am proving to myself and everyone else that I have the courage to travel. My little shop in Paris burned down. Kind members of the Guild are helping to rebuild it for me, so that I can return to it in a year or so, when I have saved some money.' He had difficulty in finishing this. He was now very tired, and his breathing was becoming more laboured.

'You have courage, lad,' remarked Henri. 'We are almost home now, and you will meet my wife, Mairie, and daughter, Hélène. Our two older daughters are married, both to farmers near here, so that we see them, and our grand-children, quite often. Before Hélène was born, two sons were born to us. One died at birth and the second at two years. So Hélène is very dear to us. Life can be very sad, as you have discovered.'

Ralph thought in silence while they covered some distance, and then said, 'Yes, but people's kindness makes up for some of the sadness.' He could have told Henri about his neighbours, about Charles and Catherine d'Albert, the Friar and the wandering scholar, but he lacked the strength to go on.

At last the little one-storeyed farmhouse stood before them, within a walled farmyard. A barn was attached to the house, and the hens ran in and out through its open door into the hay. As they turned into the track towards it, angry voices reached them. The woman's was louder. A handsome youth was talking to a very pretty girl, who obviously wanted nothing to do with him. The farmer chuckled. 'That's my daughter, turning away her suitor, as usual.' Ralph marvelled that she could reject so handsome a suitor. If only I were tall and strong, with dark hair and beard and looked like that, then surely I could easily win a wife, he thought.

Henri put his arm round his shoulders, and led him into the kitchen. 'Mairie,' he called to his wife, who was putting a pot onto the fire. 'Here is a friendly young man who needs our help. Some food, quickly, please.' He sat Ralph on a stool at the table. Ralph was too ill and tired to notice much about the neat, pretty little woman who bent over him.

'Give him milk,' she said. 'He looks too ill for meat.' Indeed, Ralph drank the milk greedily and accepted more, but could not look at the slice of ham the farmer produced for him. The kitchen-living room was large and comfortable. Another room led out of it, probably the bedroom for all three. There was no bed in the kitchen. Henri took hold of Ralph firmly by the shoulders. 'Best lie down, lad,' he said, and half-carried him through a doorway into the barn, where there was a bed of hay and a blanket for travellers.

How long Ralph lay in the hay, he did not know.

CHAPTER VII

The Betrothal

Ralph slept uncomfortably that night, tossing and turning. During one of his waking spells next day, the good farmer held a bowl of milk for him to drink from. 'Where am I?' gasped Ralph, as he finished the milk.

'At my farm.'

'What time is it? What day is it?'

'The afternoon of Saturday.'

'Saturday!' cried Ralph. 'I must get up. I must be fit to go to church tomorrow.' He struggled to climb out of the hay, but the pain from his breathing and the whole effort was too much for him. And where were his clothes? Someone had taken his hose and boots away. He lay back, defeated.

He had never seen the sea in his life, and the only ships he had seen had been the little rowing boats on the Seine. Now he was on a boat at sea, quite a large one. He was rowing hard, but he could not move. The waves forced him back. They were high and frightening, but he had to go on. He had to go on. He had to reach the shore. He had to go to the Church. He had to find the Master of Chinon. He had to make his Masterpiece. The pieces of his shoes would not fit together. He moaned in his sleep. Henri returned.

'What is worrying you, Ralph?' he asked. 'Ralph, Ralph, you have been having a nightmare.' He roused him gently.

'I have been trying to make some shoes for the Friar I met,' said Ralph. 'He was only wearing sandals, and his feet must be very cold.'

'Those fellows are a perfect nuisance,' exclaimed the farmer, 'coming round the village begging and becoming popular with the people with their amusing stories, and then trying to take away the work and influence of the parish priests.' Ralph had never heard this point of view before, but was too ill to argue.

Now he was on the boat again; but the sea was calmer. This time, the main hazard came from birds. There were so many of them, and they swooped down on him from the mast, scraping past him with their wings and sometimes even pecking him on the face. He screamed. He tried to get up but he could not. Then some people were carrying him out of danger. He was on a proper mattress and covered with something white and smooth. All night someone bathed him with a damp, white cloth. Sometimes the hand that touched him was tiny and thin, bony but very capable. Sometimes it was young and plump and soft, but very tender. A voice said, 'Should we try leeches?'

He screamed again. 'No.'

'No, lad. I don't believe in them either,' said a homely, masculine voice. Someone held up a bowl of hot liquid. Being thirsty, he drank and then discovered that it was very bitter, and stopped. A voice urged him to try again. This was repeated at intervals until, exhausted, he fell into a deep sleep. Later, he discovered that he had been given a mixture of rue leaves and grated mandrake roots, boiled in water, to induce sleep and cool his fever.

The next afternoon, he sat up. He was in the living room. There was a fire in the hearth, and Mairie was dozing on a settle beside it. She awoke when she heard him stir. 'You are better now?' she asked. Ralph could only nod. He was slowly taking in his surroundings. He was on a mattress in the corner of the room, covered by a sheet and blankets. The sheet was indeed a luxury. It was made of cotton of the kind soldiers brought back from Egypt, on their way home from the Crusades. He drank more milk and now ate a little bread.

From then on he recovered slowly. During the next few days he was able to sit up a little, and regained his appetite. He was alone with the two women of the household most of the time, while Henri was out on the farm. They insisted that he should rest in the kitchen and not return to the barn. So he watched them at their baking and cooking, and scrubbing and other household chores, and they talked with him. He found it hard to understand why Hélène spent so much time with him. His last memory of her was turning a handsome young man away. He did not realise that his own quietness and serenity attracted her, and that she was one who liked to do the entertaining and take the lead. But her parents noticed it.

It was now the end of January and still very cold, but Ralph insisted on going with the family to church on Sunday morning. His piety and perseverance made a deep impression on Henri. He was developing a secret affection for the lad, although he had mixed feelings of Ralph's effect on his daughter.

On the way home from Mass, Ralph walked rather slowly. He was still feeling weak from his illness, but he stumbled bravely along the track of frozen grass.

'Hélène,' he began. Then he paused. 'Hélène.' Hélène, who had guessed what was coming, slowed up, and gave him plenty of time to speak. 'Hélène! You are the best woman I have ever met. Will you marry me?'

She laughed. 'Yes,' she replied. 'Yes, but I don't think you have met many women. And you will have to ask Father tonight.'

As Henri always had to feed all his animals before giving his attention to anything else, they had to sit by the fire all the afternoon, talking happily until he had finished. Henri was not surprised, and had many questions ready.

'Can you afford to keep my daughter comfortable? Will your shop be ready soon, and when will you return there?' Ralph gave satisfactory answers to all these. Finally, Henri said, 'Don't forget that I am not a freeman like you. I must ask Lord Villaincourt's consent to your marriage to my daughter.'

Ralph had forgotten that. His face fell a little. Then he remembered that he had once met the young lord, and brightened. He looked forward to meeting him again. 'Please take me to see him soon,' he pleaded.

'Tomorrow,' promised Henri. 'He is a good man, and I do not think he will refuse.'

* * * * * * * * *

Lord Ranulf de Villaincourt sat in a chair of carved oak, at the centre of his long oak refectory table, on a dais at the end of the hall of his manor house. His great-grandfather had built this home for his family at the end of the last century. He had added a fireplace, made in the wall with an external chimney-stack. A fine carved stone arch held up the roof, across the centre of the square room. On either side could be seen the rafters. This was the main, and the only communal, room of the house. Lord Ranulf's unmarried men-at-arms, his servants and younger workers all ate and slept there.

It was noon and the trestle tables had been folded up after last night's dinner, the brass candlesticks packed into chests which lay along the sides of the room, the floor swept and fresh rushes laid out. Following the example of his father and grandfather, Lord Ranulf always sat in his hall on Mondays at noon to be available to his tenants, to hear their requests and complaints and to settle any disputes among them. He took his duties as Lord of the Manor very seriously. Sometimes his chaplain came too. Today only his bailiff sat beside him at the table, with his writing materials. Lord Ranulf could write slowly, and could read lists and figures, but he could not write much. He was a Knight, not a scribe. Others performed these mundane tasks for him. It was his mission to fight and lead his men into battle, not to seek safety behind a desk.

This morning, very few of his tenants had come to see him. Two had brought a dispute over the use of oxen to plough the communal strips for next year's harvest. This he had settled with some contempt. He would have liked better to have known which of the villagers was stealing his hen pheasants, which should shortly be roosting. He was just about to tell the bailiff to go, when Henri Fourneau arrived with a dishevelled and strange young man. Henri bowed, introduced his companion as Ralph the bootmaker, and waited. The young man seemed familiar. As he seemed embarrassed, Ranulf dismissed his bailiff. 'Can I help you?' he asked Henri, for whom he felt a genuine respect.

Henri and Ralph stood bareheaded in front of the Lord, while Henri explained the situation. 'I have, therefore, to ask for your permission for my daughter, Hélène, to marry Ralph who stands before you,' concluded the farmer. 'That is,' he added, 'unless you wanted my daughter for yourself.' Then he blushed in horror, as he realised he was being impertinent. This was not what he had intended to say at all, but his nervousness had got the better of him.

Lord Ranulf understood. He was not offended, and laughed. 'When I marry, my wife will be one of my Saxon mother's fellow countrywomen', he said. 'I like their fair hair, and blue eyes.' Then he went on, 'Yes, I will give you my permission to marry Hélène, but first I want to know if you have enough money to support a wife, and a house to live in.'

Ralph told him about the shop in Paris, and about the fire. 'I want to marry Hélène in about a year', he said, 'and take her back to live there. But first, I have to go to Chinon, to stay with a Master there, and make my Masterpiece.'

'Work hard while you are there,' Lord Ranulf advised him, 'and save some money. Did you say you were a shoemaker?' he asked. And he thrust forward his feet from under the table. One boot was longer than the other.

All three laughed heartily. Then Lord Ranulf rose from the table, and Ralph and Henri turned to go. 'Thank you, my Lord,' said Henri. Ralph turned round hastily and said thank you, too. After they had gone down the steps from the Hall into the walled garden, they hugged each other.

They walked past the fruit trees, which were hardly in bud, across the Lord's own farmland, and over the common strips, to Henri's farmhouse. 'The Lord had give his consent, Hélène,' cried Ralph, and kissed her. 'Oh, my dear,' cried Hélène, 'thank God for that! If only you did not have to leave us tomorrow.' And they both hugged again, and shed a few tears.

CHAPTER VIII

To Orléans

As he packed his things in the morning, Ralph felt glad that his decision at Melun to take the track to the east had led him this way. What a happy mistake! Meeting Hélène was the happiest event in his life so far. Henri gave him careful instructions to find the road to Orléans again. He was to join it at the little village of Étampes, and go south from there through Neuville-aux-Bois. He also suggested very strongly, that as Ralph had only just recovered from his illness, he should look for a lift in a cart. Farmers often passed through Étampes during the morning on their way to market. If Ralph waited at the crossroads, he should eventually find a friendly one. Henri explained, 'The keeper of the hostelry there is a good, honest man. If you have not found a lift by dark, you should spend the night there, and try again next day. Have you sufficient money to pay for a night's lodging?'

'I still have the money that Comte de Villaincourt paid me for his shoes,' replied Ralph. 'You have sheltered and fed me, and nursed me back to health. Please accept this livre as a gift.' He put up his hand to find his purse, but Henri firmly refused.

When Hélène reopened his pack to put in some bread and cheese for the journey, he took the opportunity to take out the best of the three pairs of boots he carried, and insisted that Henri should keep them. 'Please take these,' he said, so eagerly that the farmer could not refuse.

Henri had occasionally visited Étampes, rarely Neuville, and Orléans only once in his life. He remembered staying at a hostelry at Orléans near the site where the new cathedral of St Croix was being built, and suggested this to Ralph, as being a good place to stay.

At last it was time to go. Ralph embraced them all, and promised to find a clerk to write a letter for him, to send from Chinon to announce his safe arrival. They stood outside the farmhouse door in the winter sunshine to wave good-bye, Henri once again pointing out the way to Étampes. Ralph was very sad to leave them, and resolved that he too would form a family group like that one day.

As he drew near Étampes, he met a pedlar who gave him a civil greeting. They stopped to talk, and Ralph noticed that among his goods for sale was a bale of white cloth. 'What is that?' he asked, pointing.

'It came from Egypt, and was sold to me by a soldier, returning home from the Crusade. It is the finest cotton, and very valuable. Nevertheless, I will let you have it at bargain price, if you're interested, to lighten my load.'

Ralph thought again. It would be just the right present to give to Hélène to save towards their married home, but he could not carry it as far as Chinon. His spirits were still very low, and he longed to see her again. 'I will have it if I can afford it,' he decided. He was not very good at bargaining, but the pedlar was not too demanding and he finally bought it for one of his precious livres. He was rather worried about taking out his purse in front of the pedlar, but he had to do it. The pedlar showed no sign of grabbing the rest of his money. He resolved to spend as little as possible after this, in order to begin saving for his marriage straight away. There was only one thing to do now, and that was to turn back and take the present to Hélène. This meant adding three or four leagues to his journey, and he was not very well yet. His step was light in spite of the increased load. Would they be pleased to see him?

He found Hélène and Mairie in the living room, and Mairie ran to fetch Henri from the cowshed.

'Ralph,' cried Hélène anxiously. 'You have come back! You're not ill again are you?'

'Not to stay,' replied Ralph.

Then, seeing Hélène's downcast look, he went on, 'I bought you a present to remind you that I'm coming back soon. So, work hard, and sew some sheets ready for us from this cloth by the time I return.' Hélène tried to smile, but tears prevented her from doing more than giving him a hug. They finally parted and, as Ralph set out again, he felt very tired.

When he reached Étampes, it was still light. He stood still, his pack heavy on his shoulders, and looked towards Neuville-au-Bois. A sound of horses' hooves and the grating of wheels on stones made him turn round. A cart! The farmer drew up. He was lonely, and prepared to take a risk in his choice of travelling companion.

'Up you get, lad,' he said. 'Where are you going?'

'I'm going to Orléans, and intend to reach it tonight, even in the dark.'

After a few attempts at conversation, the farmer noticed that Ralph was so tired that he gave up. He hoisted him over from the front seat into the bottom of the cart. 'Cover yourself with those fleeces I'm taking to sell,' he said. This was indeed travelling in luxury.

When Ralph awoke, it was dark, and the cart was rumbling over the cobbles of the main street of Orléans. Although it was a cold winter's night, there seemed to be people everywhere. Some carrying torches. There was a general stir of excitement. The farmer called to Ralph, 'Sit up. Look, there is the new Cathedral that is being built.'

The scaffolding stood out in the moonlight. The workmen had reached the first of the two great towers on the western front. Ralph took only a brief glance. He was still sleepy, but it seemed to him even larger than Nôtre Dame, and the windows were being built in a strange pointed style, which was new to him.

The farmer called to him 'Climb into the seat beside me again. I am going to stable the horses at the hostelry near the Cathedral, and to spend the night there. Can you afford this?'

Ralph had no option, but was worried at the thought of losing a few more precious coins. He had almost a superstitious determination to keep the livres intact for Hélène. Perhaps he might not have to spend more than a few sous? Would anyone like a pair of boots in lieu of payment? So his thoughts ran on, to be interrupted by singing and ribald laughter as they approached the hostelry. Surely this could not be the same one Henri Fourneau had stayed in years ago?

He seized his pack and leapt out to hold the horse's head while the farmer detached the trappings. He was not very good with horses, but fortunately this one was quiet. Then they entered the hostelry together. A young serving woman gave Ralph a keen glance. He stood fair and square, and looked straight in front of him. Now that he had Hélène's affection, he did not care if other young women tried to embarrass him or not. The farmer was negotiating with the owner for a room. 'Fifty sous for a bed in a room, shared, or twenty sous for a place in the hay,' he repeated. Both prices were absurdly dear. The farmer settled for the room and Ralph for the hay. He thanked the farmer, who was returning to Étampes next day, for the lift, realising with some alarm that he would be on his own again next morning. Before they turned in for the night, the farmer promised to see him again before he left, and to set him on his way. Ralph turned towards the stable.

But the lads in the hostelry were not going to let him get away so easily. They shouted after him, 'A drink! Come and join us!' Although he was hungry and thirsty, Ralph knew that he could not afford to spend his money on them, so he pretended not to hear. Two of them chased him into the stable shouting insults. 'You are mean and ugly! Are you stupid as well?' When he still kept silent, one of them grabbed his pack. Together they opened it, and pulled out the pair of boots. Ralph leapt up to grab them back, but they threw them over his head to each other, roaring with laughter, calling out, 'You're too short, and too slow!'

Seeing it was useless to try to catch his boots, Ralph turned his back and made for his bed in the hay. For a time, the two rough lads went on throwing the boots to each other, and then suddenly gave up, threw them at him instead and ran off. Ralph gave a sigh.

He hoped they would leave him in peace, but back they came. This time they were carrying three pewter mugs of ale. They sat down, one each side of him, and offered him one. Now they were smiling and good-natured, as if they were trying to make up for the teasing.

Ralph drank the ale. He was surprised to find that they were not completely vicious. He took out some of the bread and cheese Hélène had packed for him and offered them some as a sign of his thanks. As he shared it out, he felt nearer to her and happier. 'My fiancée packed this for me,' he said proudly. 'I am glad to share it with you.' They thanked him in their own way with a thump on his back. Their mouths were full of ale and bread and cheese. After their feast, all three slept soundly.

It was getting light when Ralph woke. In spite of their friendly ways, Ralph did not trust his companions completely, and crept silently away to find the farmer. They paid their dues together, so no one else saw Ralph take his purse from around his neck and count out the coin. The farmer brought Ralph some bread and ale, and advised him, 'Return to the square before the new Cathedral, and wait for a cart. You have still some way to go, through Blois and Tours to Chinon.' Ralph nodded. He knew that he would have to spend another night or two on the way according to the luck he met on his journey.

He said goodbye, and another thank you, and walked down the little side street towards the Cathedral de la Croix. His way was blocked by a crowd and he could not at first reach the square. With some pushing he arrived there, to find more people lined up on either side. The King's baggage train was passing through! He had missed the arrival of the King's herald, who made the announcement. First came the carts, driven by weary servants, who doubtless had been up since dawn to do the packing. The royal party had probably stayed at a nobleman's manor on their way from Paris. The more important the courtiers were, the later they started their journey. The carts were packed high with the luxuries of life: feather beds, cushions, curtains, trunks of clothes, stools and chairs. There were at least twenty of them. They turned left into a side street from the square towards the Bishop of Orléans' palace. Then the men-at-arms followed on horseback, wearing tabards showing the royal coat of arms, and armed with lances to ward off attackers. After them came three knights on horseback, noblemen who were staying at Court to keep the royal family company.

Ralph was amazed at the numbers of the entourage. Where were they going to stay, and who could possibly afford to keep them all? A friendly fellow at his elbow greeted him, and Ralph took the opportunity to ask him these questions. 'The royal party is going to stay with the Bishop of Orléans,' replied his new companion. 'As to the expense, the King will probably give the Bishop the right to take further dues from us, the townsfolk of Orléans, to cover the cost.' This was a disturbing suggestion to Ralph, who held both the King and all church dignitaries in high esteem. Would the saintly Louis IX really cover the expenses of his journeys from the pockets of the poor? 'Is the King himself coming?' he asked.

'So they say,' the young man replied. 'Since his return from the Crusade two years ago, he had been travelling round to see his people on his own estates, which extend in this direction. Wait, and you will see!'

Indeed, Ralph could no nothing but wait. The constant arrival of more parts of the royal procession, and the pressure of the crowd, made it impossible to leave the square.

Some wagons now entered, carrying the personal servants of the nobility. The servants waved merrily, and the crowd shouted remarks at them, some cheerful, some critical, some in ridicule, all of which appeared to be accepted good-humouredly. 'This is a sign that the King will soon be here,' confided the young man. 'He keeps his personal servants near him in case of need.' Ralph was surprised to notice that there were many more women than men in the wagons; this suggested more ladies than gentlemen in the court party.

Now came a wagon of jesters and musicians, singing and playing pipes and stringed instruments. The jesters were leaping among them and generally fooling about. Two of the merriest leaped off the wagon at intervals, ran among the crowd, pretending to tickle women with their bunches of feathers, and then caught up with their comrades and leaped onto the wagons again.

At last the royal wagon came into view. Alas, it was covered over and the side windows were curtained. Undismayed the crowd roared 'Hurrah!' and 'Long live Your Majesty!' An escort of men-at-arms, wearing the royal arms and waving standards, followed. A youth from the crowd, with greater temerity than the rest, ran alongside one of the soldiers. 'Who is inside this wagon?' he asked.

'It is the queen, with her ladies,' was the answer. He learned that King Louis with his advisers had returned to Paris, and Queen Margaret, with only three knights and their ladies, had carried on to Orléans. 'Long live Queen Margaret,' shouted the crowd, as the word went round, wishing her to know that she had all their loyal support.

It was now past midday. As the excitement was over, Ralph wished to continue his journey. He was now alone, on foot, and had planned to reach Blois before dark. It was still not possible to leave the square. Pedlars were now struggling through the crowd, hoping to take advantage of the general feeling of goodwill to sell their wares. One near Ralph held a tray of silver medallions, containing the effigy of St. Christopher, the patron saint of travellers. Realising that he was looking his way, the pedlar held up one to Ralph. It was a skilfully engrave picture of St. Christopher carrying the Christ child on his back across the river. 'All blessed, all blessed!' called the pedlar.

Ralph hesitated. He did not want to spend any more money, but he still had two or three days' journey to face alone. 'Look out,' whispered his new friend. 'It is unlikely that they have been blessed at all. We have not seen a priest do so and there is no proof.' Ralph was thankful for his warning, and withdrew his free hand from his throat, where he had been fumbling for the thong of his purse.

The crowd was now thinning out, and it was possible to move away. He grasped his staff firmly. His pack still felt secure on his shoulders. Seeing he was now determined to go, his new friend gripped his shoulder warmly in a farewell gesture. 'God go with you,' he said. 'May you reach your destination safely.'

CHAPTER IX

Orléans to Chinon

Ralph left Orléans in the afternoon sunshine, grasping his staff, and firmly striding out. He felt physically better than he had done since his illness, and the sight of the royal procession, especially the knights on horseback, had been inspiring. He felt that he, too, was a knight, and that he was riding out to win his fair lady. He did not realise at this stage that his imagination was over-stimulated, partly by hunger. He had not eaten since early morning. Fortunately a little of the food Hélène had packed for him remained. The road towards Blois ran along beside the River Loire, which flows northwards from the central plateau, and turns sharply eastwards at Orléans. It was much warmer in the river valley, and, as he left the city, Ralph noticed that many houses had their own gardens in which fruit trees grew. Beside the road, after he had left the peasants' strips, were pasture lands, where cows and goats fed. Clearly this was a prosperous area. Ralph could not hope to cover the six or seven leagues to Blois that afternoon. Three was all that he could manage, and this effort brought him to the little town of Beaugency. Passing the church, he found himself beneath the great castle keep, well back from the river. It had been built over two hundred years before to defend the town, and was five stories high, an impressive and awe-inspiring sight. Two men-at-arms stood on guard, each on either side of the main gateway. For some inexplicable reason Ralph suddenly felt afraid, and hurried past. He was soon out of the little town into the country beyond, and he knew that he must now find shelter for the night. To his right lay a peasant's little cottage. He decided to approach the tenant, and spend a few of his remaining sous, if necessary. He counted out twenty, and placed them in the pocket of his cloak, so that he would not have to pull out his purse.

He walked up the garden path to the door. It was a single-storied building, containing only one room, and an adjoining barn. Obviously his footsteps had been heard. Before he could rap on the door, a deafening and frightening chorus of barking made him step back suddenly. The door opened and two dogs charged at him. They would have knocked him over, if he had not instinctively used his stick.

A tall peasant followed them and grabbed each dog in turn by the scruff of its neck, holding them off. 'What do you want?' he called to Ralph. 'It's no use trying to rob or attack us. I can set these dogs on you whenever I choose!' Seeing that Ralph was shaking, he went on more gently, 'Is it shelter for the night that you want?' Ralph nodded. 'I'll have to ask my wife,' he said, and called 'Maria!' over his shoulder, still holding the struggling dogs. The man and his wife held a brief conversation, speaking in low voices. At last Maria nodded, and her husband called, 'Come in!'

When they had banished the dogs to the barn, they offered Ralph a stool, and ladled out a bowl of soup from the stew pot over the fire. 'Do you want some bread?' asked the husband, rather brusquely.

'No, thank you, I have my own. I will not impose on you further,' replied Ralph, pulling out some bread and cheese from his pack. 'I must pay you for the night's lodging.' He offered them twenty sous. The peasant took them gratefully, and drew out a trestle bed for him. Their own stood in a corner of the room, which was sparsely furnished. Whether they were really poor, or whether they wished to give an appearance of poverty to ward off would-be robbers, he could not tell. Ralph slept soundly.

The next morning, as he drank their milk, he asked, 'Do you think I can get a ride in a cart to Blois?'

'You may be lucky,' said the peasant. 'But stick to the road. Occasionally boats pass down the river, but it is very dangerous here.' Ralph had noticed that the river was very wide and that a deep channel ran down the centre, containing a fast-flowing current. Nearer the bank on either side were sandbanks.

Thanking them, he left for the road once more. A misty haze rose from the river as he walked along. He was not lucky enough to get a lift. Although several carts passed him, they were either full or their drivers unfriendly. The happy mood of yesterday had left him, but he plodded on and was in Blois by midday. He noticed at once the tower of Foix, and the beautifully built Hall beside it, which dominated the river. They were now uninhabited, as the great family which had built them had died out. Ralph sat down by the river to eat his last piece of bread. The mist was clearing and the sun was coming out. He wondered what the afternoon held in store for him.

He was just finishing his meal when a cheery voice called out, 'Hey, do you want a lift?' He looked up to see a farmer driving his cart towards Tours. Elated by the prospect of reaching Tours before sunset, he climbed up beside the driver. It was a happy journey; his companion, whose name he discovered was Louis Deschamps, laughed and joked. He had an endless store of stories and was delighted to find a good listener. 'Have you been to Tours before?' he asked. On hearing that Ralph had not, he remarked, 'Then you may not know about St Martin of Tours?' Ralph did not. Seizing his opportunity, Louis launched into his story. 'He was a good man, a saintly man. He lived a long time ago, you know, hundreds of years ago, when the Roman legions ruled France. He was a brave soldier, and fought for the Romans, and led an army. But he didn't enjoy that kind of life. He wanted to become a Christian, and live like a monk, but his father wouldn't have it. But Martin was kind, kind to everyone. One cold day, like this one, when he was serving at Amiens, he met a beggar who was shivering in his thin clothes. Martin whipped off his cloak, seized his sword, and cut it in two, and gave half to the beggar.'

'Was half a cloak large enough to keep him warm?' asked Ralph, who wore only a narrow cloak himself.

'Of course it was,' replied Louis, displeased by this apparent doubt.

'Why is he the patron saint of Tours?' asked Ralph.

'Well, he became a Christian after that, and lived in a monastery near here. It is said that St Hilary gave him the land for it. The townspeople of Tours heard all about his kind deeds, and asked if he could come and be their Bishop. Martin didn't want this, so they captured him with a trick. They asked him to come to the city to visit a very sick woman, and when they had got him inside their gates, they wouldn't let him go.' Ralph couldn't understand how this could have been allowed, and asked what the Pope thought about it. To his surprise, Louis explained that all that happened before there was a Pope. He then hurried on with his tale: 'And that's not the end. He lived to be eighty, and spent his life helping all those he met. There are many stories told of his miracles. He was buried at Tours. You must visit his tomb. He died some distance from the city and they put his body on a boat, which carried it upstream along the River Loire, without oars or sail. As it went on its way to Tours all the people along the river bank could hear heavenly music, and, although it was the month of November, all the trees burst into blossom as it passed.'

47

And so Louis continued with his stories until they reached the great city of Tours. To add to his good fortune, Ralph learned that the farmer knew of a good hostelry where they could spend the night. He was going to sell his farm produce, mainly cheeses, to a rich merchant the next morning, and then was going on to visit his married sister, and would take Ralph with him. He promised to point out the way from there, over the bridge to Ussé, towards Chinon, saying, 'You should be able to cover this distance in half a day.'

By now they had negotiated the main streets of Tours, past the new Cathedral, and the two great towers which marked St Martin's own church, and his burial place. 'You must visit these places in the morning, while I sell my produce,' urged Louis.

The night at the hostelry was uneventful. They ate supper together, which Ralph insisted on paying for out of his precious supply of livres, and then they parted for the night, the farmer to a bed and Ralph to a humbler resting place in the stable. Louis' mare, La Dorée, slept near Ralph, and the cart stood in the yard, the cheeses carefully disguised under an old blanket. Ralph was relieved to find them still there in the morning. He set out to explore the city, and found the sundial near the new Cathedral, which Louis had appointed as their meeting place at mid-morning. He was sorry to leave such a lovely city after only a brief visit.

They set off again together. Louis wanted to tell more stories, and Ralph sitting beside him listened, although he would have preferred to stretch out in the empty cart. The fog of the previous day had brought back the pain in his chest, and he was becoming rather anxious about his health, especially as he would have to go on alone. Ignoring Ralph's low spirits, Louis asked him if he had ever heard of Charles of the Hammer. Delighted to learn that he had not, he began again.

'He is connected with Tours, and that is why I am going to tell you about him now. He was a knight and wore shining armour, and he had a band of foot soldiers, archers in shining armour too, who followed him.' Surely it was rather heavy going to walk thus armed, thought Ralph. 'His father was called Pippin and he looked after the King's affairs. Now there were wild Moors, followers of Mohammed, who had conquered Spain, and they had invaded the south of France. It looked at one time as if they would conquer all of France, too. If they had, then all of Europe might have fallen under their rule and we should not now be Christians. But this knight called Charles led his archers into battle, and after days of fighting drove the Moors back and saved France. That battle was fought at Tours in 732. After it, Charles became even more famous, and his grandson became the Emperor Charlemagne. You've heard of him, haven't you? He ruled not only France, but parts of Germany and Italy as well.'

Ralph was learning a lot and storing it all in his memory to impress Hélène when they were reunited. He hoped she would be interested. He had now made up his mind that if he was well-received at Chinon, and could settle down to work hard and save some money, and with luck get some help to make his Masterpiece, he would return in less than a year. He would join her at the farm near Maisse, they would marry and he would be back in his own house, with his bride, before Christmas. He had had enough of wandering.

They were moving along smoothly now, and quite quickly. The road between Tours and Langeais was used frequently, and the white flints which formed the road had been worn smooth. Louis pulled over onto the grass verge to let another cart pass. When he returned to the main track he began yet another story, the last, and comparatively brief. This was inspired by the great, forbidding castle keep of Langeais, which they were approaching. He pointed this out with great pride. 'That was our castle,' he began, 'until that impudent King of England, called Richard Coeur de Lion, took it. He was never in his own kingdom, always in other people's, causing trouble in order to earn a name for himself.'

Our own King has been away for a long period on Crusades, too, thought Ralph, but kept silent.

'But the English couldn't hold it for long after his death,' went on Louis. 'Our own King's grandfather took it back, praise be. And now it belongs to the French crown again.' La Dorée clattered along under its great walls as he spoke. Its height and austere aspect reminded Ralph of Beaugency, which he had found very frightening a few days ago.

It was now time for Louis to leave Ralph to complete his journey on foot, through Ussé to Chinon. The sun was still shining. He was glad of this, as he was still feeling rather poorly. But he strode on determinedly, thankful that a large part of his adventure was safely over. In Ussé he paused to sit on a grassy bank to take out the scroll addressed to the Master, to have it ready to hand him. It was now becoming colder. He made one last great effort, rose to his feet, and turned towards Chinon. As he reached the outskirts, he could just see the great towers of the fortress reaching down to the River Vienne in the gathering dusk. A few flakes of snow began to fall.

CHAPTER X

Chinon at Last

Émile le Juste was driven from his garden by a few flakes of snow. He had been looking at the aconites which bordered the stone flags of the courtyard beneath the brick wall. The fruit trees trained along the wall showed signs of buds, and beyond his orchard grew. He felt happy there.

As he entered his two-storied townhouse, his doubts about the future returned. Would he ever get through the work which was piling up? He had taken orders from several influential people he did not wish to disappoint, and a row of boots and shoes, cut out, but not yet sewn up, lay along the bench in the shop. He missed Jerome, his former apprentice, who had worked under him for seven years, and had now gone out as a journeyman. He was a very good lad, and a skilled workman, and in about a year's time would make a good Master. He hoped very much that he would return to Chinon.

About his second and junior apprentice, Leo, he could hardly bear to think at all. He was partly Italian, a likeable cheerful lad, but impetuous and wilful. In spite of many warnings, he had insisted on rowing, alone, in a borrowed boat, up the river Vienne to the point where it joined the wider river Loire. There he had been swept away by the current. His boat had capsized, and he had been drowned. His father and Italian mother had moved to set up business in Aquitaine since the English had left, and it had been difficult to find them.

'Émile, mon cher, do not look so sad,' said a voice. It was his wife, Blanche, coming into the living room from the shop. She was a native of Chinon, of a respectable merchant family. To their mutual disappointment, there were no children.

'I'm not said,' he replied, 'only thinking, and trying to find a solution which will see us through the immediate future. Come here beside me and think too.'

51

As usual, the closeness of her little round figure, with her neat dress, and the graying curls tumbling out of their braids, comforted him. They continued to sit together in silence on the settle before the fire.

Bang, bang, bang! Crash! Bang again! The shop door knocker was being used to its fullest extent, with desperate force. 'Stay here,' ordered Émile to his wife, as he seized a lantern, and lit it with a taper from the hearth. The knocking went on, but grew feeble, as though the aggressor, if he were one, was losing his strength. Blanche, ignoring her husband's command, followed him through the shop to the door.

Émile pulled back the bolts, and opened the upper part of the door, holding the lantern above his head. The small figure outside immediately slumped over the lower part, as if he could not stand upright a moment longer. 'Steady, steady,' called Émile. Blanche rushed forward and together they dragged him in, and sat him on a bench in the shop. The small man before them was poor and dishevelled. His head, shoulders and beard were covered in snowflakes. His breathing came with a rasping sound. There was no doubt that he was exhausted.

Ralph had longed to make a good impression on his arrival. This was essential if he was to be offered work with Émile le Juste. And he had failed. For the third time in three weeks, he had arrived at a strange house in a pathetic condition, first at the Priory, then at Henry Fourneau's farm and now at the Rue des Bottiers, Chinon. He lost his grip on the scroll, and it rolled towards the flames. Just in time, Blanche spotted it and clutched it back. 'It's for you,' she said to her husband, shaking her hand which had ventured painfully too near the fire.

She was able to read a little, and her husband rather more, but for the time being they placed it on the table, and began to fetch water to revive Ralph. Blanche removed his cloak and snow-covered capuchon and Émile his boots, shaking his head sadly as he did so. Who had made these?

'You must read your letter. It is important. You must read your letter,' stuttered Ralph, becoming agitated as he recovered his senses. Émile cut through the wax seal and unrolled it, reading to Blanche as he did so, while she continued her administrations. 'You have come from my old friend Charles d'Albert,' he said, 'all the way from Paris? In this weather? By the date here, you have been travelling for three weeks.' Ralph nodded. He could not speak. He watched while Blanche carried a pot through the shop. When she returned with it, he recognised the smell. It contained herbs similar to those in the brew he had drunk at the farm at Maisse.

'Do not worry, I could not send away a protégé of an old friend. At least, not in your present state.' Émile had intended to reassure him, but his words contained uncertainty which produced a violent trembling in the boy, which Blanche noticed.

'It is important to get well,' she said, 'before we begin to think of anything else.'

Indeed, Ralph did recover quite quickly this time, thanks to Blanche's capable nursing and a comfortable bed in the shop, with the warmth seeping through from the living-room.

He had promised to send a letter to Hélène, but it was three days before he was well enough to tell them so. 'Who is Hélène?' asked Émile. When Ralph explained, he looked surprised, and even incredulous. 'You, with a fiancée?' Hurt again, Ralph's anger rose.

'Yes,' he said. 'I'm affianced to the best woman in the world. I shall go back to Maisse to marry her, and take her to my house in Paris as my bride, before Christmas.' 'You with a house in Paris!' exclaimed Émile, amazed again. Now Ralph went back to the beginning and explained why he had been staying with the d'Alberts, and why he had left them, of his ambitions to prove his courage and to become a Master, and the happy accident which had caused him to meet Hélène.

While he had been talking, Émile had been examining the contents of his pack, and the two remaining pairs of boots in particular. 'Who made these?' he asked. 'The usual punishment for bad work is to make the workman consume his own goods. A brewer who brews undrinkable ale has it poured down his throat. You must wear those boots until they drop off.' Ralph's spirits sank again. Would he ever find employment? The Master looked at them again. 'The stitching is quite firm and neat,' he said. 'Indeed, if it had not been so on those you arrived in, they would have fallen off your feet on the way here. It is the cut and fitting that is so dreadful. This is what shows in the general shape and appearance.'

He thought again.

There was a line of boots in the shop waiting to be stitched, and he was the only worker available. Ralph wondered whether Henri Fourneau was wearing those he had left for him. He hoped so, if only because they would make Hélène think of him.

'Blanche, my dear,' said Émile, when they were in bed that night. 'What shall we do with him? We cannot send him away.'

'Certainly not,' replied his wife. 'He must stay here for the winter at least. You need another pair of hands to do some sewing.'

Émile thankfully agreed. 'If only he could learn to cut out as well as he sews, he might yet make his Masterpiece,' he suggested hopefully.

Next morning, Ralph was so agitated over his letter to Hélène that he felt able to assert himself. 'I must send a letter to my fiancée,' he exclaimed to Henri. 'She will be worried that I have not arrived safely.'

'I will go to the castle at Chinon for you,' replied Émile kindly. 'As it is a royal castle, there may be a chaplain there who is travelling soon to the Court at Paris. He could take a letter at least some of the way for you.'

'If he could only reach Étampes!' exclaimed Ralph. 'I'm sure the keeper of the hostelry there would take it on to Maisse. Can I send one to the d'Alberts in Paris, as well?'

Émile gave up the afternoon, when he had really wanted to get on with his work, to go to the caste to find a priest who would write Ralph's letters, and arrange for their delivery. Ralph sat in the shop by himself and began to sew together a pair of boots. As he did so, he thought how lucky he was to find such a dear couple as Émile and Blanche, and to survive that frightening journey. Now that it was over, he was beginning to realise how dangerous it had been, and how foolhardy he had been to think of it. He made up his mind that, after he had made his Masterpiece and returned to his little house and shop in Paris, he would never leave it again.

Émile returned with the good news that a priest had written his letters, and that a young clerk would take them to Hélène and the d'Alberts on his journey to Paris, which would be the next week. 'I will make him a pair of boots as soon as I can sew well enough,' promised Ralph.

'Well done! I hope that will be soon,' replied Émile. 'And now it is supper time.'

The three sat down to eat. Soon after, Ralph washed and undressed and thankfully climbed into the box bed in the shop, the traditional sleeping-place for an apprentice. 'Deo gratias. Ave Maria: Ora pro nobis*,' he murmured, and fell sound asleep.

---

* Thanks be to God. Hail Mary: Pray for us.

Part Two
Ralph's Return

CHAPTER I

Ralph's Departure from Chinon

It was a raw November morning in the year 1256. Ralph le Boeuf sat upright at the little table at the back of Émile le Juste's shop in the Rue des Botteliers at Chinon, with his possessions neatly set out before him. He had changed much since his arrival there ten months ago. Now, his back was straight, his hair and beard clean, and he displayed an air of confidence. And he was well-shod. His leather bag lay there clean and polished, beside the goods which were to go in it. First and foremost was a beautifully-made little pair of men's leather boots, the stitching perfect and the cut faultless, although they did seem rather small for a man. They were Ralph's Masterpiece, passed and recorded by his Master and other members of the Guild of Bootmakers at Chinon. The appropriate message had been sent to Henri d'Albert, Ralph's former master in Paris. Ralph was now entitled to own a business, to train apprentices and to avail himself of all the privileges of the Guild. If the pair was rather too small, only Ralph and Émile knew the trouble he had had in making the pieces fit together and the trimming and paring which had been necessary.

As he proudly and carefully packed these in first, he was aware of Hugh, the new apprentice, watching him. Hugh was only sixteen, always cheerful, amusing and cheeky. Ralph had resolved already, after a week's acquaintance, that his apprentices, when he had them, would show more respect.

'There won't be much room for anything else in your pack, will there?' asked Hugh. He was longing for a scrap of some kind, but Ralph ignored him. He picked up his pewter cup next. Henri d'Albert had lent it to him for his journey and he was anxious to return it safely. Blanche le Juste came in carrying a leather wine bottle. 'I should keep your cup in your pocket,' she said. 'You may need it on your journey. Thomas the Carter will like to share this wine with you.

57

But take care of it.' She laid an affectionate hand on his shoulder. 'You are going to marry and your children will be proud to inherit it.'

He was leaving in style in Thomas' cart as far as Étampes; they were to spend a night at Orléans on the way. From Étampes he planned to walk to Henri Fourneau's farm near Maisse, retracing the ground he had covered on that cold January day, not a year ago. There, his fiancée, Hélène, was waiting and watching for him. They had kept in touch, partly by letters read to Hélène by the parish priest, and partly by verbal messages. Pierre le Doux, who kept the hostelry at the crossroads just outside Étampes, had performed this service. Nothing had been too much trouble for him. He had listened to the messengers from Chinon who called on him and then cheerfully walked almost two leagues to the farm to pass on the news to Hélène. So, she was expecting Ralph in two days' time and was almost ready for her wedding.

Émile was talking to Thomas, who had drawn up outside the shop. After a brief handshake with Hugh and a warm embrace with Blanche, Ralph went out to try to express his deep and sincere gratitude to the Master. 'God go with you, Ralph,' said Émile. 'I'm sorry to lose you.' This was praise indeed.

Ralph leapt into the cart, Thomas covered his knees with a fleece and they were away. The mist was clearing as they rumbled through Ussé, over the bridge to Langeais and along the north bank of the River Loire towards Tours. Ralph, who tended to be silent anyway, was too happy to speak. He had accomplished so much during the last ten months, and in two days he would be reunited with Hélène. Thomas, who had been married a long time, and had children and grandchildren, nudged and winked. 'Make the most of these coming months, my lad,' he said. 'You don't know what's in store or how you will react or how you will have to adjust your ways to meet the needs of a family.'

'I am looking forward to one,' Ralph said.

'Well,' explained Thomas, 'there are the nights when you don't get much sleep because the youngest is cutting his teeth, there are evenings when they all want the same thing and all your attention. Worst of all, unless you are very lucky, there are meal times when they are all hungry and you wonder how you can afford to keep them fed. But it's worth it, at least it becomes so when you're a grandfather.' Ralph had not thought of that, and became silent again. Clip clop, clip clop, a jangling of bridles, the shouts of 'whoa', and two horsemen gained on them from behind. They wore strong leather tunics and brandished knives. One, tossing his reins to the other, leaped from his horse's back into the cart. He grabbed Ralph's pack and then the leather wine bottle, throwing them in turn to his companion. Both screamed obscenities all the while to create an atmosphere of fear. It was over in seconds; the attacker vaulted out of the cart into the road and onto his horse again, almost before Thomas and Ralph had realised what had happened, and they were away.

Thomas' horse reared and kicked in fright and it took all his strength to quieten him. Fortunately, this restored his presence of mind. Ralph just shook. Then the realisation of his loss bore on him. His Masterpiece had gone! All he had left, apart from his purse concealed round his neck, was the pewter cup in the pocket of his cloak.

For minutes, which seemed unnaturally long, they did not speak. Then Thomas turned furiously to Ralph. 'Why didn't you stop them?'

'How could I?' he replied, hurt and angry. 'They had knives and horses!' Then he remembered how angry he had been when Brother Andrew had abandoned him, or so he thought, to the Pastoureaux, on the road to Melun.

Thomas calmed down. 'Well, if I have lost nothing and you have lost all, you have only yourself to blame. We can do nothing. At least, we're both safe, and so is the mare.'

They passed small groups of cottages along the road in silence. by now the seriousness of the situation had affected Ralph deeply. He had so looked forward to showing that pair of boots to Hélène. He hoped that he was still a Master in spite of the loss of his Masterpiece. To Thomas, the worst blow was the loss of the wine, so when they reached Tours in the early afternoon, he stopped at a hostelry and gave the reins to a lad standing by. Ralph had not much knack with horses, but he did his duty in reaching for his purse. Food and drink restored them to some extent, sufficiently for Thomas to talk to the other travellers, and warn them of the danger. Endless comments and advice followed, all to no purpose. Ralph became the object of their sympathy, their scorn and their jokes. 'What are you Master of?' asked one. 'Apathy, slowness, sleepiness or cowardice?' He kept silent. There was nothing to say. At last, they went on, Thomas' good temper somewhat restored by the victuals. Ralph was too downcast to pay much attention to the sights of the city, with its many churches. He had forgotten all about Saint Martin.

They continued peacefully through Blois, and beyond. Before they reached Beaugency, Thomas stopped outside a tiny cottage resembling the one where Ralph had spent the night on his way to tours. Here he picked up a large sack, which he placed in the cart. Turning round, Ralph was surprised to see it move. It contained hens which were to be sold in Paris. Discovering this, Ralph was disturbed. He hated feathered fowl of all kinds, especially hens. His parents had kept some in the back yard in Paris, which he had inherited. They fluttered when he tried to catch them, flapped their wings, scratched and even pecked. He wondered whether these would have to be let out for corn and water, when they stopped for the night at Orléans. Would he be obliged to help catch them to return them to the sack? Unfortunately, Thomas seemed to sense his fears and laughed. 'Those will give you something to do tonight,' he threatened.

It was dark when they reached Orléans, and the keeper of the gate was unwilling to let them through, until he was satisfied that they were farming people, and law-abiding. They drove to the hostelry beyond the Cathedral. The city was quiet tonight and the hostelry fairly peaceful. Thomas left Ralph to guard the cart with its livestock while he stabled the horse. Then he returned with a supply of corn and a trough of water. Predictably, the hens scattered as he opened the bag, until they found their fodder. The problem lay in collecting them up when they had finished. Ralph tried to look helpful, but kept missing them through sheer nervousness, as they fluttered past. Thomas became exasperated, but at last the task was over, and they could go to bed. They were hungry, but it was too late to buy any food.

Next morning, Thomas insisted on taking some bread and wine before they left. The weather was clear and bright and Ralph enjoyed another glimpse of the Cathedral de la Croix in the sunshine, and believed that the first tower was higher than when he had last seen it. They drove along happily enough until the crossroads at Étampes appeared at midday. Ralph left the cart and driver, having paid his debt for the ride with scant thanks.

He felt light-hearted now, and the loss of his pack made his steps lighter, too. He sprang along the turfy path through the gorse and bracken, towards the lonely farm in the district of Maisse.

CHAPTER II

Reunion

For the past few mornings, Hélène had been rising even earlier than usual and walking beyond the wall of the farmyard, to the rising ground which gave a view of the path from Étampes. 'You won't make him come any quicker by watching,' her father always said, teasingly, on her return. In any case, she knew Ralph could not be expected before midday.

Today, Friday, was that fixed for his arrival. Mairie had prepared a meal to be taken in the late afternoon. At midday, Hélène made a second expedition to the top of the knoll. She was so excited that she had forgotten to put her cloak or sensible boots on, and tripped lightly in her slippers over the damp grass. She shivered a little as she stood at the top of the little rise in the winter sunshine.

In the far distance, she could make out a tiny square figure moving at great speed, sometimes running. He had no luggage, and his cloak streamed behind him. She ran joyfully downhill, no heavy garments to impede her progress. The other figure waved, increased his speed, and, just as he was within reach, tripped in a rabbit hole and fell full-length.

This was the moment for which he had been longing, and this was the use he had made of it. Hélène picked him up, and held him to her. She was laughing. The laughter shook her, and ran down both her arms into his. It was infectious. They stood in a tight embrace, shaking with a mixture of laughter and tears. At last they moved on, and, leaning on Hélène's arm, Ralph tried to walk. It was agony. He had sprained his ankle badly. With her help, he limped towards the farmhouse. 'What a sight I must look,' he thought. He had wanted so very much to impress Hélène and her parents with his neat appearance, his well-made boots, and his Masterpiece.

But it did not matter at all. Mairie and Henri Fourneau simply hugged him tightly, and laughed, too. Henri found a stick for him to lean on. 'How will you manage in Church on Tuesday?' he asked Ralph. 'When you lead your bride out, will you have one hand for her and the other on your stick?'

'No,' retorted Ralph firmly. 'I had sufficient courage to make my way to Chinon under great difficulties, to make my Masterpiece, and to make some money. I shall have enough courage to walk upright on my feet from Church, even if I have to bite my lips in agony.'

'Well said, well said,' exclaimed the farmer. 'That is the Monsieur le Boeuf I remember, the man to whom I gave consent to marry my daughter. But where is your Masterpiece?'

Poor Ralph. As soon as he recovered from one misfortune, life seemed to provide another, or the reminder of another. He told the story of the attack they had suffered, just before they reached Tours.

After that, they all needed food, and settled down at the long table with the open fire at Ralph's back. Mairie and Hélène served, and then sat with them. As it was a special evening, Mairie had prepared a stew of chicken and turnips with hunks of brown bread, washed down with ale.

When they had eaten, Ralph dozed off on the settle in the firelight, but Henri had livestock to feed and bed down for the night, including hens. When he came back, they all started talking. There were so many plans to make, and the arrangements for the wedding to explain to Ralph. As they went through the words of the service together, Henri asked suddenly. 'How is it that you were named Ralph? It comes from Northern stock, rather than French. It sounds like the Vikings.'

'So it is,' answered Ralph. 'My father explained the reason to me.' Turning to Hélène, he said, 'And we must hand it on to our children. If we have sons, the first must be called Ralph. Hundreds of years ago the Vikings, terrifying and wild raiders they were, sailed up the Seine in their frightening longboats. It is said that my ancestor was rowing in a very big one, with an especially horrifying figurehead. This was a serpent with teeth! Imagine such a sight. Ralph, as he was called, was tired of rowing. It was hard work and he was getting little out of it as the larger men seized most of the spoils when they landed before he could grab any. As they rowed up the Seine, it was high water and the boat was near the bank. So he let go of his oar – this was a very selfish and dangerous thing to do – and leapt ashore. No one could leave the boat immediately to chase him, so he ran and hid in a cottage beside the river. This was held by a French peasant, a farmer and his wife. They had many children, including a most beautiful daughter of marriageable age. She was impressed by Ralph's courage and spirits, and hid him in a barn until the danger of being captured by the Vikings and taken back to the ship was over. She was already promised to a fellow countryman, another peasant, but she much preferred the small, fair stranger, and they married secretly, with the help of one of her friends. When her parents discovered this, it was too late to prevent it. Ralph, who as you can tell was rather wild, frightened some poor old people into giving him part of their land, and settled down to farm. He had learnt something about growing crops in Norway, before he took part in the raids. But he was too impatient to stay on the farm for long, and began to make tools of iron on an anvil, for sale. And so he became a blacksmith and their sons became shopkeepers later. Ralph was a free man and no one could force him to be otherwise, so the family remained free and set up in a shop near Paris. Then we moved nearer the centre of the city, inside the walls, and made tools and shoes. And that is why I am called Ralph!'

'How did you get the rest of your name?' asked Hélène. 'As I am going to be Madame le Boeuf I should like to know how your family gained it.'

Ralph stretched out in pride. Ouch! His ankle gave him a sharp shout of pain. He had almost forgotten it until that moment. Hélène was concerned at once. She got up to fetch a bowl of water, and a cloth to bandage it. Ralph relaxed happily while she bathed it, and explained, 'There are two possible explanations for our name. One is that our ancestor, Ralph, was called after the animals which he tended for a time. The other is that he was so strong and muscular that he was likened to a bull. I like the second suggestion better.'

'So do I,' said Hélène. 'Is your ankle feeling less painful now?' Ralph admitted that it was, rather reluctantly. He had been enjoying her attentions.

'That's good,' broke in Henri Fourneau, 'because I want your help to set up the spit for the wedding feast. It is stored in the barn, and hasn't been used since our second daughter, Matilde's, wedding.'

'We are having a roast piglet,' explained Mairie, 'because there will be so many of us.' Ralph asked her how many. 'Well,' she went on, 'Matilde and her husband, François and their little girl Rosemairie, who is only two years old, will come from their farm near Melun, in their cart. Fortunately it is larger than most people's. They will pick up our eldest daughter Henriette, with her two little girls, Chantelle and Mignon, who will be Hélène's bridesmaids. Henriette's husband must stay at home to mind his farm. On the day after the wedding – you will spend the wedding night here – François will drive you both to Paris, to your own house.'

Ralph was very moved by all the trouble they were taking, and most grateful. He had been worrying about the arrangements, as it was usual for the groom to take his bride home on the wedding night, and clearly that was not possible. He was still puzzling over further problems when Mairie continued, 'I'm giving Hélène that oak chest over there, as a wedding present. It contains her sheets, and the rest of her trousseau, including the large bale of white cotton you gave her. Do you remember?' Ralph did and was pleased. 'François will take it and the other things in the cart. The chest is too heavy to be stolen on the way! Then, he will stay the night with you in Paris and return the next day to collect Matilde and Rosemairie. They will be nice company for me while Henri is away, driving Henriette and her daughters home.'

Henri then broke in to tell Ralph that on Sunday after Mass, their parish priest was expecting him to stay with him in the priest's house until the wedding on Tuesday. That would give Hélène a further time for quiet preparation with her mother.

'We have done a great deal already,' explained Hélène to Ralph. 'As Papa mentioned, many people will be here for the wedding feast, our friends from neighbouring farms, as well as the family. We have made a huge cake, stuffed with dried fruits, which Mama preserves every year, and marchpains of ground almonds mixed with honey. The piglet has been scalded and prepared for roasting. The stuffing is like that we made for Matilde's wedding, which everyone enjoyed so much. It was delicious. We make it from the yolks of eggs, boiled sweet chestnuts, cooked cheese and plenty of ginger.'

The intricacies of the stuffings of pigs was beyond Ralph's comprehension. He gave a loud and unconcealed yawn. 'Time for bed!' pronounced Henri Fourneau.

CHAPTER III

The Wedding

'Bonjour grandmère, bonjour grandpère, bonjour ma tante. Où est ton fiancé?' shouted Chantelle and Mignon as they jumped out of François and Matilde's cart in the misty sunshine of a mid-November morning. They turned to help their little cousin, Rosemairie, who echoed 'Où est ton fiancé?' They were brimming over with curiosity to see him.

'He is undoubtedly in church, by now, waiting for all of us,' replied Henri. 'So hurry up and get ready, and don't keep us waiting.' François carried the small wooden box, containing their bridesmaid's dresses, into the farmhouse. Henriette and Matilde followed. 'Tante Hélène, Tante Hélène,' they called. Hélène was too busy in the bedroom to reply. Mairie helped Chantelle and Mignon into their white silk dresses. These had been worn by their mother, Henriette and their Aunt Matilde at three family weddings and by countless aunties who had acted as bridesmaids in previous generations. They had been taken up, let down, let in and out to fit their various wearers at different times, and remained greatly treasured possessions. To stand still with so much excitement inside them was almost impossible. They envied little Rosemairie her freedom. She was too young to be a bridesmaid.

Hélène stood in the doorway of the bedroom. They gasped. She had not yet put on her veil, and her dark shoulder-length hair flowed strikingly over her shoulders and shone in the winter sun. She wore a long dress of green silk covered with golden thread, on which hung myriads of tiny coloured beads. When she moved the light reflected in them like countless rainbows. It had once been worn by a previous Lady de Villaincourt, on the occasion of her marriage to Lord Ranulf's grandfather. She had given it as a wedding present to Hélène's grandmother, and so it had passed into the Fourneau family.

The marriage service had been arranged to take place at midday. All the family set out to walk to church. Hélène's sisters had fixed her veil in place, but she was forced to draw it back from her face until they arrived. The bridesmaids knew they were to walk before her into church, and hurried to keep in front, lest they should miss this important ceremony. As they drew near the small Norman church, Henri smiled down at Hélène and took her arm.

From behind came a sudden thud of mighty hooves, and two horsemen caught up with the little party. François stretched out long, protecting arms towards the little girls. Matilde screamed. Brandishing a sword, the taller horseman dismounted, and tossing the reins to his follower, made as if he would wrench Hélène away from her father.

'I have come to exercise my "droit de seigneur",' exclaimed a well-known voice, and Ranulf de Villaincourt courteously offered his arm to Hélène. She recovered her shattered wits in time to place her own hand graciously upon it, as Ranulf, sheathing his sword, led her into the church porch, shooing the little bridesmaids to the front of the party.

Inside stood the priest and Ralph, standing upright in spite of his injury. A small boy held a book on which Ralph had placed the ring. On one side of it lay ten gold livres as his endowment to Hélène, and on the other, ten sous as a gift to the poor. Friends and neighbours were standing waiting as the family entered behind Hélène and Lord Ranulf. Henri Forneau moved to one side, naturally somewhat put out by the recent disturbance.

When he came to the words 'with all my worldly goods, I thee endow', Ralph could not resist a wry smile. What had he to offer Hélène? There could not be much furniture awaiting them in the little house in Paris. Not even a spinning wheel.

They all returned to the farm, where a good friend was turning the spit, and basting the piglet. The priest came too, and Lord Ranulf, while his man tied up their horses to wait during a brief visit. The men sat down to eat. Space at table was limited, so their wives stood behind them and the children raced round, too excited to sit still anyway. Ralph and Hélène sat together in the centre of one side of the table. Lord Ranulf pronounced the piglet excellent and, having washed it down with ale, stood up to leave, rather to everyone's relief. 'You're a lucky man,' he said to Ralph. 'Among many excellent qualities, your wife has beautiful little hands. Can she spin?' He was gone before Ralph could reply. The merriment then really began. They all ate as much as they could, then moved away the table and began to dance, singing as they did so. At last, as darkness fell and the fire grew dim, they lit torches from the embers, and held them high over the heads of the newly-married couple. Still singing, the guests escorted them to the bedroom. At the door, the priest blessed them both. Then Mairie insisted that they left her daughter and son-in-law in peace, and firmly closed the door. In turn all the guests, except the immediate family, left the farmhouse carrying lighted torches, still singing as they went.

Hélène brushed her flowing hair. Tomorrow she would plait it, and braid it over her head, as a sign that she was now a married woman. She folded the wedding dress carefully. It would be packed away in a chest until needed again, doubtless by Chantelle, Mignon and Rosemairie in turn.

It had been a wonderful day, thought Ralph. Tomorrow we go home, and then I must settle down to work in earnest. I shall have to make many pairs of well-fitting boots to keep such a lovely wife. He wished he had his Masterpiece to show her.

The children and François settled down in the barn for the night. As Henri came in to turn out the hens, and to make sure that the place was reasonably comfortable for them, he discovered a spinning wheel in a corner. Attached to it with pink ribbon, was a tiny scroll of parchment. As he unfolded it, Henri saw HÉLÈNE. Then there was a message which he could not read, but he could make out the initials of the signature: R de V.

CHAPTER IV

Paris Again

Mairie waited until François had negotiated the cart out of the farmyard, then she put her head on Henri Fourneau's shoulder and cried. She understood that Hélène and Ralph would only be half a day's journey away in Paris, but she realised that it would not be possible to visit them often. What worried her more was that Hélène was going into a completely strange society and into a house she had never seen, perhaps with little furniture. It might, or might not, be worthy of her. She was leaving affectionate parents and all her home comforts to marry Ralph. She was a very brave girl.

Ralph and Hélène sat in the cart on the oak chest and hugged each other, both out of affection and the need to keep warm. The spinning wheel was behind them, together with various pots and pans and cooking utensils which Mairie had known Hélène would need. François, on the driver's seat, looked straight ahead. Considering her unusually heavy load, his mare was doing well. She clip-clopped happily enough to Melun and then through the forest towards Paris. The oaks had not yet shed all their leaves and, with the pines, darkened the way. Ralph pointed out to Hélène the Priory, standing in the distance on the high ground, where he had spent his first night out of Paris. 'I didn't even know then that I was going to meet you,' he whispered.

'Wheeee! Their peace was rudely shattered. Two young men on fierce black horses overtook them, shouting and whistling to attract attention. François angrily soothed his mare, and pulled over to one side. The horsemen rode ahead, and then turned back. As they approached the second time, they shouted 'Catch!' and each hurled a leather wine bottle filled and heavy, into the laps of the two travellers. Then back they came, and repeated the exercise, twice. Their saddle bags had been filled with wine bottles. 'Vive Monsieur le Comte, vive le Comte Ranulf,' they shouted, as they rode off into the gloom of the forest.

Hélène and Ralph were too frightened at first to be pleased. Then they calmed down and their sense of humour returned. François was not so easily pacified. His mare had had a nasty fright. It is easy to be generous if one is rich and carefree!

About midday, they entered the city gates, and Ralph directed François to the Bootmaker's Street. He was wondering what they would find. 'There may not even be a bed for us.' he explained to Hélène. 'Can you face a blanket on a heap of hay?' Hélène nodded, but privately hoped this would not be necessary.

Soon they entered their street, at the end where the poorer houses stood. There seemed to be hundreds of people around. Ralph quickly picked out two of Claude d'Honnête's children, and many of those who had jeered at him round the bonfire on that cold January night. Now their tune was different. News of his success in becoming a Master had reached them. 'Bonjour, Monsieur le Boeuf,' they called.

'Bonjour, Madame le Boeuf.'

'Le voyageur est retourné, avec sa femme.' They cheered and laughed and cheered again. Hélène was a little taken aback by the noise and crowd, after her quiet life in the country, but allowed Ralph to help her out of the cart. The children encircled the newly-wedded couple just outside their own doorway, so that they could hardly see their home. Then a number of little girls appeared, and offered Hélène small bunches of winter-flowering cherry. This was blossoming so early that it was almost out of season, but Hélène made a pretty picture as she held it in her arms, standing in her everyday dress and winter cloak. The children joined hands and skipped round Hélène and Ralph, singing as they did so, 'Enchanté, Madame la grande, bienvenue à vous.' The ring they were making symbolised matrimony, eternity and fidelity, as the watching grownups knew. At length, Ralph realised what he must do. He picked up Hélène in his arms, broke through the ring towards his front door, and carried her over the steps.

Home again! This was his own house, recognisable in spite of the fire and rebuilding. The Guild members had spared no effort or expense. There was the shop counter, and the living room beyond, with its open fireplace and the back door leading into the yard. A simple wooden stair led not to one bedroom, as before, but to two! This was luxury indeed. And what a spread waited for them, on the long trestle table. Beside it stood Catherine d'Albert, clearly the organiser of the feast. Behind her, Claude d'Honnête looked after the pots on the fire.

Seeing Ralph's arrival, she immediately left her task. As he sat Hélène down, Claude simply put her arms around her, and kissed her. Catherine d'Albert followed and offered her embrace, followed by her husband, Charles, who had just arrived. He was accompanied by his son, Charles the Glover, who had left his work for the afternoon to attend the feast.

Catherine d'Albert seated Ralph and Hélène on wooden chairs in the centre of the trestle table, facing the fire. François, who had just managed to unharness his mare and tie her up to an iron bracket, was trying to carry in the spinning wheel, while two stalwarts lifted the oak chest up the staircase. The children brought in the pots and pans, and placed them in the chimney corner, getting under everyone's feet in the process.

The feast was magnificent, reflecting the influence of Parisian pastry cooks and the d'Albert's cooking! Pies and sweetmeats covered the table. Little pastry cases were filled with chopped meat, or cheese, or savoury sauce. Dishes of jelly contained eels, or chicken, or other delicacies to please the hungry, while an assortment of sweets, marchpains, dried fruits and biscuits tempted the more fastidious. Catherine d'Albert had worked tirelessly, borrowing sufficient platters and pewter mugs for the feast.

In front of Ralph was a beautiful silver dish. On it stood a small pair of men's boots, beautifully stitched, but somewhat stained. He could not believe his eyes. His Masterpiece! Charles d'Albert, who had been waiting for this moment, leaned across the table, putting his hand on Ralph's. 'Not now, my boy, later on,' he whispered. Everyone helped themselves to the food and ale. Ralph was wondering when to bring in the wine bottles from the cart, but unruly sounds from the street informed him that those who had not been able to squeeze into his house had discovered them.

Ralph's standing among his neighbours was higher now than it had ever been. The young men called to him to tell the story of his adventures. 'What kind of city is Chinon?'

'Did you get lost among the maze of streets in Orléans?'

'Which was your worst moment during the journey?'

'Which was your best?'

Ralph was unable to deal with these all at once.

'You must all come again, in turn,' he said, 'and we will tell stories by the fire.'

Seeing the alarm on Hélène's face, Charles d'Albert rose, cup in hand: 'We are here for two reasons: first to celebrate Ralph's marriage to Hélène, and secondly to welcome him as a full member and Master in our Guild, now that he has completed his Masterpiece. Let us drink to his happiness and success in the future!'

As they all rose to this toast, Claude moved nearer to Hélène, and whispered, 'Do not worry about where you are to sleep. Henri and his friends have made you a most beautiful bed as a wedding present.'

Hélène, who was near to tears with excitement and tiredness, could only grasp her hand.

Ralph realised with a pang of disappointment, as he looked round the gathering, that there was no priest to bless their first night in their own house. The person he most longed to see was not there. Perhaps sensing something of what he was feeling, Charles d'Albert went on, 'The marriage of Ralph and Hélène was blessed last night, so tonight we shall leave them here like an old married couple. Now, you lively ones, off you go. Time for home and bed.' Reluctantly, the neighbours drifted out. Claude was the last to go. 'I'll be here to help you clear up in the morning,' she said.

CHAPTER V

Catching Up

The poor mare had to stay tethered in the street all night. Early next morning, François fed and watered her and harnessed her ready for his return journey. He left as Claude reappeared.

There was a great deal of clearing up to be done. Many of the cups and bowls and knives in use the previous evening belonged to the d'Alberts or their friends. They had to be washed carefully, and put on one side for Charles to collect. Then the rushes had to be swept out, the flagstone floor washed and scrubbed, and fresh rushes laid. Hélène was grateful that the new floor was not merely of mud. That would have been much more difficult to clean. The fellow members of the Guild had been generous in every way.

When they sat down to break their fast with the remains of the feast, Ralph ventured to ask Claude about Père Jean-Pierre. He was longing for him to greet Hélène, but had looked in vain for him at the homecoming celebrations. 'I did not send you news of him,' apologised Claude, 'because I knew how fond you were of each other, and I did not want you to feel hurt while you were away from home. We all miss him dreadfully. He died last summer. It seems that he became very overheated during the warm weather, mainly through overwork. Then he caught cold, and a chill developed which proved fatal in a few days.' Ralph was horrified. He could not take this in for several minutes. Seeing that Ralph was still distressed, she hurried on, in the hope of cheering him, 'You will like the new priest. He is a very different kind of person, so do not attempt to compare them.'

'You mean he is younger?' asked Ralph.

'Not only that,' she replied, 'he came from Italy originally, I mean he is an Italian, not only trained in Rome. Before he came to our church, St

Michael's, he was assisting the Curé at the Church of St Denis, to the north of the city.'

'Surely that is a wealthy area,' suggested Ralph, 'very different from ours.'

'That is so,' replied Claude. 'And he is well-born, the younger son of a nobleman. Nevertheless, he loves people like us. He is forever talking to us, and visiting us, and playing with the children. Paul and Kate love him,' she added, turning to include Hélène.

'Who are Paul and Kate?' asked Hélène. 'Oh, I remember now, your two eldest. I saw them both last night.'

'You could not forget them, the wicked ones,' said Claude, with a little laugh. 'But Père Simon loves them just as they are, mischievous or not.'

'We must go to church soon, and meet Père Simon, mustn't we, Ralph?' Hélène asked her husband.

'Certainly I should like to go to Vespers on Saturday, as I always have done,' he replied.

They began to unpack the oak chest after Claude had left. Hélène looked forward to showing her its contents next time she looked in. She took out the bale of white cotton which Ralph had bought for her from the pedlar. 'All the way from Egypt,' she exclaimed. 'I must plan very carefully the best way to use it.'

They had barely finished when they had another caller. It was Charles d'Albert. Exerting herself for the first time as mistress of the household, Hélène asked him to share their simple meal, the main one of the day. He consented, and she busied herself getting it ready. The small pair of boots still lay in the middle of the table, on Catherine d'Albert's silver dish. Noticing that Charles d'Albert was looking at them, Ralph remarked, 'You haven't yet told me how these came to be returned to me. You know, don't you, that they were stolen with the rest of my possessions before we reached Tours? Please tell me the story. You promised to do so last night.'

Charles slowly took a pull on the cup of ale Hélène had set beside him. He smiled. 'Well,' he said. 'Well. Don't forget that almost nothing passes un-noticed in this world. Never try to have secrets: you won't succeed.' Ralph knew that if he showed any signs of impatience, he would have to wait longer.

'Please go on,' said Hélène.

'When you reached Tours,' continued Charles, 'you went into a hostelry, for a bite and a drink, and you talked, or rather Thomas talked, to all the other fellows there, because he was so angry. They listened and went on discussing it after you had left. The keeper of the hostelry heard it all. Then three pilgrims arrived, noblemen who had walked all the way from Compostella. They were returning from a visit on foot to the Shrine of St James, to expiate their sins.'

'Where is Compostella?' asked Hélène.

'It is in Spain,' replied Charles. 'After St James had been beheaded in Jerusalem, his remains were removed there, and he has become the patron saint of the Spaniards. These three noblemen were wearing badges of scallop shells in their caps to prove that they had reached Compostella. They were hurrying to reach Tours in time for the Festival of St Martin on November the eleventh, but were having difficulties because one of them was suffering badly from blistered feet. As they sat by the wayside for a moment's rest, one of them noticed a boot lying under a thorn bush. He got up to investigate and found the other one. Someone had thrown down a pair of boots. There was nothing else lying around. Why this had happened they couldn't guess. The boots were rather small, but too well-made to abandon. So they carried them with them to Tours and began to make inquiries at the hostelry where they stayed. The keeper, who had heard Thomas' story, immediately understood the situation, and together they planned to restore the boots to their owner.'

'Didn't they want to keep them?' asked Ralph. 'Were they too small to be of any use?' He was feeling a little hurt.

'They were too honest,' answered Charles. 'And anyway, they were noblemen. They would have scorned to steal.'

Hélène felt sympathy for her husband. 'How did the boots reach Paris?' she asked.

'Two travellers on horseback were going on,' said Charles, 'and being intelligent, they realised that the boots had been made by a member of the Guild of Bootmakers. Therefore, when they reached Paris, they made for our street and asked for the Senior Master. That is how they came to me!' Hélène was impressed and proud of her husband, because he belonged to such a worthy Guild and was a Master in it.

'I have something to return to you, before you leave us,' said Ralph, 'as well as all the utensils you so kindly lent us.' He produced the pewter cup which Catherine had packed for him when he set out. It had been with him all through his travels. Charles accepted it silently, with a knowing smile.

* * * * * * * * * *

Hélène clung tightly to her husband on Saturday evening as they set out for Vespers. It was her first excursion into Paris, and cities were strange to her.

Once they had arrived at the church, she felt happier. The familiar words of the Latin service were comforting.

Afterwards, Père Simon greeted them both. He had heard about Ralph and was curious to meet Hélène. In his habitually friendly fashion, he put his hand through Ralph's arm, and walked back with them through the streets.

'I want to hear about your travels,' he said. 'I, too, have moved about often, through different parts of Christendom. My home is in Florence, I was trained to be a priest in Rome, and then I came to the Church of St Denis in Paris, to help the parish priest there.'

'Isn't that a very fine place?' asked Ralph.

'Yes, it is,' replied the young priest. 'There is a great gold cross there, twenty-four feet high, and covered with jewels. It was made by Godfroix de Claire. That is only one of their treasures. Members of the royal family are always buried there, and the monuments over their tombs are very splendid, but we are expecting the good King Louis to replace them with simpler ones.

'But tell me about your adventures. Where did you spend your first night after leaving the d'Alberts? You must have felt very cold and lonely.'

'I was,' agreed Ralph, pleased to have found so sympathetic a listener. 'Charles d'Albert had advised me to stop at the Priory near Melun. It was a bit frightening, because I had never stayed at a monastery before. We had to wash often, because, the guestmaster said, the monks were following the reforms of Cluny.'

'Who is Cluny?' asked Hélène.

'It is a place,' said Père Simon, 'where some monks decided that the rules of St Benedict were not being well kept in most of the monasteries, and they set an example in theirs by adopting better discipline.'

'I know about the vows and work of the monks,' said Ralph, who loved stories, 'but I don't know much about St Benedict himself. Please tell us something.'

'He was a member of a wealthy family, who lived at Nursia, near Rome,' said the priest. 'He and his sister Scholastica had all they wanted in life and were well taught.' Hélène gave a little giggle at the name. Ralph gave her a warning look. Père Simon went on, 'There are two different accounts of Benedict. One chronicler tells us that, when he was a small boy, he ran away from his nurse, and joined a hermit in the hills near Rome. This was a very saintly man, who lived extremely frugally. He had an earthenware jar beside him containing pieces of bread which travellers had given him. The neck of the jar was so narrow that only the hand of a thin man could enter it. The hermit allowed

76

himself only as much bread as he could grasp in one handful for one meal. Benedict was attracted so greatly by this loveable character that he asked if he could stay with him. His family found him after a few days, of course, and brought him home.'

'And the other story?' asked Hélène.

'It goes this way,' continued the priest. 'When Benedict grew up, he was looked after by a housekeeper, his old nurse, who was a rather domineering kind of person. He grew tired of her ways and joined some hermits in caves in the hills to escape from her. The simplicity of their life appealed to him after his own luxurious upbringing. He was very happy with them. Then his friends discovered where he was, and asked if they could share his life. In order that they could live happily together in a community, worship God and keep healthy, he made the rules which form the basis of life in monasteries today.'

Ralph was storing all these anecdotes and accounts in the hope of retelling them one day. He would have liked to have heard more, but by now they had reached their own street. As they approached the house, Père Simon put his hands on their shoulders, and blessed them both. 'I have enjoyed our time together,' he said. 'We must talk again soon. I want to hear more of your adventures, especially how you came to the farm where Hélène lived. Meanwhile, Monsieur le Boeuf, why don't you take Madame for a walk one sunny winter's day, and go to see the Church of St Denis. It has some wonderful treasures, and you should see the monuments over the Royal tombs before the King commands that they shall be changed.'

Ralph thought for a moment. 'I'd rather stay at home,' he said.

CHAPTER VI

A Birth

Ralph's and Hélène's first son was born on St. Matthew's Day, 21st September, 1257 and given the names of Ralph Matthieu at his baptism a fortnight later. Père Simon performed the ceremony at St. Michael's Church and Hélène's parents came for the occasion. It was the first time they had visited their daughter since her marriage, and they were obviously very happy at the way Ralph and Hélène had arranged their little home.

The godparents were their very good neighbour Claude d'Honnête, Charles d'Albert and Christophe le Grand, a young man from further along the street. Ralph had found it much easier to make friends since his return, partly due to his wife's happy disposition, and party because he had gained respect by becoming a Master. His contemporaries, like Christophe, who had stood aloof from him previously, even if they had not actually jeered at him, were now pleased to be counted among his friends.

After all the excitement was over, and the grandparents and godparents had left, Hélène sat with Matthieu on her knee, facing Ralph across the fireplace. She had removed her son's elaborate christening robe, which was a family heirloom, and sent it back with her mother to be stored in the farmhouse, ready for the next new arrival. Although it was a fairly warm evening, the fire was burning steadily. It was needed for cooking, and for heating the baby's bath water. On a niche in the chimney corner stood the pewter cup which had accompanied Ralph all through his travels. Charles d'Albert had insisted on making a christening present of it and it was engraved with Ralph Matthieu's names. Less than two years ago, Ralph would never have believed that life could be so rewarding. As he was trying to express this in words to Hélène, there was a knock on the door. He opened it to let in the lively lad from next door, Paul d'Honnête. As usual, Paul was brimming over with high spirits, and came straight to the point. 'Mother says it's time I learnt how to do some real hard work', he confided, 'now that I am almost sixteen.' Ralph's heart sank; the peace and quiet of home was so very lovely, with just the three of them, and he did not want it spoiled by anybody. He could guess the meaning behind the message; it would be hard to refuse Claude anything, after her continual kindness. Not only had she been a generous neighbour to him, when he had lived alone, but her husband had helped to rebuild his house, she had welcomed him home and had been with Hélène during the birth of their child.

'I thought your father was going to teach you to make boots and shoes,' Ralph said, to gain a little time. 'Most apprentices in our craft learn from their fathers.'

'Not always,' replied Paul. 'What is your bed under the counter like? Oh, it's bigger than ours. Father says I upset Kate and the two little ones. They're so silly: they cry if I laugh at them, and sulk if I leave them alone. So we have to be parted! I'll help you bring up Matthieu,' he said turning to Hélène.

'You certainly will not,' she retorted, with unaccustomed sharpness, which surprised her husband. 'If you come to live with us, you will work hard all the daylight hours, every day except on Holy Days, and do as you are told.'

Ralph was grateful to her. 'Come back tomorrow, when we have talked it over,' he said. The door slammed, both top and bottom. The latches crashed as they closed and Paul was gone.

'We cannot refuse him, you know,' said Hélène.

'I know,' replied Ralph. 'Fortunately the work has increased so much that I can use another pair of hands. And I suppose he will bring the customary sum of money with him.'

'We cannot insist if he does not,' Hélène remarked. 'And the d'Honnêtes cannot have much money to spare. They have always been most generous to us.' The thought of the continual presence of a noisy, if cheerful, young man disturbed Ralph more than that of another mouth to feed. He would be there for seven years! He must be encouraged to visit home often, especially after dark. By now, Hélène had accepted the inevitable. To be sure, Ralph had almost more work than he could cope with. His fellow members of the Guild had been very kind in transferring some of their custom to him. She had been lending a hand with cutting out. This was strictly forbidden, of course. Now she would not have time to do so, and with luck, Paul might have inherited the knack from his father.

A BIRTH

So next morning, they told him he could start, much to his parents' delight.

* * * * * * * * * *

The next three years passed happily. Paul settled down and proved useful, sometimes working quite hard. They discovered that he was a great storyteller, and he and Ralph vied with each other in the evenings over which of them could tell the best tale. Paul's stories were amusing and exciting, but Hélène listened to them carefully, ready to call a halt at any point if they seemed frightening to little Matthieu.

On one October evening, as they sat round the fire, Paul launched into the story of St Denis, the patron saint of France. Hélène did not know this legend, but became alarmed when Paul described his death. 'He was executed,' he said, 'and then he simply put his head under his arm, and went on walking until he reached the place where the Abbey of St Denis now stands. All the angels followed him.'

'That will do, Paul,' interrupted Hélène. 'That is not a suitable bedtime story for a little boy.' She glanced anxiously at Matthieu, who was sitting on her knee, drinking warm milk from his pewter christening cup.

Paul was not easily subdued. 'Père Simon says we should tell the children the stories of the saints,' he defended himself. 'It is good for them to know about the lives of the good people who went before us, and suffered, if necessary, for their faith.'

Fortunately, Matthieu seemed quite unmoved by all this. As yet, he was too young to understand. 'I know a better story,' interrupted Ralph. 'It is about St Benedict, when he was a little boy. Do you know that once he ran away from his nurse? Wasn't that a naughty thing to do?' He went on to tell all he knew about St Benedict, and his monks. Hélène felt that all this was not much better; the work and the vows of the monks were above their little son's head anyway. Fortunately, he looked as if he were about to fall asleep. Paul visited his family for the next few evenings, to Hélène's relief.

It was pleasant to have Christophe to themselves, when he came in one evening to see his little godson. They were chatting happily round the fire, when the door burst open, and Paul charged in, breathless with laughter. His younger brother Jean, armed with a pair of blacksmith's tongs was pursuing him closely. 'I'll have you by the nose, Paul, I'll have you!' shouted Jean.

'Steady on. What's all this about?' asked Ralph in some alarm. Before they could discover, Matthieu had slipped off his stool, and was joining in the chase.

81

Round and round the table they went, until all three boys collapsed on the floor, still squealing with delight.

'Whatever is the matter?' asked Hélène. 'Come on, Jean, you tell us. You seem to be making the most noise.'

'I was trying to catch Paul by the nose,' replied Jean, as soon as he had enough breath, 'with these tongs.'

'But why?' asked Hélène.

'Because he had been very naughty, and pulled my hair, and teased me in lots of ways. So I tried to be like St Dunstan.'

'St Dunstan!' echoed Ralph and Hélène. 'What has he to do with it?'

'Don't you know?' asked Jean, showing off now. 'Why, he chased the Devil with a huge pair of tongs to catch him by the nose, to punish him.'

'Both of you are being very naughty,' interrupted Christophe, thoroughly alarmed by the proceedings. 'Jean, your brother cannot be compared with the Devil! Say you are sorry, at once. But don't pull his hair, or be unkind to Jean ever again, Paul. You are too old now for this kind of behaviour. You are an apprentice, and almost grown up. And, above all, don't come in here, disturbing this household, and putting unkind thoughts into the head of my little godson.'

'I'm sorry,' both boys said together, but Paul was still full of mischief.

'Jean,' he called, 'if you chase me like that again, you will grow a tail!'

'Whatever do you mean?' asked Christophe.

'There's a story,' said Paul, with a wicked twinkle in his eye, 'an English one, so it may not be strictly true, about a village where the people were cruel to a good man, called St Austin. They drove him out, and after that they grew tails like fishes until they repented. I can see one coming,' he called to Jean, ready to start another romp. At that, Matthieu jumped up again, and began to run around in dizzy circles to see if he were growing a tail.

'That's enough now,' cried Ralph. The boys knew that he did not often speak sharply, but when he did so, he meant it. Activities were suspended, but the peace of the evening had been broken, and Hélène had difficulty in settling Matthieu to sleep.

CHAPTER VII

An Adventure

One sunny afternoon in November Hélène decided to take Matthieu for a walk. It was stuffy in the little house, and being a country girl, she longed to get out. 'We're going to the end of the street,' she called to Ralph.

'Don't be long, and don't go far,' he replied. They were approaching their fourth wedding anniversary, and the happy memory of it made him all the more unwilling to let her out of his sight. The fact that the number of orders for boots had decreased somewhat of late made him rather more anxious than usual.

Hélène and Matthieu skipped along merrily, on the firm mud of the street, until they reached the end where the houses and gardens became larger, and a litter of crisp chestnut leaves crunched under their feet. Matthieu began to look for the shiny brown round fruit, which Hélène had to dissuade him from eating. Before they knew it, they had crossed over into a road which was paved, a sign of greater prosperity. In the distance, they could see a beggar at the next corner. He had only one leg, or so it seemed. Hélène was convinced that the other was tied up behind him, to evoke pity. As they drew nearer, another beggar appeared, also unkempt and filthy, his clothes in rags. He was about to release the bound leg of the first when he saw Hélène approaching, and hesitated. So did she. She did not want Matthieu to be frightened by them, and stopped, still staring at the couple. When she bent down to look at Matthieu, she realised he had slipped out of her hand, and was gone.

Terror seized her. He had not gone towards the two beggars, therefore he must have gone back. And there were the crossroads, and three possibilities. That to the right led towards the river. She hastened along it. The sun was going down now, and it was becoming misty. There was no sign of any small child alone. A group of mothers and children came in her direction. Agitatedly, she asked them. They had seen no one resembling Matthieu; she hurried on, too anxious to reply to their expressions of concern. The road opened out towards the path beside the river. Should she go right or left? She chose left, and then, after scurrying along it for a few moments, changed her mind, and turned. She ran past the original turning and was now almost lost herself.

Panic was threatening to take over when a youthful, upright and vigorous figure, faintly familiar, emerged out of the gathering gloom. It was Charles d'Albert's elder son, Charles the Glover. 'What brings you here, so far from home, and alone?' he asked.

Panting, and full of anxiety and remorse, she managed to gasp out her problem. 'Poor little Matthieu' and 'What will Ralph say?' she choked out between sobs, over and over again. Charles remained cool, calm and collected, a man in command of the situation. Taking her firmly by the elbow, he led her back to the crossroads. 'That is your way home,' he said. 'Go back now, or Ralph will worry that you also are lost. Just explain to him what has happened. I shall find the child and bring him back to you. You say he left you in that road, over there? Small boys often slip off, but, I understand, rarely go far. Off you go home, and leave him to me!'

Hélène, still too upset to speak coherently, and further terrified by the thought of Ralph's possible anger, ran the rest of the way home.

As it was almost dark, Ralph and Paul had stopped work, and were building up the fire for the evening meal.

'Where's Matthieu?' were Ralph's first words, and then, seeing her so very dishevelled, 'What's happened?' She told him. He was very angry.

'I told you not to go too far,' he said. 'What is the matter with our home, that you have to leave it?'

'Oh, Ralph, please, please don't. I'm so distressed,' she sobbed.

For once Paul was silent. Then, 'I'll fetch Mama,' he said.

Claude came at once. 'You may be quite sure that someone will find him,' she said. 'If Charles does not, someone else will. He is a bright little fellow, who knows his own name now, and yours, and what his father does for a living. If your Masterpiece came home to roost, Ralph, surely your son will do so.

'Those beggars! Suppose they find him? That one didn't have only one leg, after all. They could both run after him,' cried Hélène.

'Beggars, which beggars?' asked Ralph, becoming all the more angry and alarmed.

'It's not very likely that they would want Matthieu,' said Claude, in her downright way, 'they have hardly enough to keep themselves, and would not want another mouth to feed. I'll ask Henri to go out and join the search.'

'I'll go too,' volunteered Paul, 'and keep Papa company.'

'You go also, Ralph,' instructed Claude, who was becoming tired of his complaining attitude, 'while I keep Hélène company.'

Henri, Ralph and Paul set out down the street. At the end of it was a tiny figure, holding closely to a tall one, his little red knitted cap showing through the gloom. 'Papa!' it exclaimed, as Charles released the small hand. It was Matthieu.

'Thank you, thank you,' exclaimed Henri to Charles, as Ralph seemed too bewildered to do so. They all escorted Matthieu back to his mother. 'Where were you?' she asked, foolishly, because the child could not know.

'I went to pick up some of those big nuts under the trees, and then you were gone,' he answered.

They hugged and hugged, but Ralph was still angry with her.

'You had nothing else to do, and yet you let Matthieu out of sight,' he shouted, 'in a place where there were beggars, who were probably dangerous. You must have known better!' At this, Charles could remain passive no longer. This was a pretty, capable young wife, being treated unfairly by a man who left all the running of the household, and bringing up of the family, to her. He still thought of Ralph as that lazy oaf who had once lived with his parents. What right had he to so good and beautiful a wife?

'Monsieur le Boeuf,' he started, somewhat heavily. 'Your wife has suffered enough. Don't you know anything about children, not to realise that they slip away undetected at any opportunity? You are most fortunate to have a dear wife, and lovely little boy. Sit down and be thankful for this, and help your wife, who must be exhausted!'

Ralph then turned the full force of his wrath against Charles. 'What right have you to criticise me?' he asked. 'You who are not married and have no children, and lead a very selfish life, and know nothing of anxiety?'

'If I cared only for myself I should not have gone out of my way to find your son, and bring him home. But I see it is no good trying to reason with someone who is too stupid to understand.' And he left. Claude signalled to her husband and Paul to follow, and they went out, leaving Ralph and Hélène alone with Matthieu.

Hélène was still crying, and neither spoke for a long time. She cuddled Matthieu, until Ralph seized him for himself, and ordered her to cook the supper, which he then would not eat. Eventually, Hélène got Matthieu to bed and to sleep, and climbed in supperless herself. She was forbearing enough not to remind Ralph that he had told the story of St Benedict's escape from his nurse, which could have put the idea into their son's head. She did not know that the same thought had occurred to her husband. At last, he arrived in bed beside her, and whispered, 'I think you had better sew some silver bells on Matthieu's cap, don't you?'

'Certainly, if you can find some', replied Hélène.

CHAPTER VIII

To the Fair

Ralph and Hélène's second son was born at the end of August, 1261, and baptised shortly after, with the name of Robert. Sadly, it was not possible for Mairie and Henri Fourneau to come to the christening. Henri had his own corn harvest to reap, as well as his obligation to help with his lord's. Now that he was over fifty he felt much older, and it was more difficult to get the tasks over quickly.

On the first Holy Day after the christening, Ralph sent Paul home, so that they could enjoy some peace and quiet. To their delight, Christophe came in during the evening. They were discussing their recent problem of being short of money, and welcomed his advice. Thanks to Hélène's careful management, they needed to spend out very little, but some food had to be bought in the local market each week. Paul's arrival as an apprentice, almost immediately after the birth of Matthieu, had made additional demands, and now there was another child. Fortunately, Hélène's mother had made very generous loans of baby clothes, which were passed down the family for generation after generation, as well as gifts of cloth and adult clothing, which Hélène was skilful in adapting.

They kept hens in the back yard, in spite of Ralph's dislike of them, and a neighbour's cow supplied them with milk. Hélène baked their bread, visiting the local street market every week to buy flour, meat and vegetables, and candles. Ralph had to buy his own raw materials as well as firewood from visiting pedlars. Sometimes, it was possible to barter his products for these, but on the whole a pair of boots was too valuable to be exchanged for lesser stocks. Together, they explained the situation to Christophe, whom they trusted completely. 'My sales have gone down during the last year,' said Ralph. 'Fewer people are coming to me; I don't know why. They say that France is a prosperous country now. I must find more markets for my boots and shoes.' Hélène did not say what she thought, that when they were first married, the other Masters had been kind, and sent some of their own customers to Ralph, and now they judged that he should be able to stand on his own feet. The trouble was that his boots often did not fit very well. He always had trouble with cutting out, and Paul was too young to be much help in that way.

'You could take some of your best pieces to one of the Fairs,' suggested Christophe. 'If you haven't enough to fill a booth, you could carry them around, as journeymen do. That is, if you didn't mind,' he added, seeing concern on Ralph's face.

'Which Fair are you thinking of?' asked Hélène.

'There is the second Fair at Provins soon, in September, and the so-called ''cold'' Fair at Troyes, in October,' went on Christophe. 'Much trade is done at these places, but unfortunately, they are rather far off. You would need two days to reach Provins on foot, and longer to reach Troyes. A pity! There's so much fun going on there,' he added rather wistfully.

Ralph was not so sure about the fun, and he did not want to leave his wife and family. Moreover, he had had enough travel to last his lifetime. 'I've heard of a Fair at St Denis,' remarked Hélène. 'We never walked over there, as Père Simon suggested, did we?'

'I believe it is less prosperous now,' replied Christophe. 'But it is due to take place soon, at the Festival of St Denis. It's quite a distance, five leagues or so, but I expect you could stay at the Abbey. Père Simon could arrange this, if you wanted it.' Ralph did not like the idea very much, but they needed more customers. Finally, they decided that Ralph would walk over there, on one of the early days of the Fair, with his goods, and take Paul with him to help carry the load. Then he could find out if it were possible to rent the site of a booth for a few days.

'I wonder if you could share one,' suggested Christophe. 'I will make a few inquiries, if you like. Someone else may well be going from this street.'

'Charles d'Albert may know,' suggested Hélène. 'Although I think he may feel too old to sell his goods himself at a Fair. Perhaps Charles the Glover goes with his products.'

'I think that is very doubtful,' said Ralph, somewhat angrily.

He did not like the younger Charles.

'Matthieu would love to go,' sighed Hélène.

'Certainly not, not yet anyway,' replied Ralph, still a little upset. He knew he would have enough to do to keep his eye on Paul.

* * * * * * * * * *

Tumblers were racing each other down the main street of St Denis, in a series of backward somersaults. Jugglers in the square before the Abbey tossed an increasing number of balls into the air, until they dropped them, groping for them among the feet of the crowd amid screams of laughter. Pedlars, carrying their wares on trays, tried to avoid being tripped up. Friars mingled among the people, laughing at their own jokes. Apprentices helped their Masters to erect booths covered with canopies as precaution against an unlikely decline in the weather. Preparations for the Fair of St Denis were being undertaken in beautiful, sunny autumn weather. With luck, it would last from St Denis' Festival on the 9th October, until after St Luke's Day on the 18th. St Luke's 'Little Summer' usually lived up to its name. Ralph and Paul, each carrying a pack on his back containing their best specimens of boots and shoes, arrived in the middle of all this turmoil. Through Père Simon's kind negotiations, they had planned to spend the next night or two at the Abbey. Their first task was to rent a booth before they were all taken. It was already midday on the eve of the opening of the Fair, which the Governor, a local Master of high repute, was to carry out on the following day. Charles d'Albert had instructed Ralph to contact the Governor on arrival. He looked anxiously round but could see no one who appeared to be in authority. At length, he noticed a man who was instructing some of the Masters on the site of their booths and approached him. Disappointment followed. Apparently there were no sites left.

'Don't give up,' whispered Paul, who was just beginning to enjoy himself. 'We'll find a way. We'll look round this evening, and see that other people do. See that pedlar over there? I wonder how he made his tray. If we had one each like that, and walked round, we would soon sell our boots. Then we could go home; that is, after we had enjoyed ourselves,' he added. Ralph did not much care for this idea; it seemed a most undignified way for a Master to behave.

The visit to the monks at the Abbey passed very happily. That evening they both attended Vespers. The rule of silence had been lifted for the Festival of St Denis, and the brothers enjoyed the jokes and robust cheerfulness of Paul. Perhaps he is an asset after all, thought Ralph.

Before he went to bed, Paul held an earnest conversation with the guest master. After this, he disappeared for a long time, in the company of some of the working brothers. When he joined Ralph again, he was triumphantly carrying two trays, with long, brightly-coloured ribbons attached, the result of an hour or two's work in the carpenter's shop. He looked so pleased that Ralph had not the heart to dampen his spirits. Next morning, they set out with their boots and shoes displayed temptingly on the trays, which were handing from their necks. 'Who'll buy? Who'll buy?' called out Paul. Soon one or two gentlemen approached him. Paul took off the boots for them to try them on. He soon realised his mistake. One smooth-tongued, fleet of foot youth made off with a pair. 'Hi,' he shouted. 'Hi!' Ralph, separated from him by the throng, could do nothing to prevent this. Paul started to pursue the thief, scattering boots as he went. 'Stop thief!' called the crowd, while the more honest ones stopped to pick up the boots, to restore them later. The youth was gone, and Paul returned, shamefaced and out of breath to count what remained. He knew he had hurt Ralph, and was sorry.

Worse followed. In his enthusiasm, Paul had not reckoned with the ceremonial opening of the Fair. This happened every year on the first day, after Mass in the Abbey, when a procession of the Governor, the officials and Masters of the various Guilds paraded through the streets. Only after they had passed the booths, left in charge of apprentices, could selling commence. Now an official came up to Paul and put a hand on his shoulder. 'I arrest you, and your Master, for breaking the honoured regulations of the Fair,' a voice said.

'But no, why?' called Ralph.

'Because Masters and their apprentices may not behave like pedlars,' was the reply. 'You must behave like the other Masters, and hire a booth, or go home.' Someone had evidently informed against them. 'You must both appear before the Pieds-Poudrés court when it opens. Meanwhile, I must put you in prison.' He indicated a high stone wall, entered only through an iron grille, at the end of the street.

This was humiliation indeed. To be kept in prison, probably with only bread and water, was bad enough, but to be taken before the Court was much worse. It was not nicknamed Pieds-Poudrés for nothing. The lowest type of men who had travelled to the Fair were tried there, those with no boots or shoes or stockings, whose feet were therefore dusty from walking over country roads and along dirty streets. They were usually accused of mean and trivial crimes, such as cheating their customers or petty pilfering.

The officers pushed Ralph and Paul through the busy street. Although the sympathies of the crowd were clearly with the two who had been so suddenly arrested, the laws of the Fair had to be enforced. Humiliated and bowed, the

Master and his apprentice walked towards the iron grille. Innumerable thoughts passed through Ralph's mind. How could he send the news to Hélène, and what would she think and feel when she heard it? Would they be released on payment of a fine, and would the amount be within his means? If only they had friend nearby! To whom could they turn for help?

The joyous activities of the crowd, assembled in the square to await the beginning of Mass, with all the noise and colour, meant nothing now to Ralph and Paul. But the festivities were not to go undisturbed. A great black horse plunged through the lines of the bystanders. Its rider wore an elaborate surcote, bearing the four quarters of a nobleman's coat of arms. He was hatless, and his long fair hair, with a hint of red in the autumn sunshine, streamed behind him. Some of the crowd gasped with admiration, other with annoyance or pain at being thrust aside.

'Hallo, my friend the wanderer,' called Lord Ranulf de Villaincourt, as he leapt off his horse. 'You, in trouble? There must be some mistake! Let me see.'

One of the officers, angry at this turn of events, shouted back, 'He has disobeyed the regulations of the Fair, and must pay for it!'

'How much must he pay for it?' asked Lord Ranulf, putting his hand into the bag he carried over his shoulder. 'Will this do?' He flung out two silver coins. 'This way,' he called to Ralph and Paul, as he turned his horse. The officers scrambled to pick up the coins. With one hand on the bridle of his horse, he led them back along the street on foot, at a fast pace, and did not stop until they reached the crossroads just outside town. 'Now, tell me,' he said. 'How do you come to be here, and what were they accusing you of?'

'How can I thank you?' cried Ralph, overcome by the suddenness of his release. And he told Lord Ranulf all that had happened, interrupted frequently by Paul.

'Those two villains were probably cheating you,' suggested Lord Ranulf. 'I doubt very much if there are any regulations of the kind you mention. They were most likely hoping you would bribe them to set you free before the court met. Have you got all your possessions? What of the boots which were displayed on your trays?' Sadly, some of these had been lost, or stolen, but Paul had had the presence of mind to hold on to four pairs, and Ralph had some in the pack on his back. Lord Ranulf looked at a pair and laughed. 'Your work has improved greatly,' he said. 'Both feet are the same size! Do you remember the pair you sold me in your shop, several years ago?' Ralph did, only too well. Paul, who had never heard this story, pricked up his ears, but was silenced with a look from the Lord. 'You had best make your way home,' he said. 'It is midday, and you should be in your part of Paris before dark. But I will come with you. I think I may find you a customer or two on the way. My poor horse,' he continued, giving him a pat. 'You would much rather gallop, wouldn't you? But we must go the pace of these two good men for the time being.' And so, wondering what was in store, Ralph and Paul followed him.

CHAPTER IX

At the Palace

In a small room, off a spiral staircase, in King Louis IX's palace in Paris, an old man and a younger one sat playing chess. Needless to say, they were both lords; chess was a game only for the nobility in the 1260's. There was no fireplace in the room, although the sun shone through the glass of the narrow window inset in the deep stone wall. Lord Augustus de Thierry pulled his wide fur collar rather more tightly round his neck. As befitted his rank as a member of one of the old aristocratic families of France, he dressed in robes of the best quality and latest fashion. His long robe reached down to his feet, and wrapped around his shoes to give greater warmth.

His opponent, Lord François de Bohun, was younger by at least twenty years. He was descended from a famous Crusading family, who had served the Christian cause in the first and all ensuing wars against the infidel. However, he appeared more of a courtier than a soldier as he stretched out his long stockinged legs, covered to the knees in the latest fashion of breeches. Over all he wore his surcote, embroidered with ravens, the emblems of the Bohun family. 'Your move,' he said, with a yawn. He was already tired of the game, and longed to exercise his dogs in the lingering autumn sunshine. Lord Augustus put his hand on a pawn, and just as Lord François saw, with relief, the end in sight, he called out 'J'adoube'. He had changed his mind, and did not wish to be tied to his tentative effort. He knew there was no hurry to finish, because the King and Court were away on progress round the district, and the Bishop and most of the clerics had gone with him. Their absence gave Lord Augustus his opportunity to play his favourite game to his heart's content: it was frowned upon to some extent by the Church, and consequently by the King himself, as an uncreative activity.

He picked up a rook, after due thought, and moved that, thereby challenging a pawn of Lord François', which was forced to withdraw. Lord François sighed. He could now let Lord Augustus win, and the game would be over. He only played to appease the older nobleman, and as a means to staying in Paris, rather than taking part in the chilly and somewhat tedious journeys of the King and Court.

'I shall take your Vierge*,' called out Lord François, moving one of his pawns up to the little ivory figure beside the king. Lord Augustus concentrated again. He loved this game, which reminded him of his exploits in battle in his youth.

At this point, Lord Augustus' efforts were interrupted by the arrival of an unexpected guest, who swept in, his long hair streaming behind him, with all the assurance in the world. He was followed meekly by a little man and a young boy. 'Greetings, my lord,' called Lord Ranulf. 'I though I should find you here. Oh, pardon, I see I am interrupting your game. I have brought with me Ralph de Boeuf, who will sell you some boots, or measure you for some more.'

Poor Ralph! This encounter was completely unexpected. He could only hold his hat in one hand, and some boots in the other, and await developments. Paul was less easily taken aback. 'Good day, sirs,' he cried. 'What good fortune brings us to you. My Master is the best craftsman in the Guild in Paris.'

'You both need new boots in which to ride forth,' called Ranulf. 'Come now, Lord Augustus, you cannot let down your family name by going ill-shod!' Lord Augustus rode little these days, but he was a soldier, and would not let the occasion defeat him.

'I'll have some made for me,' he said, 'if this man will take my measurements.'

'What with?' thought Ralph. He could not remember if his measuring line was in the pack on his back or not. But Lord Ranulf had thought of everything. His servant now appeared with a slate and some chalk. Lord Augustus permitted Paul to remove one shoe and place his foot on the slate, round which Ralph drew a mark with the chalk.

Noticing that his master was still silent, Paul nudged him. 'Ask him how much he is prepared to pay,' he whispered. The nobleman overhead this, and made a gallant offer, and also fixed a time when his boots were to be delivered.

---

* Early name for the Queen in chess.

Meanwhile, Lord François was examining the boots which Paul had set down, and began to try them on. 'They're good,' he said. 'I'll buy both pairs. Fortunately they fit me. Do you remember those comic ones you used to wear at Court, to make us laugh, Ranulf? That must be at least five years ago!' And they both roared with laughter, to Ralph's embarrassment. He hoped that Paul, who was quick-witted, would not guess the reason. But Paul was busy on his behalf, taking some pieces of silver for the boots, and holding them out to him to put in his purse. Grateful, he bowed, took up the slate, and left.

Ralph's nervousness had now subsided, and, as he descended into the courtyard, he was able to look around and take in the scene. Lord Ranulf's horse was waiting for him, the bridle held by the strong hands of the mounted manservant. Behind these figures was the gatehouse, flanked by the living quarters of the men-at-arms. Opposite, across the flagged courtyard, lay the main part of the palace. A shallow flight of stone steps led up to the Great Hall, with living quarters on either side to complete the square.

'I have to leave almost at once to return to my country estate. You know the area,' explained Lord Ranulf. 'The King and his courtiers are dining with me to-morrow, and I must see that all is ready. But before I go, I want to take you to meet the King's Steward. He is usually to be found in the Great Hall, and may be able to help you.'

As they ascended the steps, and entered the newly-fashioned archway, Ralph was somewhat overwhelmed by the size of the building. The timbered roof resembled that of Lord Ranulf's, but the furnishings were grander. The long wooden tables remained in place, and high-backed chairs indicated the places of the Royalty. Lesser folk were allocated stools, and the servants at the far end used benches. Behind these, a screen of carved wood cut off the entrance to the kitchens, and supported a minstrel's gallery.

Ralph was so intent on looking round that he almost failed to notice a tall figure, well-dressed and wearing a golden chain, carrying a staff to indicate his office. Paul nudged him quickly. They both bowed, as Lord Ranulf explained who they were.

'This is a first-class Master and his apprentice,' he went on, with something like a twinkle in his eye. 'If any of your staff need good, stout, well-stitched boots, you can go to him. He is Ralph de Boeuf, and lives at the far end of the Rue des Botteliers.' He turned to Ralph. 'It is time you displayed a larger sign to distinguish you from the other bootmakers,' he said. 'What about a painting that indicates your name? A worthy ox!'

'I'll do it,' cried Paul, full of enthusiasm.

'You're a good lad,' responded Ranulf. 'I must leave now. But don't forget, M Steward. If you send any of your people to M le Boeuf, you can be sure of the best possible service.' And he was gone, leaving Ralph and Paul to make their farewells, and to follow as best they could. It was almost dark, and they had to find their way home. They had been away for only two days, but it felt like a week. They had sold a few pairs of boots, lost quite a number during their misadventure, and gained one definite order and the promise of more. They carried the few pairs which remained unsold, and their earnings lay in Ralph's purse. He prayed that they would not be molested on the way home.

His prayer was answered. The only incident they encountered was a crowd of students from the University, conspicuous in their little black scholar's gowns, walking with linked arms down the street, singing their own peculiar songs as they went. Ralph remembered the student, Bolognus, whom he had met years ago at the Priory near Melun, and wondered where he was, and if he were a teacher by now.

The students bore them no ill-will and simply lifted their arms to allow Ralph and Paul to pass through their rank. 'Looking for boys like me, from the town, to tease,' remarked Paul.

'How awkward it would be,' thought Ralph, 'if one of two brothers were a scholar, and the other a craftsman. Would they fight each other?'

At last they reached Ralph's front door, weary but contented. They had to bang hard and call out their names before Hélène would open it, as she was not expecting them for a few days. Her delight overcame her surprise, and they settled down before the fire to tell her all. Looking up, Ralph saw a small pair of pink feet descending the stair. Matthieu had heard the noise, and was coming down to greet Papa.

CHAPTER X

Home!

Ralph and Paul spent the winter of 1261 – 62 catching up with their orders. First, they made the boots for Lord Augustus. Ralph sent Paul to the Palace with these. He left the boots in the care of the Steward, reminding this important official that more orders could be executed. The result was that a stable lad and a young cook from the Royal kitchen arrived at Ralph's door to ask him to make boots for them. When these had been finished successfully, other young workmen from the Palace arrived. There were no further orders from the nobility. Although Ralph and Hélène would both have liked to have served the highest in the land, they learned to be thankful for any work for which they were promptly and honestly paid.

Ralph remembered Thomas' warning during their ride together in the cart, on that autumn day in 1256, when he had been on his way back to Hélène at the farm near Maisse: 'There are mealtimes when they are all hungry and you wonder how you can afford to keep them fed.' Happily, that danger had passed. All the family looked happy and well-nourished.

As the spring of 1262 approached, Ralph realised that what Hélène needed most was more fresh air. She was a country woman, and was used to helping with the poultry, and to long walks to visit neighbours, through the countryside. Conditions in their little house were rather cramped, and her outings consisted mainly of short trips to the local market with the two little boys.

'I could manage a few more hens,' she said to Ralph, one sunny day. 'They feed mainly on scraps from our meals and the eggs are useful.'

Ralph's heart sank. Hens were scratchy things and he hated them. He thought. 'I have a much better idea,' he said at last. 'Why don't we keep the hens to one side of the yard. We could fence them in, and then grow fruit trees in the other part. A plum and an apple tree would be lovely, and we could sow some grass for the fruit to fall on.'

This pleased Hélène. 'We could let them grow up the walls,' she suggested, 'and grow something else in the rest of the ground. Turnips, perhaps, or even flowers. Some roses would be lovely.' They both knew she could spent some time out of doors tending them, and this was what she wanted.

'I wish we could have a larger garden for you, and a larger house,' sighed Ralph.

'You know we cannot,' she replied. 'We talked of it before, and you pointed out that this house is yours because your family have lived in it for so many generations, that no one knows of any other family owning it. Even if we could afford the money for a larger one, it would not be wise. Someone might arrive to claim the overlordship of it, even in a city like this. After all, Claude d'Honnête has brought up four children very happily in a house of this size.' They both looked at Paul, and realised quite well what Claude and Henri's difficulties had been.

'Never mind, we have enough food, clothing, firewood, and now we shall have a garden,' agreed Ralph.

He thought of Émile le Justes's garden in Chinon, with the aconites growing in it in winter. They could enjoy a scene like that, on a smaller scale. Robert crawled over his feet as he sat opposite Hélène. Prospects for the future were good: there were promises of more orders from the Palace, Paul would not live with them for ever, next year there would be another baby, and there would be many a long winter evening of story-telling round the fire. He felt very happy in his home.

Part Three
Ralph's Family

CHAPTER I

Matthieu's Future

Ralph Matthieu seized the shoe from his younger brother as he sat cross-legged on the tiny patch of grass in the small back garden in Paris. He threw it fiercely through the back door into the workshop living room, where their father, Ralph, the Master shoemaker, was sewing shoes together, causing him to look up in angry surprise. Ralph loved to look through the doorway onto their tiny garden, especially now, in the early spring sunshine. He viewed with great pride and satisfaction his younger son, Robert, aged two and a half, who had been pretending to sew like his Papa. What a pity it was that Matthieu always spoilt the picture. He could not resist upsetting his brother, but perhaps, at six and a half, he was still too young to know better.

Hélène also looked disturbed. She loved their elder son dearly, and was often suspected of favouring him. Only the fact that Anne, not yet one year old, was crawling over her feet, prevented her from smacking Matthieu soundly. Robert cried and ran to his father. In the confusion, Matthieu escaped punishment. It was not the first time that such an incident had occurred. Matthieu resented any kindly efforts to interest him in his father's work, as much as Robert's enthusiasm for pretending to stitch shoes together, 'like Papa does'.

The two little boys were different in many ways. Matthieu moved like lightning. He was slender, moderately tall for his age, and dark-haired like his mother, Hélène. He had inherited her quick wits and ready sense of humour. He could be very kind and helpful when in a good mood, and adored his little sister, to whom he sang all the children's songs he knew in a high-pitched but tuneful voice. He had been quick in learning to talk, but clearly had great difficulty in using his hands and was not patient enough to try. This was a great disappointment to his father.

Fortunately for Ralph, Robert had been endowed with all the qualities which his elder brother lacked. He was quiet and patient, although slow to talk. He followed his father everywhere, to his great delight, and imitated all his movements as he sewed, including the use of the awl, which he was not allowed to touch.

Their house was small. Looking at her three children, Hélène wondered how they would all fit in as they grew up. There was only just enough sleeping room already. She was beginning to worry about Matthieu's future. If he did not wish to spend his time learning an honest craft, what was to be done with him? Noticing that he was scratching away the young grass with a stick, she picked him up and placed him in the hen run, behind the wooden fence. The ground there was rough anyway, and he could make what patterns he liked without doing any harm. Fortunately, the hens did not seem to mind sharing their run with him. Although her husband disapproved, she had done this before. Ralph disliked hens himself, and resented having to run the risk of their pecking and flapping when it was time to lift his son out. Matthieu continued to make shapes with his stick while the others sat in peace, until a tall figure in a dark cloak appeared suddenly in the doorway. 'Père Simon,' cried Hélène in delight, as the priest stepped into the garden, followed by her husband.

'How lovely to find you altogether in the sunshine,' cried the priest, putting out his hands to bless the two younger children. 'Hello,' he said, crossing over to Matthieu, 'safe and sound and secure, I see. What are you playing at?' he continued. Barely waiting for Hélène's nod of assent, he lifted the small boy over the wooden palings.

'I'm making patterns on the ground for the hens to jump over,' explained Matthieu.

'Let's try making signs over here, then,' said the priest, pointing to a circle of bare earth at the base of the cherry tree. 'Would you like to do some drawing? We can learn something at the same time. This is the letter A.' He seized a fallen branch, and began to write capitals. Matthieu was intrigued. This was a new game. He soon began to recognise some of the shapes the second time round. Here was someone who was ready to spend time and trouble with him. His self-esteem rose.

The two dark heads, one mature and tonsured and the other childish, grew close together as their owners became absorbed in their task. Kneeling with their backs to the rest of the family and apparently oblivious of their presence, they concentrated on the lines their sticks were making in the soft earth. Above, the cherry blossom, just breaking into flower against the background of the blue sky, gave little shade, but much beauty. After a few moments, Père Simon turned and rose from his knees with an agility which came from much practice.

Ralph watched the scene with mixed feelings. He had great respect for learning. Although he could read very little, he admired those who could. Now, his elder son was showing distinct ability. How had he come by it? It was good to see the child enjoying himself on such a worthwhile pursuit, but he hoped that it would not make him conceited.

'What you need is to go to school,' the priest was saying. To go to school! Even if they could afford the fees, could they, a humble family, send a child to school? 'You could go and learn with the monks at Nôtre Dame,' Père Simon went on. 'I expect your father could find the few pence needed every week, and it's not far to go. Or perhaps you could board there? I'll inquire if you like,' he added, turning to Ralph. 'I know some of the monks who teach there.' Ralph was too surprised to disagree.

Hélène was thinking. She was torn between her desire to keep Matthieu near her as long as possible, and the realisation that life would be more peaceful in their house if she had only Robert and Anne to care for. Paul, their apprentice, was due to leave soon, and it was uncertain whether they could afford to keep another, in view of the few orders for boots and shoes which were coming in. Then, realising the underlying selfishness of this opinion, she thought again. 'Don't you think we should talk about it to Christophe?' she asked her husband. 'After all, he is Matthieu's godfather.'

'There are one or two points I ought to mention before you consider it further,' the priest went on. 'You probably are aware of these already, but I must remind you of them. First, it is often assumed that boys entering monastic schools will grow up to become deacons, and then either monks or parish priests. Your son would not be expected to take these vows for many years. In fact, he might leave the school and never do so, but there would be a strong possibility of this all the time he was there.'

Hélène nodded. She recognised that it was a very great honour to have a clerk in the family, but was somewhat alarmed at the restrictions it would place upon her son. 'This would mean that Matthieu would have to give up all thoughts of marriage, wouldn't it?' she asked Père Simon.

The priest agreed that, if Matthieu was ordained a priest, he would have to take a vow of celibacy, that is, the promise never to marry. 'But,' he continued, 'not all men wish to marry, and there are many advantages to be gained from being single like me, one being that we can move anywhere freely without having to make provision for a family, or to consider their comfort and well-being. It is a decision which would have to be left finally to the young man himself.'

Hélène looked across to Ralph. 'He is so very young to leave home and to board at school in the monastery,' she said.

'I would, of course, help in every way I could,' offered Père Simon. 'I would bring him home to spend the Saints' Days with you, and watch over his progress very carefully. I have enough friends and influence at the school at Nôtre Dame to make this possible.'

Meanwhile, Matthieu had been practising his newly-acquired skill, and was drawing letters below the cherry tree, listening to the conversation as he did so. At this moment, he got up and turned round. 'I'd be awfully glad to get away from all these horrid boots and shoes,' he said. The shock of these cold words passed through the little group. Clearly, Ralph was very hurt.

'You must not be ungrateful for all your parents have done for you, Matthieu,' admonished the priest, as soon as he had recovered. 'Always remember that without the boots and shoes which your good father makes, you would not have food and clothes, and there could be no thought of sending you to school.'

Nevertheless, that he should go to school was now almost a foregone conclusion.

CHAPTER II

Matthieu at School

So it was arranged that Matthieu should go to the monastic school at Nôtre Dame, and board there, when he reached the age of seven.

Père Simon came to fetch him on a sunny September morning in 1264. When the moment came to leave, Matthieu was clearly more cheerful than his parents, and set out gaily skipping along the street, with his hand in the priest's. Père Simon, relieved that the parting had been so easy, began to tell him a little of what he was to expect.

'Your father will have told you about the monks,' he said. Matthieu nodded. 'They belong to the order of St Benedict, so they wear black robes.'

'And they have a white rope round their waists knotted in three places, don't they?'

'That's right,' said the priest. 'Do you know what the knots mean?'

'They are promises,' said Matthieu, 'not to have any money or anything of their own, to do as they are told by the Abbot, and – I forget the third one.'

'It is called chastity, and means that they promise not to marry.'

'Oh, yes,' said Matthieu, no longer interested. 'Is one of the monks going to teach me?'

'You are very lucky,' replied Père Simon, 'because you are going to be in the care of an especially kind master. Every master has two little boys in his charge. He teaches them and looks after them all day, and all night. You will have a small bed to yourself, and Brother Marcus will sleep in his, between you and your fellow pupil.'

'Who am I going to share lessons with?' asked Matthieu.

'With a very nice little boy,' replied Père Simon. 'The brother who is the Head Master thought about you very carefully, and decided to pair you with

Lord Augustus de Thierry, who is also one of the youngest boys. He is quite clever, and as he comes from an aristocratic family he has beautiful manners.' Lord Augustus' name and connections meant nothing to Matthieu.

'Can he run as fast as I can?' he asked.

'Oh, I don't expect so,' replied Père Simon. Satisfied, Matthieu leaped along beside him. He was just beginning to feel tired when the towers of Nôtre Dame arose above them. Passing the cathedral, Père Simon led him through a wide arched gateway into a quadrangle, onto which the monks' living quarters opened. Sounds of cheerful shouts showed them that it was the play hour before school. Some of the boys were hopping on one leg from square to square, chalked out on the flag stones of the cloister. This, explained the priest, was hop-scotch. Another group, on the grass in the middle of the quadrangle, armed with sticks, were flicking a short piece of wood from one to the other, in an effort to keep it in the air. This, Matthieu discovered later, was called 'Tip-sticks'. Others, apparently a little older, were chasing each other round and round in a game of tag. Impulsively, Matthieu slipped his sack from his shoulders and dashed off to join them. Père Simon was glad to see him accepted immediately.

After a few minutes, Brother Marcus appeared and the two adults stood chatting together until Père Simon could secure Matthieu's attention to beckon him to join them. 'Goodbye,' he said, placing his hands on Matthieu's head. 'God bless you. I will look in to see you soon and take you home on the next Holy Day.'

For the first time, Matthieu felt alone. Seeing his mouth drooping, Brother Marcus hastily took him by the hand and, picking up his sack, led him up some stone stairs to his dormitory. There, two beds away from him, sat a fair-haired, blue-eyed boy, tall for his age, his aquiline features revealing aristocratic descent. 'This is your partner in studies, Matthieu le Boeuf, Lord Augustus,' explained the monk.

The boy looked up. 'What an extraordinary name,' he said. 'I live in our castle at Thierry, where my father is the Count since my grandfather, Lord Augustus, died. Where do you live?'

'Matthieu lives in Paris,' Brother Marcus stated for him. 'As he is very young, you must help him all you can. Your mother wishes you to remember that you come from the noble family, de Thierry, and that all your family for generations have helped those who are poorer, younger or in any way weaker than yourself. This is an opportunity to prove that you are worthy to be made a Knight when you are older.'

Lord Augustus looked a little surprised at this, and not very pleased, but he thrust his feelings aside and went over to embrace Matthieu. 'Now I will unpack for you,' went on the monk, 'and then we will go down to my desk. We shall work in the cloister until becomes cold, when we shall go into the parlour.'

As they went downstairs, Matthieu noticed that the other little boy was carrying a frame, which held rows of coloured beads, ten on each line. 'What is that?' asked Matthieu when they reached the cloister.

'Do you mean to say you don't know?' exclaimed Augustus in scornful surprise. 'My mother has been teaching me to use it for a long time. Hasn't your mother taught you how to use an abacus?'

By now they had reached Brother Marcus' high desk in a sunny spot. The monk pointed to the stools on either side of it. It was still early morning, and small boys on either side were taking their places beside their masters in a similar fashion. Fortunately, Augustus was too busy watching them to notice that Matthieu had not replied.

'Do you know who first used the abacus, Lord Augustus?' asked Brother Marcus.

'Yes, of course, I did!' replied the child. 'My mother gave it to me for my fifth birthday!'

The monk smiled. 'What I meant was, do you know who invented it?' he said. 'It has been used for a very long time,' he went on, turning to include Matthieu. 'The Romans used it. It was easier to do sums by counting beads grouped in tens, than by using their complicated system of numbers. Do you know about the Romans?' Matthieu shook his head. 'I will tell you one day, when we have done some real, hard work. To go back to the abacus: the use of it spread to the East and to Western Europe. The Arabs knew about it, although they had invented their own numbers which we are just beginning to learn about.'

'The Arabs are very clever people aren't they?' interrupted Augustus.

'They are indeed,' agreed the monk. 'They are mathematicians and scientists, and know a great deal about medicine. For example, they are much more skilled at mending broken bones than we are, because they are careful to 'set' the injured arm or leg, before binding it up with a splint.'

Although Matthieu was already tired and hungry after his long walk, the abacus fired his imagination. Augustus was generous in allowing him to play with it, and he quickly learnt the basic rules of adding and subtracting, and soon caught up with his more experienced partner.

At midday, they stopped work to wash and go to the Refectory for a meal of cold meat, bread and beer. Matthieu showed that he was unused to the taste of this, and the kind monk fetched him some water. He was now very tired, but determined not to give in to his weariness.

On his way back to work in the cloister, Matthieu recognised one of the boys he had played with when he arrived, sitting with his master and partner. The boy waved cheerfully and Matthieu was horrified to see the monk rap him over the knuckles with a sturdy, round ruler. He looked anxiously at his own tutor, who pretended not to notice. The rest of the afternoon was spent learning letters, and writing them on a slate. Matthieu was grateful for the practice Père Simon had given him in these. He knew the alphabet as well as Lord Augustus. 'My father, the Comte de Thierry, doesn't write much,' Augustus confided to Matthieu. 'Of course, he can write in French, and he knows a little Latin, too, but he is too busy hunting and hawking to spend much time on it. Does your father write much?'

'No, he is too busy too,' replied Matthieu. He had sensed already that it would be wise to keep the nature of his father's work to himself, at least until he knew Lord Augustus better. Brother Marcus kept silent.

They worked until the September sun went down. Both boys were hungry again by now, and looked forward to supper. The tolling of the bells for Vespers warned them that they must join the line of small boys processing into church, and attend the service before their bodily needs could be satisfied. Once inside, Matthieu felt more at home than he had done at any time during the day. Brother Marcus, standing beside him, was pleased to hear him trying to join in the singing, and to notice that he looked happier. He remembered that Père Simon had told him that both his parents, especially his father, were very devout, and therefore the church services were familiar to him. At last supper came, a good hot meal, with little sweet egg custards to end. Bed was warm and clean and, although hard, no less comfortable than the one he shared at home. He was glad to know that the good monk was sleeping next to him, and that he could reach out to touch him for reassurance.

CHAPTER III

Lord Augustus

After the first day, Matthieu's life at the monastic school of Nôtre Dame fell into a pattern. On the whole he was reasonably happy, although there were some unwelcome activities such as frequent washing. He suffered too, from becoming very hungry, and then eating too much at the next meal. He discovered some irritating habits in Lord Augustus, although fortunately his own mind was quicker. If he drew too far ahead of Augustus in their joint studies, he had to endure his small partner's air of superiority, and his critical remarks. Lord Augustus soon discovered the social differences between them, and, if provoked, made unkind comments, in spite of his mother's warnings to behave tolerantly.

Matthieu always enjoyed the playhour before school, when he could escape from Augustus, and run round and round the quad with older boys at top speed. One morning he raced faster than ever, excited at the prospect of going home for a few days on All Saints' Day. He bounced over to Brother Marcus' desk to find Lord Augustus already seated, and drawing on a slate. The childish drawing was difficult to make out, but as he looked again, he saw it was a four-legged creature, with wings flapping out of its head, and a large tail falling from its mouth towards its front feet. Another tail, very small, hung down at the back.

'What is it, a huge bird?' asked Matthieu, rather scornfully.

'Of course not. It's a beast,' explained Augustus, who was hurt by his tone. 'It is an elephant. My father helped to escort it across the sea when our King Louis sent it as a present to King Henry of England.'*

---

*Louis XI sent Henry III a present of an elephant in 1255.

113

'Why didn't it use its wings, and fly over?' asked Matthieu, who didn't believe him.

'It cannot fly. It is much too heavy,' explained Augustus, very seriously. 'If you came near it, it would certainly dislike you, and squirt water all over you from its trunk.'

'That is nonsense,' said Matthieu scornfully. 'There is no such beast. You have copied it from the margins of one of the manuscripts.'

'Indeed I have not!' Augustus was very angry now. 'I am always truthful. Are you calling me a liar?'

Matthieu knew he was, but he was not going to apologise.

'Say you are sorry at once, do you hear?' shouted Augustus. 'My father is a count and one day quite soon I shall be a knight. Knights do not lie. But you do not know this because you come from the streets of Paris.'

At this, Matthieu lifted his hand and struck the other small boy across the face. He gave out a scream of pain and rage, just as Brother Marcus came across the grass to them. He had seen it all happen. He took Augustus on his knee to comfort him. 'What is all this about?' he asked Matthieu, who, seeing the affection that his rival was receiving, immediately felt isolated and unhappy. Tears came, and through his tears, he tried to explain, with many sobs and false starts. Brother Marcus gradually sorted it out. 'You are both going home in two days' time,' he said. 'Meanwhile, you will stay on your bed in the dormitory, Matthieu, and only leave it for meals. Augustus will have lessons alone. What happens after that, we will decide when you return from your home visit.' Matthieu struggled up the spiral stairs still in tears. It was only that night, when he saw Brother Marcus beside him, that he realised he was lucky to be going home at all.

* * * * * * * * * *

Ralph and Hélène walked home from Mass with their two small children, through the early morning mists on All Saints' Day. Robert and Anne could only walk slowly, and Hélène was worried that they would not get the fire rekindled before Père Simon brought Matthieu home. She had just got a fire blazing when the street door opened. Hoping to catch Matthieu for a warm embrace, she leaped towards it. It was not Matthieu, but Claude d'Honnête, their next door neighbour.

'Has Paul come to you to spend the day?' asked Hélène. 'We told him to run home directly after the Mass, so as to make the most of this Holy Day.'

'Yes, he is with us,' replied Claude, 'and talking happily to his father. I came to tell you some interesting news we heard from a pedlar yesterday, who had walked from your home district at Étampes to sell his cloth in Paris.' Hélène was waiting for her son's arrival far too eagerly to pay much attention, but Claude went on. 'Your former overlord, Ranulf de Villaincourt, has just left on a visit to England. It is said that he is going to arrange his marriage to an English lady.'

Ralph, who had been showing his tools on the bench to Robert, turned towards her. 'When I went to see him, with Hélène's father, to ask his permission for my marriage,' he said, 'he told us that when he wished to marry, he would choose an English woman because he liked their looks. His mother was English, as you can see from his fair hair and long limbs.'

'It is not a very good moment to sail to England,' Claude went on. 'A courtier who came to us for shoes told us that their King, Henry III, is having trouble with the barons. Our King, Louis, tried to help him to make peace, but did not succeed. A French nobleman, Simon de Montfort, is encouraging the nobles to demand the right to be heard, by force of arms if necessary. I am not sure exactly what they want from the King, but Simon de Montfort is known to be upright and truthful above all things, and would not lead them to ask for anything unjust or dishonest.'

'We heard from one of the Palace cooks who came here for shoes,' interrupted Ralph, 'that Simon de Montfort is said to have a very quick temper, and therefore may be acting more rashly than wisely.'

At this moment two figures appeared in the doorway, and with a cry of 'Mama', Matthieu threw himself into Hélène's arms. He had not seen his mother, or any female figure, for six whole weeks, and was overcome by the moment. He burst into tears, and refused to stop. Père Simon followed him in. Claude left quietly.

'Matthieu is very tired,' explained the priest. 'He has worked hard and behaved beautifully, until a day or two ago, when, most unfortunately, he had a quarrel with the little boy he studies with, and struck him in the face.'

Ralph was horrified, and wanted to know why. He looked at his son who was still very tearful, but before he could say anything, a glance from his wife stopped him.

'Most small boys fight each other,' she said. 'It is natural. But you must be more careful, Matthieu,' she went on, putting her arms round her son. 'Never strike someone who cannot defend himself. You must say you are sorry the moment you see him on your return.'

Noting a very stubborn look on the small boy's face, the priest gave him a solemn warning. 'As I told you, you are very lucky to have Brother Marcus as your teacher. You may have seen how some of the other masters beat their pupils. They are allowed to, if they judge it to be right.' Matthieu had indeed witnessed this. 'If you do not apologise, and settle down to work with Lord Augustus, you will be sent to another master, and you will not find one so kind again.' Turning to Hélène, he explained, 'The Comtesse de Thierry came to see the Abbot yesterday, in her covered wagon with two servants. She threatened to take Lord Augustus away to work with a tutor at home unless your son promised to behave better.'

He gave rather a wry smile. 'I understand that she also asked if Matthieu was a freeman's son, as it would have been insufferable if Lord Augustus had been struck by a peasant.'

Nothing more was said, and, by the afternoon, Matthieu's confidence had returned. He wanted to show Robert and Anne what he had learnt, but he had left his slate at school, and the fragment which Ralph produced for him didn't provide room for many letters. Robert wasn't interested, he preferred to learn to stitch shoes like his father. But Anne, who was just two years old, was intrigued by her big brother's activity, and wanted to copy him. So he drew the alphabet for her. As Ralph sat and worked, he watched his family with pride and affection. 'You are getting on well, aren't you?' asked Hélène. 'You will soon be able to write properly, not only in single words.'

Matthieu, who by this time, was showing some signs of conceit, explained that the next time he came home, he would be writing in Latin. 'You see, we don't learn to write French, that is not important,' he said impressively. 'But Latin is, because the Church services are in Latin, and the King does all his business in Latin.' Ralph was suitably impressed, and thought perhaps the school fees, which he struggled to find each week, were worthwhile after all.

* * * * * * * * *

Matthieu's return to school was happier than he had expected. He found Augustus was also ready to apologise. His mother had used her influence to good effect. After this, the two boys became firm friends, and remained so. Augustus had more difficulty than Matthieu in settling down to hard work, especially where Latin grammar was concerned. Matthieu was intrigued by the whole structure of the Latin sentence. The verb came at the end! However had the Romans managed to talk to each other? With his quill, he practised writing in

Latin on parchment, using the style of letters known as miniscule. Brother Marcus had told them that the great French Emperor, Charlemagne, had encouraged scholars to write at his court, where they had developed these clear, round letters. The Germans, on the other hand, wrote pointed letters, known as Gothic, which were much more difficult to read, and, as the monk explained, they were lucky not to have to learn them.

During their lessons, Matthieu tried to help Augustus, and Brother Marcus, who was always seated between them, encouraged him to prompt his partner over the difficulties of parsing a Latin sentence. By the time he was eleven, Matthieu had a very good command of the language, whereas Augustus was still struggling, and not always very hard. He knew that when he was twelve, he was going to leave school, and train to become a page, and then a squire, and finally a knight.

One warm day in spring, when they were working in the cloisters, Matthieu's eyes strayed toward the trees in the quadrangle, whose bare branches were just beginning to show a hint of green against the bright blue sky. He was brought back to earth by a sudden burst of song from Augustus:

'Here ends the Romance called "The Rose",
Where all the art of love's enclosed:
And Nature laughs, it seems to me,
When joined at last are He and She.'

'Lord Augustus! Wherever did you learn that?' exclaimed Brother Marcus, shocked, while Matthieu began to laugh.

'Oh, it's a verse my father had set to music, and taught me,' answered Augustus. 'It comes from a story which a Frenchman, called William of Lorris, began years ago, and hasn't yet finished. It is called "The Romance of the Rose".'

'Then you had better keep it to yourself until you leave,' admonished Brother Marcus, rather sternly. 'And then, when you are a page, do not sing until your Master bids you do so. And make sure he approves of the song you have chosen before you sing it to other people.'

'Certainly,' replied Augustus, who was still feeling cheeky. 'And I won't have to wait long, because I'm leaving you at Easter. I'm going to be trained at the household of my father's old friend the Comte de Venables, who, my father says, enjoys a joke!'

'I am sure you will never carry a joke too far, Lord Augustus,' remarked the monk, 'because you normally have good manners. I expect your father has given you some idea of what your duties will be.'

'Yes, indeed. For one thing, I must put down a sheet beside my lord's bath every night, wait on him until he gets into bed, put on his night-cap, turn out the dogs and cats, if he has any – and I'm allowed to clout them if necessary – bow, and withdraw. At table I must stand behind my lord, not speak unless I am spoken to, and never claw my flesh with my nails. I never do that, anyway.'

'Indeed not,' Brother Marcus exclaimed. 'But it is most important to remember that you will be trained in obedience, because only by learning to obey yourself can you learn to exercise authority over others when you are grown up.' All this time, Matthieu had been listening attentively. He was beginning to think that, if he were going to become a scholar at the University of Paris, as he was hoping, his life would be much freer and easier than that of a page.

The monk's last remarks had made Augustus realise that he had been rather rude, so he added hastily, 'Of course, I shall be very sorry to leave you. You have been very kind to me, and Matthieu, too. He will make a good scholar, if he decides to become one. My father says we can only do what we are meant to do, according to our position in life, and we had better train to do that as early as possible. This is what he told me: "A man may rarely be a good clerk who does not begin in childhood, any more than he may be a good rider, if he does not learn young".'

After that speech, Brother Marcus insisted that they returned to the translation of Cicero into French until it was time for the midday meal. As usual, this was taken in silence, and the season being Lent, it was rather frugal. There was fish and cheese, followed by the remainder of last year's apples, which had grown rather soft. Augustus' face expressed disapproval, but he could not comment. Sunday however, was a 'talking day'. 'I'm awfully tired of this beer,' he said. 'It is brought in from farms, isn't it? Now, my father always has wine served with his meals. There are vineyards nearby at Champagne. We don't have it here.'

'Lord Augustus, you are most fortunate to have any beer at all, especially during Lent! Our saintly King, Louis IX, detests beer, but he drinks it all through Lent in preference to wine. Think of the wonderful example which he sets us. And in other ways, too. He gets up in the middle of every night to say Matins with the monks, and goes to Confession every Friday. He often invites beggars from the streets of Paris to come and eat at his table.'

118

'So does Papa,' interrupted Augustus, 'at least, not beggars, but the poor people from his estates. Phew! The servants have to leave the door of the Great Hall open!'

'Then you, too, have a good example to follow,' went on the monk, and they resumed their meal quietly. In spite of all his faults, Brother Marcus was sorry to see Lord Augustus leave on Easter Monday. His father sent two servants and three horses to collect him and his baggage. After affectionate farewells, Augustus mounted a little uncertainly, as he had had little practice in the saddle since the age of eight. He waved jauntily, and set off. 'We shall miss Lord Augustus very much,' said Brother Marcus.

CHAPTER IV

At Ralph's Shop

The door of Ralph de Boeuf's shop in Paris closed behind Gerald the Cook, who was returning to work at the King's palace. He carried a pair of boots under his left arm and swung a second pair in his right hand. One pair was for his assistant in the royal kitchens, and the other for himself. Neither pair was very elegant, but they were made of good leather and would last a long time. Gerald was grateful for his break from work, and had tried to prolong it by asking Ralph to mend the pair he was wearing on the spot. Ralph had refused, saying that members of the Bootmaker's Guild made boots and shoes, but did not carry out repairs. Nevertheless, Gerald had stayed to talk for some time, and had given Ralph's family some news to discuss.

In the shop living room, Hélène and Claude d'Honnête sat on a bench near the fireplace, while Ralph sewed at his work bench. His second son, Robert, now eight years old, was totally absorbed in waxing the thin leather thongs with which his father stitched shoes together. His small sister, Anne, was sitting on a tiny stool at her mother's feet, pretending to learn to sew, but her eyes wandered frequently towards the open back door into the yard, where the hens scratched. It was a warm day in June, but the small fire was essential as it provided the only means of cooking the midday meal.

Hélène was joining together the seams of a tunic for Matthieu, ready for his next winter at school. Lessons in the cloisters in the autumn could be chilly affairs. It was a beautiful blue colour. She had spun the wool herself, and sent it to a neighbouring weaver to be turned into cloth.

Beside her, Claude chatted, glad of a short rest. Now that she was well over forty she tired more quickly, although as only her husband and younger daughter, Jeanne, were at home, she had less to do now. Her elder son and daughter had both married and moved away, and her second son Paul, Ralph's former apprentice, was travelling as a journeyman through the Loire valley, following the route which Ralph had taken before his marriage. A lock of greying hair escaped from Claude's coif as she relaxed in the warm room.

'It is strange that Lord Ranulf de Villaincourt has not married yet,' remarked Hélène, commenting on the gossip from court that Gerald the Cook had supplied them. 'When he is not at Court, or travelling to England to visit his cousins, he must be very lonely living in his manor house in the country.'

'Such a beautiful and courteous knight is bound to marry one day,' replied Claude, who cherished secret admiration for the handsome Ranulf. 'I'm sure he must be popular with the ladies, and he will need an heir to his estates. English women must be strange creatures to lack affection for such an attractive person. I wonder why an English nobleman does not arrange for his daughter to marry him, and insist that she consents to the worthwhile match.'

'When the steward came last time from Court, to order boots for his servants,' said Hélène, 'he told us something about those English ladies. Some of the French nobles, who had visited the English King's court, came back with amusing stories, which the servants overheard and repeated. It seems that the English ladies who are descended from old Saxon families are very haughty, and even when their ancestors have intermarried with the Normans their pride remains. Above all they value their independence, and expect complete command over their households when they marry.'

'So do French ladies,' interrupted Ralph, with a laugh.

'Yes, but the English ladies do so, openly,' smiled Hélène. 'We heard that, when Lord Ranulf visited friends in England four years ago, the lady who was the centre of his affections took a dislike to him because of his overbearing manner and ways. Not even his good looks and exploits as a horseman could win her round. When her parents tried to insist on arranging their betrothal, the young lady grew very angry, and shut herself up in her chamber. No amount of coaxing, bullying or threats could make her change her mind. Even a diet of bread and water had no effect. Therefore, he was forced to leave her, and return to France. If you ask my opinion, I think Lord Ranulf will go back to England one day to find another English lady. He admires their kind of beauty.'

'I wonder what happened to her, then?' asked Robert, who had just finished his task.

'I expect she married an Englishman of her own choice,' suggested Claude. 'What strange goings on there are in England! No sense, no law and order anywhere. When Lord Ranulf was there, there were more wars between the King, Henry III and the barons!'

'Don't forget it was a Frenchman, Simon de Montfort, who stirred up most of the trouble,' said Ralph. Meanwhile, Anne, realising that no one was noticing her, slipped into the yard.

'Yes, and look what he did then,' said Claude. 'He called an Assembly, Parliament is the name they give it in England, and invited not only the nobles to attend, but ordinary men from the towns as well!'

'Thank goodness our good Louis IX does not govern that way!' exclaimed Hélène. 'Since he put down the rebellion of the barons a very long time ago, when he first came to the throne, he has governed the country himself, and only asks advice of the nobles when he chooses.'

They were interrupted by a knock at the door, and the parish priest stepped in. He noticed the happy, domestic scene, and was sorry that he had some unwelcome news. Before telling them this, he decided to discuss Brother Marcus' plans for Matthieu to go on to the University of Paris in about a year's time. If he did not talk about this at once, it would be more difficult to do so later.

They all rose to meet him, and Ralph placed a chair for him beside Hélène. 'Your son, Matthieu, is still doing well at Nôtre Dame,' he began.

'Yes, and he is happy,' agreed Hélène. 'We are both grateful to you for all you have done for him.'

'There is still one more think for me to do,' said Père Simon. 'I must persuade you to help him to go to the University next year. That will mean fees for lectures, and he will need money to keep himself while he is there, including a few books and writing materials.'

'We have been expecting this,' said Ralph, 'from all he has said when he has been at home. How long will this study take?'

'It depends how far he wants to go,' replied Père Simon, somewhat uncertainly. 'He shows a desire to enter the Church. If he becomes a cleric, he will stand a good chance of a fine position in life. Our King uses clerics to do most of the business at court for him, and then throughout the country in many ways. For example, he sends them to collect taxes from the royal lands.'

Seeing that this impressed Ralph, he went on, 'Matthieu would spend three years at the University of Paris, and then should pass his Bachelor of Arts examination. For this he would study Latin, Rhetoric and Logic.' Ralph was puzzled; he wasn't sure what kind of studies the last two were. 'These are the first three subjects of the seven liberal arts,' went on the priest. 'The remaining four are arithmetic, geometry, music and astronomy. But before going on to these, he could be ordained as a deacon. Some young men travel all over Europe to complete their studies, but the Archbishop does not like his deacons to wander about as scholars do so often, picking up bad habits, like excessive drinking. He would be lucky if he could study the last four subjects at the College which has recently been founded in Paris by Roger de Sorbon. Some very fine Masters teach there, and they are especially famous for their lectures in Theology. Matthieu would enjoy these, and he is very likely to become a priest later, as well as scholar. Will you talk to him about this, and find out what plans he has for his future?'

Poor Ralph! He dearly wished to be a good father, but he wasn't sure what was meant by Theology. 'I'd rather you talked to him,' he said, looking towards Hélène for support. She smiled and nodded in agreement.

Père Simon turned to Claude, 'Madame d'Honnête, you are an old friend of the family. Try to persuade them!'

Ralph was thinking. In a few years, Robert would be his apprentice, and he would not have to pay a lad from another family to help him. He was very proud of his elder son's ability, and wanted to encourage him. 'He could earn enough to pay his fees by cleaning rooms for richer students, if he is prepared to do this kind of work,' the priest went on. 'Then he would need money only for his food and books.'

Hélène smiled, 'I don't think he would enjoy that, but if he is keen enough to study, he will do it.'

Robert looked up. He was tired of all this talk of study. It was very uninteresting. He had hoped the Madame d'Honnête would tell them a little more about Jeanne, who was twelve years old. Her family were already considering whom she might marry. He admired her very much. She was much older than he was, but kind and nice, and pretty. He, too, escaped into the garden.

Now the priest came to his own personal news. He explained that, as the King was getting older (he was now over fifty), he needed more help at Court. Père Simon's friends among the monks at Nôtre Dame had suggested that the would be helpful to the King as a Royal Chaplain. He could not refuse such an honour, which was, in fact, a royal command. The outcome was that, in a few weeks, he was leaving St Michael's Church to serve the King personally. His own sadness as he told them was reflected in their faces. He had not been not only their personal friend and adviser, but had helped them in so many different ways. It was to him that they had brought their letters to be read, or written, while Matthieu was at school. It was he who had advised them the prices to charge for their boots and shoes, and who had delivered their son's school fees to the Abbot each week.

Père Simon loved all Ralph's and Henri d'Honnête's families dearly and felt real concern for their future, especially for their children. Of these, he was most anxious for Robert. Matthieu would do well as a student and later as a cleric, he was sure. Anne and Jeanne were both likely to marry into families similar to their own. But Robert le Boeuf would stay at home, continue his father's business and probably marry, so that he would have the responsibility for his parents as they grew old, as well as his children. These duties would interrupt his work as a shoemaker, which he had already shown signs of enjoying. But all that lay in the future.

Before the priest left, he looked into the small garden at the back of the shop to say goodbye to Robert and Anne. Robert was lolling sulkily over the fence of the hen's run, but Anne was scratching letters in the earth, in imitation of her elder brother. 'Many girls learn to read and write these days,' remarked Père Simon to Hélène.

'Let Matthieu teach her next time he comes home.'

'He does that already,' replied Hélène proudly.

CHAPTER V

Lord Ranulf Returns

It was a beautifully sunny June morning in the year 1268 when Lord Ranulf de Villaincourt led his bride, the Lady Ethelburga, onto the small sailing ship which was to carry them over to Le Havre.

A week ago, they had been married at the little village of Ashby-en-Houte, near Lichfield. After the ceremony and the wedding feast which her father. Lord William, had provided, they had left on horseback to begin their journey to Portsmouth, where a ship had been chartered for them. The journey, with Lord Ranulf's two grooms, and Mary, Lady Ethelburga's personal maid, and all their horses, had taken longer than Lord Ranulf had anticipated, and he was anxious to return to his estates in the Loire Valley. They had spent two nights rather uncomfortably at hostelries, before reaching the nunnery at Abingdon. Here, the guest mistress had insisted that they rested for two whole days, before moving on to the Benedictine Nunnery at Romsey. Lady Ethelburga had been all too ready to spend time at Abingdon. Not because she was tired, she was never tired, but because she was thrilled to be staying at the Nunnery where Queen Matilda had once stayed, when she was fleeing from her cousin, King Stephen.

Arriving at Romsey, Lord Ranulf had tried to insist that his party left immediately after Mass the next morning. The guest mistress had pretended not to hear, but when the servants brought the Lord and Lady's supper to their private room in the evening, she had come with them to see that all was well, and pointed out that the Abbess never allowed ladies to leave in the mornings before they had broken their fast, and a light meal would be served to them before departure.

At last they were on board. Fortunately, there was a light breeze, which promised an easy journey. One of the grooms led Lady Ethelburga's mare on board, and down a sloping plank into the hold. She had refused to abandon her horse, although her husband had assured her that fresh horses awaited them at Le Havre. As there was only room for one horse in the little ship, Lord Ranulf had had to leave his on the shore, contrary to his wishes. A priest came on board, blessed the newly-weds, the sailors and the ship, the men heaved up the anchor, set the sails, and they were off. As Lady Ethelburga did not wish to go below to rest in her cabin, Lord Ranulf stood beside her on the deck. Why did the English love the sea so much, even when they lived inland, he wondered? He looked at his bride's long limbs, her fair hair streaming in the wind, her blue hood tossed loosely back on the shoulders of her light cloak, her blue eyes intent on the gleaming water. Their servants stood at a respectful distance. The ship rose up and down over the waves in the light breeze. Lady Ethelburga was enjoying herself. He looked at her again. This time, her generous mouth seemed rather too large and too full of perfect teeth, rather like a horse's, in fact.

Suddenly it happened. He was violently sick, and only just reached the rail in time to vomit into the sea. As he reeled backwards, he fancied a look of amusement on his lady's face, which was reflected in the smile of her maid, who revealed a row of uneven black and crumbling teeth. There was no escape. The Lady Ethelburga had decided to stay on deck all night to watch the moon on the water.

Next morning, they were rewarded by the glorious red glow of the sunrise. They disembarked, found fresh horses waiting for them, and just managed to reach the monastery at Rouen without incident. Here they were treated with great respect, as the name of Lord Ranulf was well known.

From now on, the journey became easier. At the hostelry at Pontoise, Ranulf and Ethelburga were given the best guest room while the two grooms slept below, and in turn watched the baggage. The next day they passed through St. Denis on their way to Paris, where they were to spend two nights as the guests of the King and Queen. They rode into the courtyard of the Royal Palace, where Lord Ranulf had stayed so often as a young man. A servant took the news of their arrival to Queen Margaret, who came at once to greet them. She embraced Lord Ranulf, and then kissed his bride warmly on both cheeks. Lady Ethelburga looked a little surprised. English ladies usually offered one cheek, rather coldly.

They were taken to their apartments, where her maid prepared her to go to dinner. This meal was to be taken with the King and Queen in a small upstairs room, a most unusual practice, as King Louis loved to eat in his Hall surrounded by his family, courtiers and subjects of all kinds. However, he had waived his usual habit in order to give all his attention to the newly-married couple. Ranulf was pleased to see how beautiful Ethelburga looked in her full-length gown of blue damask, which had been woven for her specially at her mother's request. Her hair was braided with gold thread, and she wore a girdle of gold. The Queen, like the King, was dressed very plainly in sombre colours. She spoke kindly to the bride. 'I hear you come from Lichwood, near Lichfield,' she said. 'I have not been there, although I have visited England to see my sister, Eleanor, who is King Henry III's Queen. How is it that you have kept an English name and title, when most English nobility lost their rank after William of Normandy conquered England?'

'My ancestor, Earl William, owned much land when the Norman Duke arrived,' explained Ethelburga. 'He had just lost his wife, whose name was the same as mine. Shortly after this, one of the Norman lords, Henry de Courcey, died of a fever, and then his wife, who had only arrived in England a few weeks ago, became a widow. King William, as he became, was very fond of this lady, and to ease her sorrow arranged for her to marry the Earl William. He allowed him to keep his title so that their children should be members of the nobility. That is how my title has been passed down to me.'

The Queen looked pleased. Meanwhile, Lord Ranulf had been discussing more serious matters with the King, who now turned to Ethelburga. 'My lady,' he said, with his usual courtesy. 'you have indeed been fortunate in your choice of a husband. Lord Ranulf is a valiant knight and a valued counsellor to me. May you be blessed with many children to follow his example.'

'We have been blessed with six sons and five daughters,' explained the Queen. 'Their education and marriages have been a great responsibility and caused us much concern.'

'I have taught them all their catechism, and the main teaching of the Christian faith, personally,' said the King. 'I do commend this practice to you, Lord Ranulf. It provides the best way of knowing your children and of making sure that it is well done.'

'Oh, I think I shall want to do that myself,' interrupted Ethelburga. Her husband looked rather taken aback.

'Well said!' exclaimed the Queen, and Ranulf gave her a grateful look. It was a first real moment of understanding which had passed between them.

'You will see that all your children will have different abilities,' said the King. 'Now my eldest son, Philip, who will succeed me, was very slow in learning the Creed, and the Ten Commandments. Little Agnes, on the contrary, is very quick indeed to learn. Robert was very competent, too. I think the younger ones learnt a great deal from the others.' He went on to talk of the new monuments which were being built in the Church of St Denis which held all the Royal tombs.

The next evening they all ate in the Great Hall. Early the following morning, Ranulf and Ethelburga, with their attendants, set out for the de Villaincourt estates near Étampes. They arrived just before dark, both a little tired. But their spirits rose when they saw all the villagers, servants and men-at-arms lining the path to the Manor House. Ranulf introduced each one to Ethelburga as she rode along on her mare. Among them were Henri and Mairie Fourneau, the parents of Hélène le Boeuf. Ranulf had a special word for them. They had always ranked very high in his esteem. The Great Hall of the Manor was decorated with flowers and foliage, and the long tables were weighed down with dishes of all kinds. Even Ethelburga would have preferred to rest, but they let the feast go on until the villagers had clearly had enough, and then allowed them to escort them to their bedroom with lighted torches.

*   *   *   *   *   *   *   *   *   *

Ranulf's and Ethelburga's son was born in May, 1269. They chose the name Ranulf William Louis. The godparents were the baby's own parents, Ethelburga's father William, and King Louis of France. The christening was arranged to take place in June. Unfortunately neither William of Lichwood nor King Louis could attend, but each sent a nobleman to represent them. The nurse carried the infant Ranulf William Louis along the path from the Manor House to the little old parish church, followed closely on foot by Ethelburga and Ranulf, nobles, friends and servants. The villagers were already assembled to witness the ceremony. The priest was waiting for them at the font, and began the prayers to exorcise the devil from the devil from the baby. He then anointed him with Holy Oil, with the words 'Ego in linio oleo salutis in Christo Jesu Domino nostro, ut habeas vitam aeternam.'

He then changed his purple stole for a white one as a sign that the most joyful part of the service was to begin.

He handled a small white robe to Ethelburga, who managed to slip it over the baby's head as he struggled in his nurse's arms.

'Accipe vestem candidam,' commanded the priest. He then baptised the child with water from the font, and finally handed Ethelburga a lighted candle to hold on her son's behalf, saying, 'Accipe lampadem ardente. Vade in pace, et Dominus sit tecum.'

At this, the party left the church to return to the afternoon sunshine, and made their way to the christening feast. Standing at one side of the main door to greet the villagers, Lady Ethelburga looked across at her husband. Lord Ranulf stood tall, smiling with delight at the birth of his son and heir.

CHAPTER VI

Matthieu the Clerk

It was a sad morning on the whole, although the September sun of 1270 was shining. Paris had just heard the news of the death of France's greatly loved King, Louis IX. At the age of fifty-five he had embarked on a second crusade, against the wishes of his family, his counsellors, and the whole nation. His party had landed at Tunis, on the way to the East, and there he had suddenly become very ill with a fever. Death had come quickly at the end of August, and news of it had reached France some days later. The people were greatly impressed by the message he sent to his son, who was to succeed him as Philip III: 'The first thing I teach thee is to mould thy heart to love God; for without that, no-one can be saved.'

It was also a sad time for Ralph and his family. They had suffered a serious family loss, the news of which had reached them the previous day. Hélène's dear father, Henri Fourneau, had died suddenly on his farm. He was over seventy years of age, and had worked hard until the last moment. Hélène's brother-in-law, François, had come to tell them this, and she had returned with him in his cart to comfort her mother, taking their little daughter Anne with her.

It was an especially disappointing day for Matthieu. He was to be made a clerk in Holy Orders by the Bishop at the Cathedral, together with nine other young men, just before the beginning of the University term. He had been looking forward to this for a long time, and had wanted all his family to be there on this important occasion. Ralph was pleased that his son was to be a clerk, not only because it would very likely be the first step towards ordination as a priest, but because he would have the protection of the Church and special privileges of the clergy when he became a student.

The three of them set off together towards Nôtre Dame, Ralph, Matthieu and Robert. Matthieu carried his candle, and the white gown Hélène had made for him, which he would need during the service. 'I expect Mother is as disappointed as I am,' he said, 'and I should have liked Anne to have come.' He sighed.

They saw that there was plenty of room as they entered the great west door. The ceremony of ordaining clerks was a very frequent one. As Matthieu left Ralph and Robert to stand in the nave, he noticed with delight the shafts of coloured light falling from the great Rose window in the north transept, which lit up the heads of the people standing beneath. He joined the other young men and waited for the arrival of the Bishop and his clergy. Soon they entered, and the Latin service began.

The Bishop took a pair of scissors and a basin from his serving boy, and one by one the new clerks stood before him. He cut each one's hair in four places, on the forehead, at the back of the head and over each ear, carefully placing the locks in the basin. The he placed the young man's gown over his head, handed him his lighted candle and told him that he had now been made 'de foro ecclesiae'. This meant that if he was in any difficulty he could claim special privileges as a churchman. The Bishop warned him not to disgrace himself in any way, as this would mean the loss of those benefits.

The ceremony meant a great deal to Matthieu, especially as he was to leave his family almost at once to enter the Hall of the University, where he would live in term-time. He parted from his father and brother outside the Cathedral, after an affectionate embrace. He had already left his books in the dormitory he was to share with four other students. The Master had explained that they would all be French. It was arranged that he would keep the room clean, and in return would receive a small fee to help pay for his lectures.

He found it empty, and stood wondering what bed he should take. As a poor scholar, should he sleep in the most uncomfortable, by the unglazed window? Fortunately, there were shutters for use in winter. His thoughts were interrupted by the arrival of another small, dark-haired lad, even shorter than himself. 'Hullo,' said the newcomer. 'I am Roger from Brittany. Who are you?'

'Ralph Matthieu,' he replied. 'My father works in Paris, but I am descended from, and named after, a Viking, who landed on the banks of the Seine long ago.' Then, realising that he was boasting, he stopped.

'I'm glad we're all Frenchmen in this house,' said Roger. 'I know the lectures will be given in Latin, and I can speak it, but I'd rather speak French when I'm not working.'

'The Masters tend to keep us in groups with our fellow countrymen,' explained Matthieu. 'I'm not sure why. I should think young men would give less trouble if they were of mixed races. They wouldn't plan escapades so easily.'

At that moment, a rush of heavy feet broke into their friendly conversation. 'Hey, hey,' shouted four voices all at once. 'This is what we do! This is what we do to newcomers,' and they seized Roger without hesitation and hustled him down the rickety stairs. Matthieu was wondering whether to follow to try to help, or to hide himself, when another band of students appeared and seized him, too.

Outside in the courtyard was a horse trough. A loud splash revealed that they had thrown Roger into it. He gasped and spluttered, then they let him heave himself out, dripping in the autumn sunshine. He was shaking himself as Matthieu was thrown into the trough. He was frightened and furiously angry as the cold penetrated his tunic and hose. He shouted, 'Stop this at once! Stop this!' Fortunately his vocabulary was too limited to contain any stronger words. The more he shouted, the more they laughed, and plunged his head backwards right under the water. The smell of the slime was horrible. He was shaking and choking as they pulled him out.

'This is how we treat all newcomers,' one of them said. 'It cools their ardour, and puts them in their place.'

'You'll be doing it next year!'

Never, thought Matthieu, dashing upstairs to the dormitory, in hope of escaping his tormentors.

There he found Roger, still in the middle of a dripping pile of clothes, rubbing himself dry with a towel. 'It's lucky it's a warm day,' he said. 'I suppose this is part of what is called an initiation ceremony to welcome new students. There wasn't room in that pond to swim, not even one stroke!'

Matthieu searched for his towel, leaving pools of water behind him as he moved, still trembling with fear, cold and anger. He hadn't the Breton's love of water and swimming. Moreover, he had to mop up the pools in the room after they had dried themselves, as part of his work.

The floorboards were still damp, but they had finished tidying the room when the third occupant arrived, another Frenchman of similar appearance, but a little older. 'I am Raymond, nicknamed the Traveller,' he announced. 'Tell me your names.'

'Beware of the trial by water,' cautioned Roger. 'There is a trough in the courtyard, and bands of unruly students are looking for newcomers like us, and the Master is out.'

'They won't dare to try any tricks on me,' replied Raymond. 'I am no newcomer to learning. I have spent a whole year at Cordova already, studying the skills of the Moors, and now wish to learn the Arts of Paris.'

'Where is Cordova?' asked Roger. He was surprised to learn that it was near the southernmost tip of Spain, in the region of the Great Rock, on which the chief of the Moors called Tarik had once landed from the northern shores of Africa, and led his followers to conquer Spain. Both boys were fascinated by Raymond. He was clearly highly intelligent, and displayed the self-confidence which came from his experience of studying and travelling.

'How long did it take to reach here?' asked Matthieu, remembering his father's story of his great journey before his marriage, and wondering if the distances were comparable. He was appalled to hear that, whereas his father's journey to Chinon had taken only a few weeks, Raymond's journey from Cordova to Paris had taken a year.

Their new friend went on to describe a few of his many adventures. He had walked over the mountains of Spain, often hungry, sometimes in danger from robbers, frequently barefoot when his shoes had worn out, but fortunately never alone for long. He had spent nights in the villages, relying on the hospitality of the natives, and had met up with other students doing just the same. They usually had to beg for their food, and tried to repay their debts by singing student songs, or playing a stringed instrument if anyone in the party had managed to keep one. When times were bad, they cheered each other along. Even big, strong young men often cried through sheer homesickness. Matthiew thought of Anne and Hélène, miles away at Étampes with his bereaved grand-mother, and felt sad.

Roger, noticing this, changed the subject of their conversation. 'I hear that there is a famous tree in Spain called the olive,' he said. 'I understand that some wealthy people use its juice for washing as well as for drinking. But it is a luxury we could not afford where I come from.'

'Indeed, that is so,' replied Raymond. 'The lower slopes of the mountains are covered by these trees. The sun shines brightly there, and their shadows make patterns in straight lines across the light-coloured soil. From a distance, these orchards resemble a tapestry. But what I love more are the orange trees. Do you know that in Cordova, the fruit and flowers are on the trees at the same time, and one can stoop to pick as many as one can eat?'

'There are also some in the southern parts of France, in Provence, I think,' remarked Matthieu, remembering some of Lord Augustus' stories about his luxurious home. 'Orange trees are spreading northwards now.'

'You should try to go to Cordova to study,' went on Raymond. 'The University there was founded by the Arabs.'

'Are there many Arabs left?' asked Matthieu.

'Yes, quite a number. The Spaniards, who reconquered the south of Spain from them, dislike them, but are forced to admit their skill, especially in science and building. You should see the Mosque! It is so magnificent, and has been standing for five centuries.'

'What is so great about it?' asked Roger, somewhat disbelieving.

'Its size,' explained Raymond. 'It is far larger than Nôtre Dame, and its arches are more rounded, and decorated with bands of colour, usually red. Although the windows are too small to let in much light, the whole scene is most impressive.

Mathieu was not feeling very happy. He had been taught carefully by those he loved and respected not to question his own faith, and therefore thought he should not be listening to any stories about a heathen religion, not even a description of a building. 'Let us go and buy some supper,' he suggested. 'There is an excellent pastry cook near here, where we can buy delicious cakes and custard pies.' He was waiting to test his new-found freedom after so many years spent in a monastic school. As yet, the two remaining students who were to occupy their room had not arrived, so the three made their way into the street, where the students were already gathering. 'We must cook our own supper in our Hall tomorrow,' cautioned Roger, 'unless you are both richer than I am.'

'By no means,' laughed Raymond. 'I have only the few coins I earned by telling stories, and singing my way through France. When that has gone, I shall be hungry!'

They linked arms and strode along singing, rather inappropriately:

> *'Fluxit Labor diei,*
> *redit et quietis hora,*
> *blandus sopor vicissim*
> *fessos relacat artus.'*

> *'The toil of the day is ebbing,*
> *The quiet comes again,*
> *In slumber deep relaxing,*
> *The limbs of tired men.'*

CHAPTER VII

Adventures

The next morning, work began in earnest. Roger went off to study Grammar, while Raymond and Matthieu made their way to a small Hall, where they were to listen to Bernard of Chartres lecturing on dialectics. This meant that they would listen to the Master's discourse on the ideas of Aristotle, discuss and argue about them. When they arrived, Bernard was already seated on a platform in a wooden chair, with a writing board across its arms, on which was placed his parchment containing his notes. About twenty students sat informally before him on the floor. Parchment was less expensive than it had been, and this meant that they each spread out their pieces, with quills and ink. Raymond and Matthieu found it difficult to find a place to lay out their materials.

There was much talking, and Bernard made several false starts to gain the students' attention. Matthieu felt sorry for him. Unless he discovered a way to control them, Bernard would find himself without an audience, and lose his position. He came from the famous school at Chartres, where standards were high, and behaviour was good. Raymond was used to his fellow students' methods of interrupting the lecturer as they wished. Matthieu, after his quiet education in the monastery, was appalled by them.

However, Bernard had one good story to tell which took everyone's attention. He was speaking of Reality, and used an example handed down by the famous Welsh scholar, Giraldus, who had become famous both at Oxford and Paris fifty years earlier. 'There was a young scholar who had six eggs, and he tried to persuade his father that in reality he had twelve eggs. "All right," said his father, "put them on the table." Then the father ate all six eggs and, turning to his son, said, "You may eat the other six!"' The laughter which followed was so tremendous that he had difficulty in resuming. A group of long-legged, fair-haired, blue-eyed young men were the worst offenders. "Bravo, bravo," they shouted in their native tongue, forgetting that Latin was the only language used in the lecture hall.

Finally, Bernard's ordeal was over, and the students broke into groups to walk along the river bank, to discuss what they had learned and to buy some food before returning to the afternoon session. Stalls along the Seine sold eggs and fruit. Raymond and Matthieu spent a few precious coins on hard-boiled eggs, only to find that they were bad. Afterwards, they learned that this often happened, and eggs in Paris were best avoided. On their way back to the Halls to find their lecture on St. Augustine's 'City of God', they met Roger. He told them that he had enjoyed a very peaceful morning, and some worthwhile instruction in Latin Grammar. He was aiming at becoming a priest, and needed this before he could go on to study Theology. Raymond and Matthieu found Father German's lecture on St. Augustine gave them much useful information, even if it was a little dull. Most of the students listening to it were from Bologna and Padua, and took their work more seriously than the group from Oxford, which they had encountered earlier.

Then they returned to the Hall to prepare their own supper of broth and bread that evening, they realised that the other two students had not yet arrived. 'They may not ever come,' said Raymond, hopefully. 'Anything may have happened to them.'

'What kind of things?' asked Roger, who showed more concern.

'Well, they may have run out of money, and cannot pay for their lectures. That is very likely. Or they may have been attacked, and robbed, or injured on their way here,' suggested Raymond. Naturally, they all rejoiced at having more room to spread out their books and notes.

During the next few days, they all became more and more aware of their hunger, which was preventing them from putting out their best efforts. Matthieu decided to take one friend at a time to his home. He knew that his parents were poor, but he was sure that they could not refuse to give them a meal. On the second Saturday of the term, when they were free, he set off with Raymond to the shoemaker's shop. He knew nothing of his friend's background, except that he had travelled a great deal, and had suffered hardship. These experiences had helped him to settle down happily in any company.

At length they reached the more humble end of the shoemakers' street, and Matthieu pointed out the sign of Ralph Le Boeuf over the shop door. Ralph was just taking the money from one of the Palace servants for a pair of boots as they entered. Robert, as usual, was sewing neatly, with much concentration. Hélène was cooking the midday meal in a great stewpot over the fire. There would be plenty. Turning suddenly, she saw Matthieu enter, and embraced him with a cry of delight and surprise. Her warm greeting was quickly extended to his friend, and they were soon all seated at the table.

When they had eaten, Hélène and Ralph wanted to hear all about Matthieu's adventures, but Robert remained stubbornly silent. On hearing about the noisy discussions, and the interruptions during lectures, Ralph looked very displeased. This was something he had not expected, and was quite outside his experience. Hélène, however, was more tolerant. She did not expect young men to remain silent, and was more concerned about their lack of food. 'I will pack some loaves for you to take back, and you must have some fresh eggs from our own hens,' she said. Matthieu wanted to hear news of Anne, who had remained at Étampes to keep her grandmother company. 'I am sure she is very happy there, or I would not have left her, so do not worry about her,' said Hélène. 'And the parish priest will help her to write, so that your efforts to teach her have not been in vain. Next time you come home, you may find a letter from her.'

Then they went back to talk about the University again.

Matthieu repeated Giraldus' story about the six eggs, which Bernard had told them, and this made Ralph laugh. But it was difficult to make him understand how men could learn by talking and questioning, rather than by rote memory. 'This is a fairly new way of teaching,' Raymond told him, 'which was developed by Peter Abelard.'

Ralph did not find this remark very consoling. Their new parish priest, an Italian, Père Francesco, had told him something of Peter Abelard, and he did not approve of him. 'Peter Abelard drew literally thousands to listen to him,' interrupted Ralph. 'Père Francesco told us that he was so popular that he drew away all William of Champeau's students. And then, as if that were not enough, although he was a churchman, and therefore had vowed never to marry, he fell in love with a lady called Héloise and wished to marry her, thus causing the disgrace and ruin of them both.'

Knowing that Raymond admired Abelard greatly, Matthieu said quickly, 'But all that happened a very long time ago. I heard an amusing true story of something very recently. You had great respect for our late King, Louis IX, didn't you, Papa? He encouraged learning and often invited well-known scholars to eat at his table in his palace in Paris.'

'Yes, I have been told so,' answered Ralph.

'Well,' went on Matthieu, 'the great scholar, Thomas Aquinas was invited to dine there. As he was very shy, he was thankful to be placed at a corner of the table, where he did not have to talk to people, but could pursue his thoughts. In the middle of dinner, he suddenly thumped his fist on the table, making all the cups and plates clatter. 'That will settle the Manichees!' he called out. The King, realising that the scholar had found an answer to an argument, was not in the least angry but told his secretary to take writing materials over to him to write it down before he forgot it!'

And so they went on talking through the afternoon, forgetting that, as they had not yet purchased their scholars' long black gowns, they ought to get back to their Hall before dark. The rules of the University forbade them to walk the streets at night without them, as they were thought to give some protection.

Matthieu could not afford to purchase a gown, even a secondhand one, for another week, and Raymond not only could not afford one, but had not given it a thought. Seeing that Robert was very quiet, and feeling out of the conversation, Raymond now tried to interest him by telling him some of his adventures wit the Arabs at the University of Cordova.

'Do you ever suffer from toothache?' he asked Robert. 'The Arab students had a wonderful cure for it. You take the tooth of a dog. I'm not sure how you do this if the dog is still alive. Then you grind it down to dust, make it into a paste and put it on your aching tooth. If you cannot find a dog, the brain of a partridge will do as well.'

'What would happen if I had caught a fever?' asked Robert, now more interested.

'You would go to a Doctor of Medicine,' replied Raymond. 'There are many things he could prescribe for you. The best remedy was thought to be inside the little worms with many feet which are found in the bark of trees. You would have to swallow them in a cup of water, or, if you were lucky, in wine. Alternatively, the blood of foxes or the livers of vultures are believed to relieve a fever.'

Both Hélène and Ralph looked distressed, especially Hélène, who had been brought up on herbal remedies on the farm. Then, when Raymond went on to talk of magic in which the Arabs had some belief, Ralph and Matthieu both decided that these stories must stop. Fortunately, Hélène moved to get them some supper, and they drew up again to the table.

It was quite dark when they left, linking arms to reassure each other. The visit had been a great success, and they were happy until some singing through the darkness warned them of the approach of a large band of students. They were singing troubadour songs, in French, with a zest which suggested that they had been doing a considerable amount of drinking. Raymond and Matthieu pressed themselves instinctively against the wall of a house in shadow, until they had passed. They were both frightened of being mistaken, without their gown, as sons of merchants, or 'the town', traditional enemies of students, or 'the gown'. They would have been heavily outnumbered, and bound to have got the worst of a brawl.

As they approached their Hall, a now familiar figure, in gown and square black cap, advanced down the other side of the street. It was their Master, Dr Charles le Peau. If he saw them as they were, they would be liable to pay fines they could not afford. Dr le Peau held his head high. He knocked firmly on his own door until his servant opened it, and then crossed the threshold, looking neither to right nor to left.

CHAPTER VIII

Success

During the following weeks, Matthieu and his friends got to know Docteur Charles le Peau better and they heard their fellow students talking about him in a way which confirmed their own views. Everyone had said he was strict when necessary: excess drunkenness, stealing or violent behaviour, he punished immediately by fines or imprisonment, but youthful high spirits he was ready to ignore. Sometimes he came up to the dormitory in the winter evenings of 1270 and talked to the three boys.

'You are lucky to have so much room to spread yourselves,' he said on more than one occasion. As the term went on, he remarked, 'It is very likely that two more students will arrive after Christmas. You will have to pack up some of your possessions, but you may gain by the light of two more candles. Three do not give a great deal, but five will give a bright light, if you are sensible and do not try to economise too much.' He came from a family who had made their fortune from making parchment at a time when it was dear, and was very matter-of-fact about money. He was concerned about all three boys, and soon gained great affection for Matthieu, whom he knew hoped to be ordained as a priest later. He had had good reports of him and his family, both from Brother Marcus and Père Simon, and watched his progress at his studies, giving him every encouragement. Raymond had not so far declared what his plans for the future were, but as he was extraordinarily intelligent, and a good talker, most people expected that he would become a Master at one of the Universities. Roger, too, hoped to be ordained, and like Matthieu would probably become a parish priest in due course.

When Matthieu returned from his Christmas holiday at home, he found Roger and Raymond already in the dormitory with two other young men, both red-headed and long-limbed. He guessed that they were not Frenchmen, and approached them with open arms, and the greeting of 'Saluté'. He was right in assuming they would have to use Latin in conversation for the time being.

The young men, whose names were Peter and John, were both English, although their red hair, and the fact that they were both from eastern parts of England, suggested that they were descended from Danish invaders. All the boys spoke fluent Latin, but it was often difficult to find words in a classical tongue to describe the homely details of their lives, so they all made great efforts to learn each other's languages. The best time for conversation was during the evening, when they shared the cooking utensils in the Docteur's kitchen, while his servant rather dubiously left the place to them.

Peter lived near Cambridge and had studied at the University there. He was attending the same lectures as Roger, beginning with Grammar. Raymond asked him what he missed most about England. He replied, 'The open country and the great wide fields, divided into strips, where the wind blows over the oats, or wheat or barley, according to the chosen crop that season. I feel restricted in the streets of Paris, and long for the narrow ones of Cambridge which are much nearer the countrywide, with its homely red-brick cottages and farmhouses.'

'I miss the sea,' interrupted John, whose family lived at Whitby, in Yorkshire.

'What is it like?' asked Matthieu, 'I have never seen it, and am always rather frightened by the thought of it. Did you feel alarmed when you crossed it to come here?'

'It can be frightening in winter,' replied John. 'When the wind howls and the rain pours down, and the waves are so high that they threaten to crash over the mast and decks of the ship. In summer, it is wonderful, when the sun sparkles upon it. But I love it most from the beach on a calm winter's day, when it comes in in great green rolls, which are almost transparent, and then, when they hit the sand, change into white lacy patterns of froth.'

'Now that you have overcome the danger of crossing it, will you stay over here for several years?' asked Raymond.

'No, just long enough to learn something of grammar and dialectics, which are so well taught here,' replied John. 'Then I shall return to Yorkshire, and continue my studies as a monk. Not at first, of course. It takes time to become a monk, but eventually, at one of the great Cistercian abbeys in Yorkshire. Fountains, perhaps.'

The three Frenchmen knew little of the Cistercian monks; their experience had been only with the Benedictines. 'Please tell us more,' said Matthieu.

'I admire them because they work so very hard,' went on John. 'They believe in the dignity of human labour, whereas the Benedictines, forgive me, I'm not being critical, believe that they are meant to do more important things and hire labourers to work for them. The Cistercians are mainly employed with farming sheep in the Yorkshire dales, and shear them themselves, to sell the wool to keep their community going. Some of it they weave to make their own habits, which are white. They speak to each other when it is absolutely necessary, hardly at all.'

'That wouldn't suit me,' laughed Raymond. 'And what are you going to do?' he asked Peter.

'I hope to stay here for some time, perhaps even long enough to complete my Master's degree, and then return to Cambridge to become a Master myself,' he said. 'I must put up with the limitations here to fulfil my purpose.'

'You may not find them so great after all,' suggested Raymond, deciding that he would show Peter how to enjoy life in Paris. The smell of the beef stew boiling over the pot drew their attention, and all serious conversation ended.

*   *   *   *   *   *   *   *   *   *

The group of five soon developed strong bonds of friendship, broken only when John left them after a year to enter the great abbey of Fountains as a novice. They missed him very much, and afterwards tended to split into two pairs: Roger and Peter worked together, while Raymond and Matthieu talked, argued and encouraged each other over the three years leading up to their examinations to become Bachelors of Arts.

The main part of the examination was in the form of an argument with the Masters of the subjects they had chosen. As this took place in public, and as any students could come along to listen, cheer or jeer, it was a two-fold ordeal. Matthieu had selected the works of Plato, Aristotle and St Augustine to discuss. There were not many books available by the two Greek authors, as they had only reached France during the past century, but St Augustine was well-known by all scholars.

The 'disputation', as the examination was called, was fixed for a morning at the end of June. In spite of his own prayers, his awareness of being surrounded by so much goodwill, and the kindness of Raymond, Matthieu had spent a sleepless night. His confidence had been shaken by Raymond's account of his own performance on the previous day. Although he had passed the test, and could now call himself a Bachelor of Arts, Raymond had come back exhausted, and haunted by the feeling that he could have done better if only he had stopped to think before he answered back.

Raymond walked down the street with him as far as the door of the Hall, which was already crowded with noisy students. At length the three Masters who were to examine him arrived, and he was summoned in. He knew only one of them, Docteur le Martineau, who was known, but not loved, for his quick wit.

'Monsieur le Boeuf,' this Docteur began. 'Can you tell us which author has contributed more to Christian ideas, Aristotle or St Augustine?' An easy beginning!

'Sir, Aristotle lived before Christ,' replied Matthieu. As the argument about the relative value of their works went on, Matthieu gained confidence, and became aware of the support of the crowd behind him. Many of his replies were warmly applauded. He managed to avoid the temptation, however, of trying to be too clever, or to show too ready a wit. At the end, his steadfastness was rewarded. The three consulted together. Then Docteur le Martineau spoke. 'M le Boeuf,' he announced. 'We proclaim you a Bachelor of Arts!' The crowd of students surged up, and followed Matthieu into the street, clapping their hands, and calling out messages of good will. Matthieu tried to make his way to find his good friend, Raymond, but before he could do so, a small group from the rowdier element appeared, and were seen to be carrying a blanket by its four corners. Two or three of the strongest seized Matthieu, and flung him into it, and the tossing began. At the third toss, he was aware of his stomach rising up, almost into his mouth, with a sickening sensation. He let forth a cry, and was immediately dropped into the gutter, where he vomited loudly and sorely. He lay there for a moment to recover, his neat tunic splashed with his own filth. This was the punishment of success!

* * * * * * * * * *

That evening, having been wiped, dried, congratulated and consoled by Raymond, Matthieu made his way alone through the streets to tell his good news to his parents. Raymond had reminded him, thoughtfully, that his brother Robert might find this difficult to rejoice over. His work and interests were so very different, and perhaps it was easier for Matthieu to understand Robert than it was for Robert to understand Matthieu. Realising that this was sound sense, Matthieu took the advice in good part.

He knocked on the door of the shop, which was closed for the night. When Ralph let him in, before announcing his success immediately, Matthieu looked round for Robert. He wasn't there. Noticing his surprise, Ralph gave him a broad wink. 'Next door,' he said. 'He's growing up. Some boys marry at his age, and Jeanne is even older, and a fine lass!'

'Hélène hugged him. He smiled at her, and nodded. There was no need to say more. Even Ralph had guessed his triumph. He brought out three cups and a flagon of ale. 'I'm sorry we have no wine, son,' he said. 'but you know you are always welcome to what we have. How is that good lad who comes here sometimes with you? Raymond?'

'He is a Bachelor of Arts, too,' said Matthieu.

'Mon Dieu! A Bachelor of Arts!' said Ralph. Then he produced a scroll. 'Please read us your sister's letter from the farm.'

Matthieu was pleased to see how well Anne was writing for one so young. 'She says she and Grandmère are well,' he said. 'She loves the farm, and helps with the cooking and the animals – especially the hens! Pierre le Laboureur helps them, and does all the heavy work, like ploughing.'

'That's good, I'm glad they have some help,' remarked Hélène. 'Anne is doing well for her eleven years, isn't she? I hear that Lady Ranulf de Villaincourt thinks highly of her.'

'What are you going to do now?' Ralph asked Matthieu, although he already had some idea.

'I should like to go on studying for my Master's Degree, and spend the next three years at the college Docteur Sorbon founded. It is a wonderful place. Not only is the teaching excellent, but the students have to behave well. No drinking! Then I hope to become a priest.'

'How wonderful,' cried Hélène. Behind her enthusiasm, Matthieu noticed for the first time some signs of tiredness. Her skin appeared suddenly more wrinkled, especially around the eyes. Her face was thinner and the gray hairs predominated over the dark ones. He looked at Ralph and was relieved to find him robust, and little changed. He remembered that his mother was a countrywoman, and had never really flourished in the city. He was glad that he was now due to spend a few weeks at home, and would be with her.

CHAPTER IX

Anne

In the autumn of 1273, Matthieu returned to his studies. This time, he went to live in a Hall for the Sorbonne College. This was near his former Hall, and he did not feel at all strange. He was to live there for three years, at the end of which he hoped to become a Master of Arts, and also a priest.

Robert was soon to become a Master of a different kind, one of the Guild of Shoemakers. He had almost finished his Masterpiece, a beautiful pair of shoes with long, pointed toes, and was about to be accepted by the other members of the Guild. Ralph was justly proud of him.

Meanwhile, Anne was still living with her grandmother, Mairie Fourneau. Like her mother, she was a country girl at heart, and soon learnt how to tend the farm animals, as well as the way to manage a household. From their loyal friend and helper, Pierre le Laboureur, she learnt how to milk the cows, watch the sow to make sure that she did not lie on her piglets, and find the nests of hens who layed out in the hedgerows. This last task she did not enjoy much. Like her father, she disliked the way hens flapped and pecked. Noticing that she was an exceptionally intelligent child, Mairie had asked the parish priest, Père Jean, if he would help her with her writing, as well as instructing her in the Catechism. This he was pleased to do.

Anne walked to his house next to the village church one afternoon each week for her lesson. On her way home one warm autumn afternoon, she met Lady Ranulf, riding her palfry. Anne stepped aside, and curtsied. 'How is your Grandmother?' asked the lady. 'And where have you been?'

'She is well, thank you, my lady,' replied Anne, 'and I am returning from my lesson with Père Jean.'

'Oh, yes, I hear you can both read and write,' said Ethelburga, who was feeling a little bored. She was having to rest more, before the birth of her second child, and found this irritating. 'You must come to visit me, and we will read together. I have some beautiful books of verses. We could sing them. Do you play an instrument?' Anne, of course, did not, but the lady invited her to come to the Manor House the following afternoon. This was a command which had to be obeyed, but Anne found she enjoyed the time she spent in Lady Ethelburga's solar, or small private room, upstairs. She did worry, however, about leaving her grandmother so long alone, and over the jobs left undone on the farm.

Lady Ethelburga taught her to sing some of the romantic songs of the time, which described the heroic adventures of the knights:

> 'Chascun de soy armer se peine
> D'armeures neufves et freches.
> Li un y porte unes bretesches
> En son escu reluisant cher,
> Cil un lyon, cil un cengler,
> Cil un lepart, cil un poisson.'*

Then they read stories of romantic heroes together, Ethelburga encouraged Anne, and helped her to pronounce any unfamiliar words.

Lady Ethelburga's second child was born just before Christmas 1273 and named Eleanor, after the sister of the Queen of France who had become Queen of Ethelburga's own country. Anne enjoyed helping to bath and dress the baby, and learnt how to play with her. 'She would make a good nurserymaid,' thought Ethelburga.

'I suppose your Grandmother could not manage without you,' she said one spring day to Anne, as she threaded her needle to put through her embroidery frame.

'Indeed, no,' replied Anne, who was always completely truthful. 'She is wonderful, but she is becoming very frail, and needs my help. That is why I have given up going to Père Jean for my weekly lesson,' she added. She did, indeed, miss this time with the parish priest very much.

'I see,' said Ethelburga. 'But what will you do when you are eventually left alone on the farm? You will not want to leave the country to return to your parents' shop in Paris.'

---

*Each strives to arm himself with new clean armour. One has a tower shining brightly on his shield, one a lion, one a board, this man a leopard and the other a fish.

ANNE

Anne knew the answer, and therefore was completely unperturbed. 'I am going to marry Pierre le Laboureur,' she said.

Lady Ethelburga was horrified. 'But you are not old enough to marry,' she said. 'And Pierre is utterly unsuitable. Indeed, he is a good man, and a hard worker. When I am out riding, I can see which strips of land he cares for, because the furrows there are straighter than anywhere else. But he cannot read or write! And what would you talk about?'

'The cow and the pigs,' said Anne.

'Has he asked you?' demanded Ethelburga.

'No, but he will,' replied Anne. 'Next year. I shall be old enough.'

Ethelburga thought to herself: I could stop this marriage. Pierre will have to come to Ranulf for permission to marry, because he is only a peasant. If I ask Ranulf to refuse to give it, he will do so. She said nothing. Anne, seeing her displeasure, rose from her footstool to go home quickly.

'Perhaps you were unwise to speak so openly, before Pierre has declared his love for you,' said her grandmother when Anne told her about it. 'But I am very pleased to hear that that is how you feel. If Lord Ranulf is willing, and I can see no reason why he should not be, you and Pierre could go on farming here after my time. There is nothing for Pierre at his home. He has too many brothers and sisters.' She resolved secretly to hurry Pierre up, before Lady Ethelburga made any alternative plans.

Ethelburga had second thoughts. She liked her own way, but she was a fair and honest woman. She decided that if Pierre and Anne did get married, she would be their most generous benefactor, and help them all she could. Thanks to some promptings from Anne's grandmother, Pierre managed to find the right words on the evening of Easter Day, when they were going round the animals together, to shut them up for the night. Mairie was delighted when she heard what had been agreed, and suggested that Anne's thirteenth birthday, in the coming October, would be a suitable day for the wedding.

Anne set out to tell the Lady Ethelburga the following week. The news was not unexpected. 'Have you a wedding gown?' asked Ethelburga, and was delighted to learn that the family possessed one which had once been the gift of an ancestor of Lord Ranulf. 'And bridesmaids?' when on the lady. 'Have you any younger relations?'

'My aunts' children are all married already, and their daughters are only babies. I do not know who to ask,' replied Anne sadly.

'Then I will find you someone suitable and supply her with a dress,' promised Ethelburga. 'My younger sister, Elfrieda, is coming to visit me in the summer, and will bring her maid, who has a small daughter. I will tell her to bring the little girl with her, and she can look after you at your wedding.' The fact that the little girl probably spoke only English did not trouble her.

Anne settled down to write a long letter to ask her parents' permission for her marriage, and to tell them of her plans. Then she had to wait until someone reliable was travelling from Étampes to Paris. Then Hélène had to wait until Matthieu paid them a visit until she could read it. The news was not unexpected, and Hélène was pleased with the arrangement, especially as the prospects of farming there were good, and she knew that her mother liked and respected Pierre. She insisted, however, in the reply which Matthieu wrote for her, that the wedding should be put forward to early September. Neither she nor Ralph felt able to make the journey, but she wanted Matthieu and Robert to be there. For that reason, it must take place before term began again at the Sorbonne. Matthieu's studies must not be interrupted. Matthieu and Robert were delighted at the plans and decided to walk to the wedding, and spend a night at the Priory of Melun on the way, where they knew their father had once spent a night on his famous journey. Matthieu would have liked to have spent several days there, especially as he had just heard that the famous scholar of the last century, John of Salisbury, had stayed there, and could have left some of his manuscripts in the Priory. But Robert insisted that he could not leave the shop for long, and that he did not wish to walk alone, so Matthieu could only agree.

* * * * * * * * * *

When Matthieu and Robert reached the farm, they found that their aunt, Matilde, with her husband François, had already arrived. Their married daughter, Rosemarie, could not leave because her own daughter, Elizabethe, was too young to travel. Chantelle and Mignon, who had been Hélène's bridesmaids, were there, with their husbands. So were Chantelle's small daughter, Jeanne, and Mignon's lively little boy, Henri, who at the age of four promised to get into every kind of trouble on the farm. The wedding was arranged for the next day and they were all spending the night there.

Mairie had not seen Matthieu since his christening, and she had never seen Robert. She embraced them eagerly with much affection, and many tears. Matthieu was troubled to see how frail she looked; after all, she was over seventy years of age. He could understand why Anne had not been able to leave her to return home. Then, as they all sat down to supper, and she took control of

160

the situation, he forgot her tiredness and noticed only how closely she resembled his own mother.

Robert was busy, storing up everything to tell Hélène. He was especially eager to see his sister in the wedding gown which his mother had worn.

The next morning, the little English bridesmaid, Elizabeth, arrived in good time with her mother. She was a little shy, but curtsied to Mairie, and said, 'Bonjour Madame' very nicely. For a moment, Mairie felt a pang of jealousy when she looked at the little girl's dress. Lady Ethelburga had ordered a length of beautiful white silk from Lyons, and it had been made into a full-length gown with long sleeves, and a blue girdle. This was rather hard on the bride. But Anne was so happy that it did not matter, and Mairie quickly put all resentment from her.

They all made their way to the village church, where Pierre was waiting. Mairie had helped him to find the customary dues for the poor, and the dowry, to be offered at the ceremony. They all had to wait at the door until the Lady Ethelburga arrived on her mare. She handed the reins to a manservant, and at last they were able to begin the service. Afterwards, Mairie breathed a silent sigh of relief, as the lady explained that she must return to the Manor at once, as Lord Ranulf was away and there was much business to attend to.

At the farm, the neighbours had prepared a splendid feast. There was a piglet turning on the spit, plenty of fresh bread, little custards and pies of all kinds, and a whole cask of wine which had arrived mysteriously in their absence. The men sat round the table tightly packed, and ate while the women stood behind them. The younger people moved out as soon as they had finished and chased each other round the courtyard. Chantelle and Mignon and their husbands joined in the fun, and tried to divert little Henri from the pigsty. Forgetting her wedding dress, Anne seized little Elizabeth's hand and ran with her round and round the well, until both were dizzy. Henri leaped upon her with a piece of crackling from the pig, an especial present. The grease fell all down the front of her green brocade dress, and passed unnoticed in the fun. Watching, Mairie wondered whether either of the dresses would ever be the same again, and decided that it did not matter. At length, it was time for the neighbours to harness their carts, for Tante Matilde and Oncle François to say goodbye, and for Anne and Pierre to be left alone to start their married life in the home of their much loved grandmother. Matthieu and Robert prepared to spend the night in the barn, and to start early next morning to walk as far as Melun on their way home.

CHAPTER X

The Family Goes On

Farewells next morning were very sad affairs, as the brothers did not know when they would see their family again. Mairie had packed a liberal amount of food for their journey, knowing that they would have to leave the monastery at Melun next day before breaking their fast.

'I do like Pierre,' said Robert, as they walked along.

'So do I,' agreed Matthieu. 'He is completely honest and very hard-working.'

'And he will look after Anne, he is very fond of her,' said Robert.

They reached Melun during the afternoon in good time for vespers and the evening meal. 'I don't expect you were here nearly twenty years ago, when our father spent a night in this monastery,' said Matthieu to the young guest master, who laughed. 'That would not have been possible,' he replied. 'But after Vespers I will take you both to visit Brother Jacques in his cell. He was the guest master for some time, and might remember. What is your father's name?'

Brother Jacques did indeed remember Ralph le Boeuf. 'And he must be married,' he exclaimed in some surprise, 'because he has two sons!' There was no time for further talk as they were due to go into supper, but the old monk sent a kind message of remembrance to Ralph before they left him.

They left after Mass in the morning, and sat down on a mossy bank to eat the food Mairie had given them, before they went far. 'Were you happy in the monastery?' asked Matthieu of his brother, knowing that it was his first stay in one.

'I didn't mind for a short visit, and because you were there,' his brother answered him. 'But I wouldn't want to do it often. I shall be glad to get home.'

'Papa can manage the shop quite well without you,' said Matthieu, who had enjoyed his stay at Melun very much, and would have liked to have spent some time there. 'But perhaps there is another reason why you are in a hurry?'

'I promised Jeanne d'Honnête I would not be long away,' admitted Robert.

'She is certainly a pleasant lass, and a good one,' said Matthieu kindly. 'I imagine you are going to marry her?'

Robert looked a little embarrassed.

'I should like to,' he said at last.

'Then you must ask her as soon as you can,' advised Matthieu. 'But talk to Papa about it first, because she will have to come to live with you all, and it will mean more mouths to feed. And don't forget that it is polite to ask her father, Henri d'Honnête, if he is willing, before you ask Jeanne.' Robert looked a little overcome by all this good advice. Seeing this, Matthieu went on, 'Just do things one at a time. Ask Papa tomorrow, Henri the next day and after that, you will have to ask Jeanne!' They both laughed, and Robert felt encouraged.

In due course, he did just as his brother had advised, but it took him several days to pluck up courage. Meanwhile, Matthieu returned to his studies at the Sorbonne. Ralph and Hélène were both very pleased by the proposal, and by Jeanne's acceptance. They had naturally been expecting it for some time. The wedding was fixed to take place soon after Christmas, and their own priest, Père Francesco, agreed to marry them in his own parish church. Hélène was particularly pleased. Ever since her arrival as a young bride, she had loved the whole family next door dearly. Now that she so often felt tired, and suffered from a pain in her chest, she was relieved to know that Jeanne would there to help look after the menfolk. She and Claude had many details to discuss. Could Claude retrieve the family wedding dress from her married daughter in time to make the necessary alterations? Who could be a bridesmaid? Fortunately, Claude was equally delighted at the prospect. She admired Robert's steady and purposeful ways very much. He would be a good Master craftsman, and a kind and loyal person, who would make an ideal husband and father.

All these thoughts were going through her head, as she sat beside Hélène on the settle by Ralph's fire. She was startled by a cry, as Hélène fell forward in great pain. Ralph, bewildered, ran to her side, and together they managed to lift her back on to the settle. Claude ran to her husband for help, and Henri went immediately to fetch the apothecary. He could not be found, but Henri was caring and resourceful as always.

Robert, when he returned, was horrified at the scene before him, but Henri at once advised him to fetch a trestle bed from his house next door. Together they placed Hélène on it. Slowly her breathing became more regular, and some colour returned to her cheeks. At last the apothecary arrived, and suggested a brew of herbs, which Claude made for her. 'Above all,' said the apothecary, who had seen many similar cases, 'she needs rest.'

That night, Ralph refused to sleep alone upstairs, and occupied the bed under the counter which former apprentices had used. Robert went to warn Matthieu of the unfortunate news. He found his brother in the room he shared with other students at the Sorbonne. Fortunately, he was alone, studying. He had realised for some time that his mother was far from well, and, thankful that she was still alive. Before Robert left him, Matthieu promised to come to see Hélène the next day. In his prayers that night, he gave thanks for all the mothers of the world, who had given their complete lives to the care of their husbands and children, without the knowledge that they had done so.

It was agreed that Jeanne and Robert's wedding should not be postponed. Indeed, Hélène needed Jeanne's help in the household more than ever. It took place quietly, just before Christmas 1273. Claude prepared a modest meal in her house to be taken afterwards, but Hélène was not well enough to leave her bed, and Ralph stayed with her. It was very cold in January 1274, as it had been twenty-two years earlier, when Ralph had set off on his famous journey. As they lay in their beds downstairs one night, Ralph and Hélène watched the firelight flickering on the shutters, and listened to Robert and Jeanne talking together above them. They both were profoundly thankful for their presence, and their continual kindness, and hoped that there would be children to succeed them perhaps another shoemaker?

In their concern with Hélène's illness, the family had almost forgotten Anne, although Matthieu had written to her to tell her about Hélène's illness. Just before Easter, a merchant travelling from Étampes to Paris knocked on Ralph's door, with another letter. Anne and Pierre had a daughter, whom they had decided to call Mairie, after her great-grandmother. Ralph wished they had chosen 'Hélène', but his wife reminded him that they were living with Mairie. It was a pity that they were all too busy to go to the christening.

'You will call your daughter 'Hélène', won't you?' Ralph asked Jeanne.

'No, he will be Ralph,' interrupted Hélène. And sure enough, in September a son was born to Robert and Jeanne.

'I do feel old, with two grandchildren,' sighed Ralph.'

'Nonsense, you are not yet fifty,' said Jeanne firmly. 'Now, just hold little Ralph while I prepare the dinner.' And this he did, knowing that it would be the first of many such occasions.

'Matthieu can christen him, can't he?' suggested Hélène.

'Certainly!' they all replied, and Hélène sat up in bed to take the baby from the arms of her husband.

Part Four

Ralph's Descendants

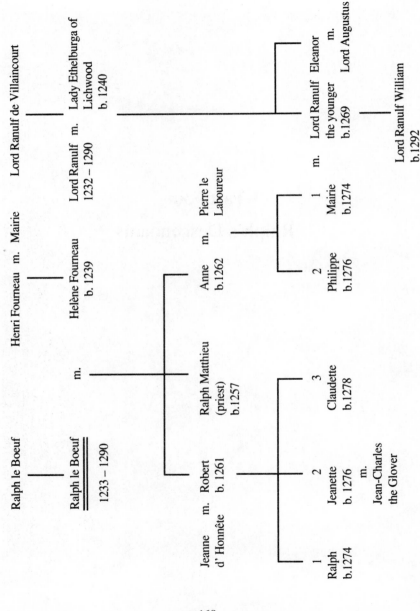

Ralph le Boeuf

Ralph le Boeuf
1233 – 1290

m.

Henri Fourneau   m.   Mairie

Helène Fourneau
b. 1239

Lord Ranulf de Villaincourt

Lord Ranulf   m.   Lady Ethelburga of
1232 – 1290   Lichwood
                              b. 1240

Jeanne   m.   Robert   Ralph Matthieu   Anne   m.   Pierre le   Lord Ranulf   Eleanor   m.
d' Honnête   b. 1261   (priest)   b.1262   Laboureur   the younger   Lord Augustus
                              b.1257   b.1269

1   2   3   2   1   m.
Ralph   Jeanette   Claudette   Philippe   Mairie   Lord Ranulf   William
b.1274   b. 1276   b.1278   b.1276   b.1274   b.1292
              m.
              Jean-Charles
              the Glover

168

CHAPTER I

Mairie

Anne sat in the farm kitchen at Maisse with the letter rolled up in her lap. She was thankful that she had learnt enough to read it herself, and did not have to ask anyone to break the sad news to her. She had read it to her daughter, Mairie, now aged sixteen, who was sitting on a stool by the fire, and seemed strangely unmoved by her grandfather's death.

'Grandpa le Boeuf was a good man, wasn't he?' she asked.

'Of course, a wonderful person,' replied Anne. 'I can remember sitting on his knee by the fire in our shoemaker's shop in Paris.'

'But you were quite young when you left, weren't you?' asked Mairie.

'Yes, I came to live with your grandmother, Mairie, here, as you know.' replied her mother.

'Well, you could not have known your parents for long, and you did not appear so upset when your mother, Hélène, died a few years ago,' went on Mairie. 'Grandpa le Boeuf was a free man, wasn't he?'

'Yes, and greatly respected.'

'I have never understood why you married a peasant,' exclaimed Mairie, very bitterly. 'You must have known that it would make Philippe and me peasants too.'

Anne was too near to tears to explain to Mairie that, if you loved a person as much as she had loved her husband, Pierre, it did not matter what his status was. 'Why can't you be like Philippe?' she asked at last, with a sigh. 'He is very happy as he is, and is now walking with his father, up and down one of our strips in the field, learning to plough. Why must you be so discontented? Well, go now to the priest for your lesson. You are no help to me!'

171

Mairie rose. She knew she was being very obstinate, and even unkind, but she could not manage to say so. She walked quickly out of the house, through the open land in the October sunshine, towards the village church. By now she was too disturbed to go straight to the priest's house for her lesson, and entered the church, where she knelt on the bare flagstones. The grinding hinges of the heavy church door drew her attention, and, swivelling round on her knees, she found herself looking up into the handsome face of Ranulf the Younger, the Lord of the Manor's son. He had just completed the ceremony of knighthood. He stood tall and straight, with his reddish hair, which was cut just above his shoulders, gleaming in the ray of sunshine which penetrated the church through the eastern window. On his gloved wrist perched a hooded falcon, preening herself under the caress of his fingers. Outside, the pawing and neighing of two horses revealed the presence of young Ranulf's man servant with their mounts.

'Good morning,' he said. 'I have never understood why your hair is this wonderful colour,' he remarked. 'All the rest of your family and the people round her are dark.'

'My mother always says we are descended from the Vikings, who used to invade France. My grandfather was a free man,' she added proudly. 'He has just died.'

'Oh, I'm sorry to hear that,' said Ranulf, now formal and polite. 'Is that why you're here, and not at your lessons?'

'How did you know I was going to my lesson?' asked Mairie, as Ranulf offered his hand to help her to her feet. 'I must go now.'

'My ancestors are mixed too,' said Ranulf, walking with her to the door. 'As you know, my mother, the Lady Ethelburga, is English, and so was my father's mother. This is why I look like this,' he said, holding his head high.

He left her and mounted his horse, which he did easily and swiftly, still balancing Chérie, the falcon, on his wrist. Mairie went into the priest's house to explain to him about the loss of her grandfather and her mother's grief. 'Tell your mother that we will pray for the repose of the soul of Ralph le Boeuf at Mass on Sunday, and on every day for some time. All will be well,' said Père Jean-Baptiste. 'I expect it is too far for your mother to go to the burial. I will tell her not to worry about that.'

The priest's obvious sympathy sent Mairie home in a more considerate frame of mind. She kissed her mother and hoped that this would be accepted as a sign of repentance, which it was. They all sat down to the midday meal of soup and bread and cheese.

'I met the young Sir Ranulf on my way,' remarked Mairie. Anne looked at Pierre, who was eating ravenously after his long morning with the plough and oxen.

'Did he speak to you?' he asked with his mouth full.

'Only to say "good morning". He was riding with his falcon, and his manservant was with him,' replied Mairie, who had learnt when to withhold details.

'Philippe did well this morning,' mumbled Pierre. 'He will plough as straight a furrow as his father does before he is much older. Even now, I could leave all the ploughing to him, if I wished.'

'I like your friend, Pierre, Joseph's son,' Anne remarked to Philippe. 'Like you, he is a good workman and has hard-working parents. And he is so handsome! He is a little older than you, isn't he?'

Mairie went on eating in silence. These hints had been made often before, and she preferred not to hear them. 'Yes, he is a good fellow,' agreed Philippe. 'Don't you like him, Mairie?'

Stung out of her silence, Mairie almost lost the calm frame of mind she had only recently acquired. 'At least he's better looking than Catherine le Court,' she replied bitterly. 'Catherine's so short and fat that she is bound to have a family of children who will be almost dwarfs. You wouldn't like that, would you?'

Anne sighed. Why did Mairie always spoil everything with these outbursts? Unfortunately, Philippe, who was usually so very calm and happy, took this badly. 'What do you know about children?' he asked. 'Isn't it time you married and produced a family?' Anne, who had stood up to serve Pierre with some more food, took control of the situation. 'Go back to work, both of you,' she said. 'Pierre, harness the oxen for this afternoon's ploughing, and Mairie, go and collect the eggs. If you are still hungry, it is your own fault. And do not return to supper until you can speak kindly to each other!'

Nothing could have suited Mairie better. This gave her freedom for the whole afternoon. Like her parents, she loved animals and being out-of-doors. Gleefully she seized a wicker basket, and made off to the hedgerows in search of the nests of the hens who had layed outside. The afternoon sun shone warmly as she took the same path as she had taken that morning. Suddenly a whirl of wings startled her, as a bird with a tremendous wingspan just failed to touch the top of her head as it skimmed across. With a swoop, it all but grazed the ground before it rose again, carrying a small creature in its hooked beak.

'Well done, well done,' exclaimed a well-known voice. A tall figure emerged from the scrub to offer his gauntletted wrist to the falcon. 'Here, a piece of meat. This is your reward,' said young Sir Ranulf, and he put his hand into his leather bag to take out a titbit for the bird, as she dropped the fieldmouse at his feet. Then he deftly placed the hood over her head, and the jesses on her legs, while she chewed up the piece of meat. 'That secures you, my lady,' he exclaimed proudly. Then he became aware of Mairie approaching. 'I didn't mean to address you in that way,' he said, with a laugh. 'That comment was meant for Chérie.'

'Of course,' replied Mairie, who by now was feeling a little jealous of the falcon. 'What a beautiful bird. May I hold her for a moment?'

'I can't let you do that,' Sir Ranulf said emphatically. 'Just look at her talons! They would tear pieces of skin off your wrist, and what would your mother say to that?'

'Certainly, that would be difficult to hide,' thought Mairie, to herself. She was disappointed that Ranulf had not offered to lend her his glove. 'Do you breed falcons, as well as train them?' she asked, not wishing to go away just yet.

'I hope to, but it's not easy, because they will not breed in captivity,' explained Ranulf. 'Chérie is a fine bird, and I hope to find a suitable tercel for her, that is, a male bird, but they will only make their nests in freedom, on the edge of a cliff, or on the side of a sand or gravel pit. When the time comes, I must watch where she lays her eggs, and wait my chance to take the young ones from the nest to train. I do not want to run the risk of losing the mother in the process.'

The sound of horse's hooves moving at a gallop interrupted them, and Lord Ranulf the elder rode into view.

'Good, I like the way you are controlling your bird,' he called out, as he reined up beside his son. Ignoring Mairie completely, he went on, 'We must take some more eyas* to be trained while you are at home. You might give some lessons in falconry to your friends later on.' And he rode off without another word. Saluting Mairie, the young Ranulf left her, and strode over the turf in the wake of his father.

---

* Young falcons from the nest.

CHAPTER II

Young Ranulf's Journey

Lord Ranulf rode up to his manor house and handed his horse to a manservant. 'Where is Henri?' he asked.

'With the falcons, Sire,' replied the man.

Lord Ranulf strode into the shed where two falcons perched, their heads hooded and their legs free from jesses. 'What are you doing here, Henri?' he asked. 'Your work is to attend to your young master.'

'Sir Ranulf said he wished to be alone with Chérie,' replied the man, humbly. 'She is easier to train that way.' Making no reply, Lord Ranulf turned towards the house.

On the way he met his daughter Eleanor, taking a walk with her maid. Eleanor walked upright with her head held high, her long dress of dark blue reaching her feet, covering but not concealing the shapeliness of her limbs. A white headdress fell to her shoulders. Happiness shone from her eyes. 'My lord,' she said, and curtsied.

When I am married, and have children, she was thinking, they will curtsey to me. I can afford to show some courtesy now. Her father was pleased. 'Is your mother upstairs?' he asked.

'She is sewing with her maid,' replied Eleanor, and added, 'The cloth has just returned from the weaver's and they are making my dresses.'

As he climbed the stairs to the solar, Lady Ethelburga's maid passed him as she went down on an errand. Good, he thought. His lady rose to greet him. He bowed, and they sat down.

'Eleanor is very happy,' he remarked, 'The prospect of her marriage to Lord Augustus is welcome to her.' Lady Ethelburga agreed. Although Eleanor was marrying before she was twenty, at times she had chafed at not being allowed an earlier match. But her mother was convinced that her partner was one worth waiting for. Also, she had wanted her daughter to have some time to be carefree at home before taking on the responsibilities of wife and mother.

'Lord Augustus is a dear man,' she said. 'Full of humour and good nature.'

'He is not much of a horseman,' laughed Ranulf. 'I only hope he will not meet with an accident while riding.'

'His education at the monastery did not include horsemanship,' replied his wife. 'It is not his fault if he does not ride as Ranulf does.'

'I met Ranulf with this falcon just now,' went on his father. 'He is a wonderful trainer of birds, and interested in everything on the estate. My lady, it is time he thought of finding a suitable wife.'

Lady Ethelburga raised her eyebrows. Gossip from her maid had reached her. She knew precisely what her husband had in mind.

'My lord,' she remarked, 'Eleanor's wedding is to take place at Easter. We must soon send an invitation to my old father, and my married brother and sister. We must be careful to choose a reliable messenger. It is a long way to the centre of England, and especially difficult in winter.'

'I am sure Ranulf would undertake this for us,' suggested her husband. 'He could take Henri with him, and we can ask our chaplain to write letters of introduction, which we could send in advance.'

Lady Ethelburga clapped her hands. 'Excellent, my lord,' she exclaimed. 'There is no need for Ranulf to hurry home. It is time that he enjoyed some company of his own age, and I am sure my brother will arrange that.'

Accordingly, Lord Ranulf put the plan before his son that evening. Young Sir Ranulf was somewhat surprised, but, as he was always eager for adventure, he agreed to make the journey. Lord Ranulf spoke to him again, as he had so often before, of his own journey from England with his bride, including practical advice on the hiring of a ship and the roads he should take through England. Ranulf, who had never crossed the sea, became very excited. 'Find a ship which will be large enough to take both your horses,' cautioned his father.

* * * * * * * * * *

It was late October when Sir Ranulf and Henri reached the port of Le Havre. As they had rested their horses and themselves frequently at monasteries on their way, they had all stood the journey well. The horses carried packs containing changes of clothes for their riders, and presents of golden cups for their host. Le Havre had been developing as a port for some time; there were moorings for ships along the jetties, and merchantmen were unloading their cargoes. Ranulf and Henri sought the masters of those flying the red cross of St George, and found some ships bearing the inscription 'of Portsmouth' or 'of Dover'.

Ranulf approached the captains with the words his mother had taught him. 'To England?' At first he was unlucky. All the ships had been chartered already. Then Henri noticed one bearing the flag of St George which was unloading a cargo of clay in earthenware pots. It bore the words 'De la Pole.' The captain replied to Ranulf's question by beckoning them on board. A seaman led his horse below decks, while Henri followed with his, removed the packs and harness and haltered them to their stalls. He was to sleep near them, while Ranulf was led to the cabin which was the Master's own. He came in to see that Ranulf had all he needed, and exchanged a golden livre for a bag full of silver English pennies. Both men were a little apprehensive, as a stiff breeze was blowing. They realised that their journey would be the swifter because of it, and this comforted them. The ship was a two-master, and larger than most. It set sail during the afternoon, and, after a very uncomfortable night of tossing and turning, they reached Pole* the next morning.

'Shall we break our fast?' suggested Ranulf. 'There should be an English inn which can supply some bread and wine.' Henri was feeling the worse for wear, and had been very sea-sick. He was still suffering from the sensation of being on the boat, but could not disagree with his young master.

They led their horses up the sandy lane from the harbour, along a street of overhanging houses of lathe and plaster, looking for an inn. Without warning, a douche of very dirty and smelly water landed on Ranulf's head, drenching his hair and shoulders. Startled, he looked up. A scream of unpleasant laughter followed the water, and a word he did not know, which sounded like 'for-in-ers!' followed by 'Gardez loo!'

'The devil take you!' shouted Ranulf, losing his temper and looking for shelter. He noticed an open door, above which jutted out a pole with a branch of leaves at the end, marking the entrance to an ale-house. 'This will do!' he called to Henri, who was still feeling too poorly to be fully aware of what was happening.

Henri held the horses while Ranulf entered. 'Some bread and wine, if you please,' he asked. A buxom lass stood before him, carrying mugs brimming over with ale to a group of stalwart men. They all turned towards him, and then

---

* Now known as Poole.

began to nudge each other and laugh. 'O, pardonez moi,' said one. 'Parley vous?' At that they all seized the mugs and gulped down the ale, with much belching, laughter, and jokes beyond Ranulf's understanding. He was a knight, and he stood his ground.

'Wine?' said the lass. 'Wine? What is wine?' and they all laughed again.

'Then bring me some water for the horses,' commanded Ranulf. An older man, who appeared to be the innkeeper, moved from the background and led Ranulf outside again, round to a yard where there were halters fixed to the wall and drinking troughs. Henri tied up, and they returned to the inn. The older man said something which might have been an apology, and motioned them to a table. The girl put some bread and ale before them. One mouthful and Ranulf pulled a face. It was dreadful! Bitter, sharp, undrinkable to Frenchmen. Angry now, Ranulf produced two pennies and threw the contents of the mug through the open door. This display produced a shocked silence.

'Give my horses some oats,' he commanded the innkeeper, and hurried out into the yard, with Henri following. He stamped impatiently until a boy came out with two nosebags of oats. While the horses were eating, he found the map in his saddle bag, and placed it before the innkeeper. He had expected to land at Portsmouth, and wanted to make sure of the way from Pole to New Sarum, where they hoped to spend the first night. The man pointed the way through the little town of Wimborne onto the drovers' track. At one point, he paused and made circles with his finger. Ranulf dismissed this as a foolish gesture. When they were ready, he pointed the way through the streets of Pole towards the open country.

As they went, Ranulf noticed a lane leading to a small Norman church. Two figures in black were walking along it. 'Look,' he called to Henri. 'There are at least two monks in the Godforsaken town.'

'Thank God for them,' replied his servant.

'With luck we will spend the night with the monks at the new Cathedral at New Sarum,' went on Ranulf. 'I expect they also are Benedictine, and wear black robes.'

'Don't all monks dress in black?' asked Henri, who, although very devout, knew little of the world outside his own village.

'Some wear white,' explained Ranulf. 'They work very hard, mainly rearing sheep. They are called Cistercians. I believe they have some houses in England, but mainly in the country. Not in New Sarum, I'm sure.'

The sun was beginning to shine, and it was pleasant riding through the countryside on the October morning. Their journey lay across scrub and moorland to pleasant farming country. 'Look!' cried Henri. 'A spire!'* The tower of the great church of Wymbourne Minster stood out, over the houses of the little town. 'Should we not go in?' asked Henri, who knew that knights often stopped, even on their way into battle, to say a prayer in a church or at a shrine.

'We must press on,' replied Ranulf, who was never unduly bound by convention. As they rode up the hill on the other side of the town, a hooded figure approached, tinkling a bell. Behind it stood a solid building of red sandstone, whose pointed arches suggested that it had been erected recently. Beyond this lay a settlement of tiny huts.

'Dear sirs, dear sirs, can you spare a penny?' called out a sad voice from under the hood. The fingers which held the bell were white and deformed. Ranulf drew rein. His good nature prevailed. 'Allez-vous en!' shouted Henri, who was aware of his duty to look after his master.

The man did not understand. He drew himself up tall. 'Our own good King Edward has given us the right of "Rogamus",' he said with dignity. 'Do you not know that this means "permission to beg"?' Neither Ranulf nor Henri could follow this.

'Give him a halfpenny,' commanded Ranulf. 'This will buy him a loaf, or even a chicken, but I don't suppose he could cook one. Do not touch him, but do not fling it at him. He is one of God's creatures, as we are.' Nevertheless, he shuddered as he used his spurs to get away. He was beginning to dislike England.

A mound of concentric circles appeared on the plain before them. 'That must be the place the innkeeper meant,' exclaimed Ranulf. 'We are on the right road.'

'Does anyone live there?' asked Henri.

'Not now, I think,' replied Ranulf. 'They may have done so in earlier days, though.'

Soon they struck the drovers' track across the downs. 'I hope we are not delayed by a flock of sheep,' remarked Ranulf. They were fortunate, and the going was good. By early afternoon they had the town of New Sarum in sight. The cathedral with its squat tower† and lovely pointed arches stood before

---

* In the middle ages church towers were known as 'spires'.

† The spire of Salisbury Cathedral was not built until the 14th century.

them. The masons had been working on it for nearly a century, and it was almost finished. They made their way along the straight streets of the new town towards it. As they went, a huge stone just missed the back hooves of Henri's mare, and yet another cry of 'For-in-ers' greeted them. Ranulf sighed. He did not want any further trouble.

They rested their horses on a wide green swathe, and looked around. Before them stood the new cathedral in all its splendour, greenish white in the late afternoon sun. Behind them lay some houses of considerable size, perhaps finished before the cathedral. 'Hold Fleur while I find the gateway into the monks' quarters,' commanded Ranulf, now a little puzzled. There was no evidence of monastic buildings of any kind. He walked towards the great west door, not pausing to take in the beauty of the pointed arch.

At that moment, a canon of the cathedral came out. Ranulf saluted, and he responded. 'Can you tell me the way in to the monastery?' asked Ranulf in rather faltering English.

'Êtes-vous francais?' responded the priest. 'Moi aussi.' Relief flooded Ranulf's face as he described their journey and needs for the night. 'There are no monks here,' explained the priest. 'It is unusual, and therefore a natural mistake for you to make.' He looked at Ranulf. His speech alone told the priest his lineage. 'Your servant and horses are over there? I do not think you would be happy in an alehouse. My fellow canons and I live in a house across the grass. We can offer you hospitality for a night, I am sure.' Thankfully Ranulf followed him, beckoning to Henri to follow with the horses. Henri caught up with them, not understanding what it was all about, but relieved that his master had found a solution.

CHAPTER III

New Sarum

The Canon, whose name turned out to be Father Samuel, led them round the new Cathedral to the north side, where some houses were built, with gardens leading down to the river. The materials in use were stones, which, Ranulf discovered later, had been brought down in carts from the abandoned town of Old Sarum.

Two or three houses were finished already, and into one of these Father Samuel led his guests.

'We live in much the same way as monks do,' he explained. 'That is, as a community. We have taken the same three vows of poverty, chastity and obedience, and we say the daily services in the Cathedral. But we are not under the authority of the Benedictines, or of any other monastic order.'

'So you do not do any manual work?' asked Ranulf.

'As to that, the reformed Benedictines don't, do they?' replied Samuel. 'Our work is to maintain the services in the new Cathedral, among other duties. Come now, I will show you and your servant where to sleep, and then we will go to supper. Your horses will be stabled over there.'

There were four canons seated at the long refectory table at supper. Ranulf sat between Father Samuel and Father Victor, who was the senior canon. He spoke excellent French. 'How do you like England?' he asked. 'I have lived here for three years without getting used to the climate. We do not have mists and fogs like this in Italy.'

'It is the manners of the natives which disturb me most,' confided Ranulf. 'Already, stones have been thrown at us without provocation. And what is that word for-in-ers, which everyone shouts as an insult?'

'Do not take that too seriously,' the Canon said. 'You may know that, not so long ago, this small island was divided into several kingdoms. Anyone visiting from a neighbouring kingdom was called a stranger, or foreigner.' He spelt it out. 'The custom has gone on. Indeed, the customs and tongue, certainly the pronunciation of words, vary so much from one part of England to another that it is difficult to understand a visitor. Fortunately, you are French. Since William I the great conqueror came, many French words have found their way into the language, especially among the nobility.'

'My mother has taught me English also,' replied Ranulf. 'As to the many divisions, we too have differences between the provinces of France. It is only since the reign of the great King Louis IX that we have felt ourselves to belong to one great country, and the English have been expelled.'

'Let us hope they will keep out,' exclaimed Canon Victor. 'To turn to more practical matters. We have a chapel in the crypt in this house. In this we are most fortunate. Such chapels are consecrated only with the Bishop's special permission. Tonight we shall say Compline there. Tomorrow morning, Mass will be said in the Cathedral. Will you join us? Boys of the song school have been singing the chants since the good Bishop Osmund founded their school near the first Cathedral at Old Sarum, in the time of the Conqueror.'

Supper was a simple meal of eggs, bread, cheese and fruit. Ranulf was most thankful that wine was served with it.

After Compline, on their way out of the crypt, Father Samuel beckoned Ranulf into the parlour. He took a map from a chest, and spread it on the table. 'Let us find your route for the morning,' he said. 'I suggest you go this way. Take this road out of Sarum. You will pass a very strange sight of enormous stones set upon the plain by the Druids many centuries ago. We do not know how they did it. From there, you will go straight across the plain to Malmesbury, where there is a monastery. There you may spend the night, unless you wish to go on to Gloucester. But I do not recommend such a long journey this time of year.

'Your next stop may be at Tewkesbury. I have been told that the Abbey there is beautiful. The Normans built it, as you will see by its great round pillars. You may need to spend the next night at Worcester, or you may reach Shrewsbury. You will then be near the borders of Wales. The Welsh are unruly, but, since the great King Edward subdued them, they should not raid the English lands or molest travellers. From Shrewsbury, you will be within easy reach of Lichwood. The Abbot will direct you, and you should reach your Grandfather's estate the following morning.'

184

Ranulf went over these directions again with the canon, and did his best to commit the route to memory. He had no writing materials with him, and, in any case, copying to him was a laborious art.

Henri, who had eaten and slept with the servants in the canons' house, was pleased to see his master walking over to the Cathedral to Mass next morning. He followed him in silence, as was customary. After the service, another canon, Father Martin, approached them, and spoke to Ranulf in French. 'Before you go,' he said, 'you must take a walk round our magnificent cathedral.'

All three walked down the Nave and turned to look back towards the Choir. 'It's like a forest.' whispered Henri, deeply impressed. On either side of them, lines of sandstone and marble rose towards the lofty vaulted ceiling, surmounted by a clerestory. Ranulf had only a rather dim memory of Nôtre Dame; the light and simplicity of Salisbury contrasted with the dimness and ornateness of the cathedral he had visited as a child in Paris.

'Look up,' whispered Canon Martin, pointing at a series of little heads carved high on the slender shafts of the clerestory. 'See their faces?'

'Who are they?' asked Ranulf. 'Surely they are very unusual?'

'Yes, indeed,' replied the Canon. 'I believe they were an idea of Canon Elias, who helped to superintend the building of this Cathedral. They are carved to honour the kings who encouraged its construction. That one may be Henry III, our King's father, and that may be the present King,' he pointed out, as he moved along. 'Some of the others are Bishops, some just ordinary people – like us. It is a pity I cannot show you the Chapter House in the other side of the cloisters, but the canons are meeting there now to consider the business of the day. Over the stone seats round the walls are stone engravings, telling stories from the Bible. But I must leave you, to join the others. Before you go, do look at this tomb of William Longspée. He was descended from a noble line of Norman knights, and was the first person to be buried in the Cathedral.'

Ranulf and Henri were both deeply impressed by the stone figure of a knight in full armour, which was beautifully gilded, and shone in the early morning light. The tunic was painted in bright blue, as was the shield, emblazoned with six rampant lions.

'What did he do to win such a reputation?' asked Ranulf.

'He was Lord of the neighbouring manor of Canford,' replied the Canon, 'and a strong supporter of the young King Henry III. It was he who laid one of the five foundation stones of this Cathedral, and his wife, the Lady Ela, laid another. Shortly after that he went to fight in Gascony, and a rumour came home that he had died there. It is thought that this rumour was started by a jealous noble, who wished to marry the Lady Ela himself. However, he came home triumphantly, but sadly died a few weeks after. I believe he was poisoned by the same person.'

'And what happened to Ela?' asked Ranulf. 'Did she marry him?'

'Certainly not,' came the firm reply. 'She founded the Abbey of Lacock, where she became the first Abbess and did much charitable work. But I must leave you.' Still he could not tear himself away. 'I should tell you about William Longspée's son,' he went on. 'He was a valiant knight like his father, after whom he was named. He took a small force of the English to Egypt, to fight under your own dear St Louis against the Saracens. He was badly muti- lated. First they cut off his right foot, and then his right arm. Although he was dying, and in great pain, he went on fighting, and, with his sword in his left hand, he killed many Saracens. At last, he collapsed and died.

'His lady mother received the news in a dream. She had a vision of a knight ascending into Heaven, and recognised her son's device on his shield. But it was not until a month later that a crusader came home with the news.'

At last he left them to take his place in the Chapter House. Ranulf and Henri went across the grass to collect their horses.

As they mounted, they found themselves surrounded by little people. The boys from the song school had just broken their fast, and were running all over the green. They rushed up to bid the travellers God speed, their faces rosy in the morning sunshine, their noses running in the cold air, their hose torn from play, their tunics splashed with grease and mud, and their brightly coloured hoods tossed askew. Above all this, good will prevailed, and they sang snatches of popular songs as they waved goodbye, making a colourful picture in front of the Cathedral. Both Ranulf and Henri felt greatly moved by their farewell.

On their way to the road towards the north, they found themselves riding down a street named Bakers' Row. The smell of freshly-baked bread was irresistible. Ranulf reined up to buy two small loaves which they ate, still in the saddle. He realised that they might not find another shop until they reached Malmesbury, and they had not yet broken their fast.

Thirst was now a problem. They both detested English ale. Ranulf decided to ask for water, but they received some unexpected kindness from an ale-house at the end of the row, where the landlord gave them milk.

'Are there no gates or walls?' asked Henri, as they left the town behind them.

'I don't think they have been built yet,' replied Ranulf. 'It's a lovely morning to be out riding,' he remarked, partly to cheer his servant and partly to restore his own spirits. He was beginning to feel a little fearful that they had so far to go in a strange country, and two or three nights' lodgings to find before they reached Lichwood. 'Wouldn't you rather be here than cleaning out the stables at home?'

'I'm not sure,' replied Henri cautiously.

Ranulf remembered he was a knight, and must not show his feelings. He touched the flanks of his mare lightly with his spurs, urging her into a gallop. 'Allons,' he cried, and away they sped.

CHAPTER IV

Mairie in Paris

Anne sat spinning by the fire in the farmhouse. She adjusted the spindle and guided the thread from the distaff onto it, before handing both over to Mairie. 'We will have some fine woollen cloth ready for the summer, so that we can both have new dresses,' she said. 'It may not be possible to buy a bale of cotton. We cannot rely upon pedlars coming this way.'

Mairie nodded. Although she disliked most forms of manual labour, she was prepared to learn to spin. After all, most ladies did it. Look at the Lady Ethelburga. Anne went on, 'It is not possible to save much money, because we do not sell very much from the farm. Much of what we need we get by exchanging things like honey with our neighbours. But I am putting back some coins to buy a loom, when we can find someone who can make one for us. Then you can learn to weave, and we can make our own clothes here.'

Mairie pouted. She didn't want to weave. 'Won't it take up rather a lot of room?' she asked. 'Oh, it can go in the bedroom,' replied her mother, stirring the pot over the fire. 'This stew smells good. We'll eat as soon as your father and Philippe come in.'

'I'm not hungry.' said Mairie.

The great wooden door to the farmhouse, left unbolted for the menfolk, burst open. A figure in black tripped over the step and stumbled into the candle-lit room. Both women retreated in terror, then 'Matthieu!' cried Anne, as the tonsured figure became visible. She ran and put her arms round him, and then stood back and studied his face. 'It's years since you came, but you are just the same!' She thought he looked older, and thinner, and there were specks of grey in his circle of dark hair, but the ready smile and the lively eyes were the same.

'Mon oncle!' cried Mairie.

She ran to put her arms round the handsome stranger, ready to kiss him. But he held her back gently. He hardly knew her: she had been a small child on his last visit. 'How are you, how are you? You must stay for days, as long as you can. Have you still a parish in Paris?' Words tumbled over each other.

'I am well, I can stay two nights, I have the same parish in Paris, and I must not leave my people too long,' replied the priest. His joy at seeing his sister again was all too obvious. 'How are your husband, Pierre, and your son, Philippe?'

'We are all well, thank God,' replied Anne. 'Sit and rest. No, first we will find some hot water for you to wash. Then you must tell us about our brother, Robert, and his wife, Jeanne, and their children. Are they all well? Is his business going well?'

They went on talking until Pierre and Philippe joined them, and they ate, and talked again.

'It is wonderful to see you again, Matthieu,' said Anne. 'And you say you walked, and spent the night at the Priory at Melun, as you did when you and Robert came to my wedding?'

'And I shall do the same on my return,' Matthieu replied, 'which brings me to my main reason for coming, as well as to see you. There is a gap in the house in the street of shoemakers since our father, Ralph le Boeuf, died. Both Robert and Jeanne miss him greatly. If Pierre could spare you, do you think you could come back with me, Anne, and stay with them for a few weeks? You have not seen Robert since your wedding, and you have never seen Ralph the Younger and his two sisters.'

She would have loved to go, but a glance at Pierre's face told her that he would miss her too much. She looked across at Mairie. The girl seemed so unhappy lately, that perhaps a visit would do her good. 'I can't leave, Matthieu,' she said decisively. 'Perhaps Mairie would like to go?'

Matthieu was taken aback, and none too pleased, but he replied kindly. 'Yes, certainly, she can come back with me, if she would like that.'

Mairie brightened. What fun it would be to go to Paris. Then she hesitated. 'Yes, please, I'd like to come,' she said. 'But I must be home again for Christmas.' This reply was unexpected, and pleased Anne very much. 'If you could wait until a few days after Christmas,' suggested Matthieu, 'I could bring you back. During the twelve days of feasting, there is less to do, and I could leave my parish after Holy Innocents' Day for a short while.'

* * * * * * * * *

Two days later, they set off. It was a frosty sunny morning in early November. Mairie was a strong girl and managed the walk to Melun easily by nightfall. Matthieu carried her bag of possessions, as well as his own, strapped across his shoulders.

At the Priory of Melun she had preferential treatment, and was given a cell in the guest house reserved for the nobility because she was the sister of a priest.

It was already getting dark, and she was tired, when they entered the gate into Paris the following day. She was aware of overhanging houses, made of lathe and plaster, with candles and lanterns shining from them, and a gutter containing rubbish running down the centre of the street. 'Beware,' warned Matthieu, taking her arm, 'that you do not slip, and also of water which is sometimes thrown from the upper windows of houses. But, seeing you with a priest, I do not think anyone will molest you.'

The stalls outside the shops were closing, and the shutters going up, but one baker still had goods in his windows. Guessing that Mairie was hungry, Matthieu bought her a little cake filled with honey. It tasted delicious. 'This is Paris,' said Matthieu.

As they approached the line of chestnut trees near the river, they could see by the light of the rising moon the outline of the two great towers of Nôtre Dame. The leaves were falling and making a damp, squelchy mass under their feet. 'We're nearly there,' said Matthieu. Then they arrived at the doorway of the little shop, with the sign of Ralph le Boeuf swinging outside. Jeanne, answering her brother's knock, was surprised to see a young woman with him. 'Where is Anne?' she asked. She soon took in the situation, and made Mairie feel at home. The living room, which also served as a shop, was even smaller than the farmhouse kitchen, Mairie noticed.

'You can share our double bed,' offered Jeanette, the elder daughter. 'It has a feather mattress and is beautifully warm.'

'I'll take your things up,' offered Claudette, the younger daughter. 'Come up and wash when you're ready.'

Robert, who had been arranging a shelf of boots and shoes, now came forward and took Mairie's hands. 'Welcome,' he said. 'This is my son, Ralph, my valued helper in my work.'

The excitement of being in Paris cured Mairie of any tiredness next day. Claudette took her to visit Claude, her mother's mother, who lived next door. She was now a widow, and lived with her son Paul and his wife. She was busy spinning when they went in. 'Come in, Jeanette,' she called out.

191

'I'm Claudette,' the girl responded.

'So you are. You've grown so tall that I don't know you from Jeanette,' her grandmother said. Mairie sat politely and listened to the old lady, while Paul went on with his work. She was longing to see the sights of Paris.

The next day Jeanette took her round the neighbouring streets. Mairie was fascinated by the stalls displaying little cakes and tarts, candied fruits, apples and little sweets. They went down a street where children's toys were made, including model houses, carts and dolls. Then there were bales of cloth, some of cotton brought back by pedlars from Egypt, and some of woollen homespun. 'We must collect the length of cloth from the weaver's for Mother.' explained Jeanette. 'She will make herself a dress from it.' It was a length of warm wool for winter, dyed a most wonderful green. Mairie looked at it with silent admiration, and then down at her well-worn homespun of brown under her dark cloak.

Jeanette led the way down a street of the glovers on the way home. They paused to look at the counter inside the open window. 'There are some beautiful gloves here,' said Jeanette. 'You must take a pair home to your father.'

'Oh, they are rather grand for the work he has to do.' sighed Mairie. Then she saw a strong pair of gauntlets in good leather. 'Surely they are made for hawking! It is a long time since I saw any like them,' she thought wistfully.

There was only a young apprentice boy in the shop. They did not linger longer, and Mairie was too excited to notice that Jeanette seemed rather quieter than usual, and disappointed.

One day Matthieu took Mairie to see Nôtre Dame. Outside the great west door, with its impressive pointed archway were grouped numbers of beggars. She involuntarily clutched her uncle's arm. Some had a patch over one eye, some had their heads or limbs bandaged, some were covered in sores as the result of scratching their dirty skins.

All were whimpering and holding out begging bowls. One shouted to Matthieu, seeing that he was a priest, and becoming angry at being passed over.

'Fold your hands and say nothing,' commanded Matthieu, 'and look straight ahead.' They entered the church. Mairie did not know enough about architecture to admire the building properly, but Matthieu told her what to admire, especially the great rose windows.

When they came out, he led her to the left bank of the Seine, and the College of the Sorbon. 'This is where I studied,' he told her proudly, 'after I had left the monks' school attached to Nôtre Dame.' He was interrupted by a group of young men, who were kicking a ball made from a pig's bladder in their direction. Other students were just leaving the lecture halls, going in search of food, still wearing their lengthy black scholars' gowns.

'Did you enjoy yourself?' asked Jeanne when Matthieu brought her home.

'Oh, yes thank you,' replied Mairie. After her uncle had gone, she admitted that she liked looking at the shops best.

Jeanne had noticed that she was very pretty, beautiful, in fact, but her clothes were worn to the point of shabbiness.

'You will be with us for Christmas. Would you like a new dress for a Christmas present?' she asked.

'You won't want to go back to the farm at Maisse, will you?' teased Claudette.

'Oh, yes I shall. I shall want them at home to see me in it,' responded Mairie rather quickly.

When the three girls lay in bed that night, they began to talk of Jeanette's forthcoming marriage. 'You are a very lucky girl,' her sister told her. 'You are only fourteen, and you are going to marry a man who is already a Master. What is more, he is very tall and handsome and kind.'

'What does he do?' asked Mairie.

'Jean-Charles is a glover, like his father,' replied Jeanette. 'He has a shop near here. And his grandfather was a Master shoemaker, like our grandfather. But he was older, and Jean-Charles' father also called Charles, married late.'

Mairie found all this talk of marriage somewhat disturbing.

'Have you got a man at home?' asked Claudette, who sensed her cousin's disquiet. Mairie gave her a tremendous kick on her shin. Claudette screamed.

'I'm sorry, I always jerk when I'm about to go to sleep,' said Mairie sweetly.

'Mairie is spiteful, yet you are giving her your own length of cloth for a dress!' exclaimed Claudette to her mother, the next day.

'Yes, she must have it, and also a new pair of boots,' agreed Jeanne. 'Your father wishes it, and so do I. She is our guest.'

'Is she staying here long?' asked Claudette.

'Only until Christmas,' replied her mother. 'Oncle Matthieu will walk home with her during the twelve days of feasting. Let's see again how many things you have collected for your home,' she went on, changing the subject as Jeanette came in, followed by Mairie.

Jeanette went to her little oak chest and began to take out her things with much pride and joy. There were some knives and spoons, a ladle and some mugs. 'What is that?' asked Mairie, now very interested as a new object appeared.

'It is a gridiron,' replied Jeanette, 'from my friend. And look, this is very precious!' She held up a silver salt cellar, shaped like a boat. 'My future mother-in-law, Katharine la Grande, gave it to me. To us, I mean.'

'What else do you think you need?' asked her mother.

'A set of lavers*,' cried Claudette, and they all laughed.

---

* A stand holding wash bowls and towels to be used before and after meals.

CHAPTER V

Ranulf's Arrival

Lord William of Lichwood walked out of the great doorway of his manor house into the courtyard. The sun was already breaking through the mist, and warming his old bones. At seventy he felt the cold, and although it was not yet November, he was wearing his surcote of sheepskin, with its wool lining. The bright blue of the sleeves of his tunic and his breeches contrasted with the surcote's sombre hues. He waved to his daughter-in-law to join him.

Lady Mary was just leaving the kitchen buildings across the courtyard, where she had been instructing the cook in a recipe for pudding. Although it was inconvenient in many ways to have to carry the food across the courtyard into the Great Hall in cold weather, this system had its advantages. Lady Mary was a noblewoman from Northumbria, of Norman descent. Her husband, Richard of Lichwood, had taken over the management of his father's estates, and since the death of her mother-in-law a few years ago, she had been her father-in-law's chief confidante.

'Come with me to see the stranger's horse, my lady,' called out Lord William, and led the way to the stables. The horse, a large grey, was standing on all his feet and appeared well. 'Yes, it has healed well,' commented Lord William, lifting a back hoof. 'That fool of a messenger should have waited longer before replacing that shoe. Moreover, he should have noticed that the old shoe was loose much sooner.'

'He was in a hurry to reach you with his letter,' replied Lady Mary.

'Nonsense!' was the reply. 'You read the letter to me, and all it tells us is that my grandson, Sir Ranulf, is to visit us as soon as he can get here. He could just as easily announce himself!'

'The messenger is also in a great hurry to return to France,' Mary remarked, 'and he wishes to keep out of sight as far as possible. I am sure he wants to get away before Ranulf and his servant arrive. Now, why does Lord Ranulf urge us to keep his son with us as long as possible? He must know that he is very welcome to stay as long as he can. And then there was a suggestion that he would enjoy younger company!' Lord William merely shrugged. Mary went on, after some thought, 'Do you think my brother-in-law wishes to keep him away from home for some time? Do you think he is in danger of making a mésalliance?'

'Nonsense!' said William again. 'The de Villaincourts have too much sense. No de Villaincourt would contemplate an unsuitable match.'

'Men do not understand these things,' thought Mary, but she remained silent. They walked together through the outer gate, onto the riders' track, into open pastureland.

'Look!' cried Lord William in great joy. Two riders were approaching at a steady trot. One was wearing a surcote bearing the de Villaincourt arms of three ravens, one in each of three quarters, with a white owl in the fourth. The other, clearly a servant, rode a little behind, and carried a pennon fluttering in the breeze, a sign that he was serving a knight.

Sir William recognised the owl as a symbol from his own coat-of-arms, bestowed upon his daughter, the Lady Ethelburga, on her marriage. His heart warmed. His grandson!

Sir Ranulf sat upright in the saddle. They had only ridden a short way that morning, their fourth in England, and he was feeling fresh and active. At their last overnight stop, at the abbey of Sandwell, his servant had supplied him with the family surcote, kept clean for this occasion. It had been made for his father on his marriage to the Lady Ethelburga.

In the distance he could see the fortified manor house of stone, with its outside stairway and small round-topped windows, and glimpsed the paved courtyard through the huge gateway in the outer wall. To his joy, two figures were approaching on foot, a bearded old man, still upright, and a tall lady in a homespun dress and white veil. His grandfather, and maybe his aunt. He sped towards them, then bridled his horse, and swung off, tossing the reins to Henri and making a low bow, almost all in one movement.

'Sire,' he said. 'Grandfather, Lord William of Lichwood,'

The old earl embraced him. 'Lady Mary, my son's lady.' he said. Ranulf bowed again, and kissed her hand. Lord William was delighted. A most handsome and well-appointed young man and, moreover, with beautiful manners!

Ranulf signalled to Henri to lead both horses, and they walked towards the house. 'First we will stable your horses. Then tell me news of my daughter,' commanded Lord William.

As they approached the stables, a servant appeared to take them. 'There is room beside the lame mare,' suggested the earl.

'My lord, the French messenger took his horse and departed, a few minutes ago,' replied the man.

'What, without saying goodbye? And isn't his horse still lame?' cried Lady Mary.

'I think the horse is well again,' remarked the servant, and fell silent.

'Which French messenger is this?' asked Ranulf, now curious.

'The man your father sent to announce your arrival,' replied his grandfather.

'I see now why you recognised us so easily,' said Ranulf. 'But I do apologise for his lack of courtesy in leaving so suddenly. I wonder why he did not wait to see me.' The matter was forgotten in the excitement of showing the Manor House to Sir Ranulf.

He liked at once the homeliness of the Great Hall. 'I have had a fireplace built in that wall,' said his grandfather proudly. 'When I inherited the house, the only fire was in the centre of the room here, on the stones, and the smoke went out through the roof up there. The holes are covered up now. It is much warmer in winter.' Ranulf looked up at the rafters, blackened by smoke, and then at the heavy long refectory table across the width of the room at one end, and at the screen at the other, and the gallery above it. 'We don't have minstrels now,' sighed Lord William. 'I miss them. But there are no young men capable of making music. I have only four men-at-arms who sleep in here, and are ready to follow me and my son into battle, and lead the labourers, if a call should come. This may happen if the King decides to go into Scotland, as some people expect.' And he glanced at his armour hanging on the wall. There were cobwebs over the heavy helmet, and the dusty suit of chain mail.

'Where is my uncle?' asked Ranulf.

'Richard is hunting with his dogs today,' was the reply. 'He will be back for dinner, tired, hungry and sleepy. There is not enough to occupy him; it is most unfortunate that I lost my other manor and lands in Northumbria, for my part in sending men to fight for Simon de Montfort against Henry III. That is all over now, of course, and our good King Edward has forgiven me, as he forgave others. But I have lost most of my lands.'

They went on again, up the sturdy stone stairs into the family bedrooms. There were only two, the outer one which Mary and Richard shared with their

197

two small sons, and the inner, where Lord William slept. There stood a large double bed with a clean white sheet folded neatly down, and comfortable pillows. A tester, surmounted by a canopy, gave it a dignified appearance. Ranulf was a little perturbed to find that he was expected to share it with his grandfather, but recovered quickly. He remembered that a knight must look cheerful under all circumstances. Gloom was a sign of bad manners. He washed and prepared for supper.

At supper, Sir Richard Lichwood appeared, hungry and impatient for food. 'Did you have a safe journey?' he asked Ranulf, after he had eaten most of the plateful of rabbit set before him.

'Quite safe, sir,' replied Ranulf. 'We did not meet any wolves.'

'I don't think there are many left in this part of the country,' said Sir Richard. 'I expect you noticed that the woods and thickets have been cut for many yards on either side of the roads. There is nowhere for robbers to hide.'

'That is a rule of our good King Edward,' explained Lord William, who was seated on the other side of Ranulf. 'He is a great admirer of your King Philip IV's grandfather, St Louis. From him, he has taken the motto ''Keep Troth''. You do not remember St Louis, of course.'

'My father has told me about him,' replied Ranulf, dipping his fingers into his bowl, as roast beef replaced stewed rabbit. He was glad to discover that his father had been right in his description of the habits of Lord Lichwood's household. As Lord Ranulf had explained to him, Lord Lichwood was partly French and partly English by descent, and his French ancestry accounted for his civilised manners.

The meal went on for a considerable time. Root vegetables and a hot pudding accompanied the beef. Then meat pies followed, and finally custards and candied plums. 'We cannot grow peaches here,' apologised Lady Mary, 'but I think you will find these English plums are very good.' Across the table, her two small sons, William and Richard, were almost asleep.

At last the family went into their private sitting room behind the Hall. There was no fire here. The two little boys revived in the colder air, and began to play with their toys. These were tops, which they wound up with cords and chased as they spun away, competing to see whose could keep going longer. Then William, the elder, went to a wooden chest, and took out a model of a farm wagon. Ranulf was astonished to see how beautifully it was made, complete with four wheels, and shields to keep the hay in place. A painted wooden horse stood in the shafts, and the whole did not measure more than two feet long.

'Look at mine, too,' called Richard, who was only four years old. He fetched a model sailing ship with a square sail, and little oars. 'That goes on the sea,' he said, 'Did you come in one like that?'

'One very like it,' replied Ranulf, and he told them about the sails, and the poop-deck, and his cabin, and the stable for horses below. 'Are you going to school one day?' he asked.

'No,' they replied in chorus, and with vigour.

'They will be pages in the household of a friend,' replied their father. 'Before they go, their mother will teach them enough. She went to school in a convent, you know. They don't need to read much. After all, they are going to be knights, and fight. You were a page, weren't you?'

'Yes,' said Ranulf, 'at the household of the Comte de Venables. He was a dear old man, and had a great sense of humour. There were three of us pages, and what he didn't teach us, we taught each other: that is where my sister's future husband, Lord Augustus of Thierry, was a page, before me of course. He is older. I hope you are coming to her wedding, my lord?' he said, turning to Lord William.

'I doubt whether I can attempt the journey,' replied the Earl. 'But is it not due to take place until Easter, is it? You must stay here as long as you can. In a few days we will ride over to visit my younger married daughter, Elfrieda, your aunt. Her husband Lord Harold of Uttoley's manor is only a few hours' ride away, and we will stay for a night or two. There is so much to show you. But now, the boys must go to bed and so, soon, must we.' And he called to a servant to bring in the torches.

CHAPTER VI

An Excursion

A few days later, they all set out for Lord Harold's manor: Lord William, Sir Richard and Lady Mary, Sir Ranulf de Villaincourt, and a retinue of grooms-men and servants. Like Lichwood, the manor house stood in its own courtyard and was fortified by an outer wall. But it was far larger, by a moat, and entered by means of a drawbridge. The Hall was larger and loftier, with an inner staircase to the solar, like Sir Ranulf's home. Along the walls hung stag's heads, their antlers making a pattern of shadows in the firelight during the evenings.

Dinner, which was ready soon after they arrived that afternoon, was a very grand affair. They were served by two pages on bended knee, and Lord Harold's squire. Lady Gwenned of Caernarvon sat next to Ranulf. Lord Harold had explained to him earlier that she was an orphan, and his ward until she married. Meanwhile, he was managing her vast estates. Ranulf, whose English was still a little limited, found her Welsh lilt very difficult to follow, and she would have been happier in her native tongue.

'Do you ever go home to Caernarvon?' he asked her.

'Why yes, look you,' she replied, fluttering her dark eyelashes over her little brown eyes. 'Harold takes me to look at my manor, where the bailiff has charge and to see my lands. But most of all, I like to see the progress the builders are making to the castle.'

'Is it very new?' asked Ranulf.

'Oh, no. The old Norman keep has been there a long time. The English King Edward keeps adding to it in the newest style, that is, to provide circular walls all round it. His son, the Prince of Wales, was born there nearly six years ago.'

'I've heard about it,' remarked Ranulf. 'Did you attend the ceremony when the King placed the baby in his shield and showed him to the people?'

Gwenned giggled. 'Good gracious. I was too young! My father went. He died soon after, you know, killed by the arrow of an English noble. It was an accident. Lord Harold has care of me now. You are hunting tomorrow. You must take care.'

'I have learnt to be skilled in the chase,' replied Ranulf, somewhat severely. She did not intrigue him. She had confided in him too soon, and she had no appeal. He turned to Lady Mary. 'Do you hunt, my lady?' he asked.

'I follow the hunt with my groomsman,' she replied quietly. 'It is a sport I do not care for, but my husband goes, so I follow, partly because I am concerned for his safety, and partly because it is my duty as the wife of an English nobleman to be interested in all that happens on our estates. You hunt frequently in France? Boars or stags?'

'Both, my lady. Like you, my lady mother follows the stag, but not the boar. That would be too dangerous, and is considered suitable for men only. You realise that we must dismount, and slay the boar on foot, and he is a very fierce animal, with an ability to charge at high speed.'

Lady Mary nodded. 'And jousting,' she said. 'Our King Edward has introduced that here. It is an impressive scene, with two knights in full armour, with their surcotes showing their coats of arms, thudding towards each other on their horses, bearing lances. But I do not care for it. Although it is supposed to be only a game, there have been many fatal accidents as a result of a blow being dealt in a vulnerable spot. Nevertheless, I have to accept it, and have sometimes been asked to give the prize, usually a silver goblet, to the winning knight at the end of the event. Does Lady Ethelburga preside over these tournaments?'

'My father will not have them in his territory,' Ranulf said gravely. 'The Pope disapproves, you know, because they result in unnecessary loss of life of noble knights.'

'I did not know of the Pope's views,' commented Lady Mary, as she paused to help herself to a portion of food from a dish offered by a page. Ranulf followed her example. It was a mixture of fried chicken and pork, bound together with egg, ginger and other spices, and smelt delicious.

'Have you been to King Edward's court to pay your respects?' asked Gwenned, who by now was feeling left out. 'Do you like him?'

'I have not met him yet,' replied Ranulf politely, 'but I have heard he is a true, honest and gentle knight.'

'Do not be so sure of that,' Gwenned replied. 'I have heard that he has a fierce and sudden temper. Have you not heard of the cleric who went to see him with some plea or other, and was so terrified by the King's wrath that he collapsed and died?'

'No, I have not,' said Ranulf.

After dinner, the servants and men-at-arms folded away the trestle tables where they had been seated, and everyone joined the dogs round the fire. 'A game!' cried Lord Harold. 'Come along, Rufus,' he called to his squire.

'What shall we play?'

Rufus, who was as jolly and amusing as his red hair suggested, grinned all over his face, and replied, with a naughty twinkle of his blue eyes. 'Hoodman Blind!'

Everyone clapped their hands and cried 'Yes, yes, Hoodman Blind.'

'Be careful, sire,' urged Henri to Ranulf, who had joined him after supper.

'I must join in everything as a guest should,' was the answer.

Lord Harold seized a serving man's hood and bound it round his squire's head, blinding him. 'Now, Rufus,' he cried. 'See what you can do.' And they all laughed at the joke. The men-at-arms seized Rufus and spun him round, and then sent him hurling off to find a captive. As he went, all the young men whacked him gleefully with their knotted hoods, but managed to avoid him. Only when he drew dangerously close to the fire did they intervene to save him, and then the yelps of the dogs warned him first. At length he seized Ranulf, which everyone had been expecting, and guessed his name from his height, and the length of his beard.

Henri was forced to watch his young master being made sport of. He felt humiliation for him, and wished for the hundredth time that they had not visited this barbarous island. Ranulf, blinded as he was, ran about courageously. Someone thrust a lady into his arms. Her build made it obvious who it was. 'Cedric,' cried Ranulf, naming a serving man. They all roared and cheered, and demanded more.

At last Lady Mary saw he had had enough, and intervened. 'It's Mary,' she said, hugging him. 'I will take your place.'

'Enough, enough,' responded her host and called for ale. They all collapsed onto benches of the floor round the fire, until someone started a song. 'Will you hunt in the morning, Sir Ranulf?' Lord Harold asked.

'They do insist on titles, these English,' thought Ranulf, and consented.

'Can I lend you a horse?' went on his host. 'Yours has had enough of travelling, I think. And a cross-bow?'

'Thank you, I will just follow with my servant,' Ranulf suggested.

In the morning, they assembled in the forecourt. As Ranulf mounted the horse the groom led to him, Sir Richard appeared, accompanied by Lord Harold's squire, who was carrying his long bow and quiver of arrows. 'You are not hunting, sire?' he asked. A little malicious grin spread over his heavy face. These Frenchmen could not do everything, even the graceful and handsome.

'I shall follow also, on my mare,' said a voice at his elbow, as old Lord William rode up to them.

The followers on foot, with their lymer hounds on leashes, were ready. The huntsman mounted and blew his horn, the stragglers, mounted or on foot, got ready, and the hunt moved off.

They covered some scrubland outside the bailey, and rode towards the forest. The men released the lymers, who sifted round the heather. Soon a pair of antlers appeared, and in full cry the pack moved on, seeking to intercept their prey before he reached the cover of the trees. There was no water handy to throw off the scent, and the dogs caught up with the stag just before he reached shelter. Sir Richard seized an arrow from Rufus, and raised his crossbow. 'Ping!' The arrow found its mark in the beast's neck, and another followed.

The hounds moved in, tearing at the neck and sides of the fallen beast, who, in his agony, tried to maul them with its antlers. Several of the dogs were bleeding. The huntsman signalled to Richard to shoot again to end the struggle, and called off the dogs, so that the stag's carcase could be brought home in triumph.

Ranulf turned to look for Lady Mary. She was resting her horse some distance away, accompanied by her groom. He rode up to her. 'I have to spare myself this sight,' she explained.

He nodded. He was younger, and undisturbed by it, but he understood. 'What a pity,' he was thinking, 'that all ladies as good and beautiful as this are married already.' He was forgetting that she belonged to another generation. He felt tired of England and longed for home.

'You must go riding often with Richard,' Lady Mary was saying.

'My lady, I know that my Lady mother is expecting me home in time for the Feast of Christmas,' he replied gently. 'I must find a ship before the worst of the winter weather sets in. But I hope my Grandfather will understand. I should be deeply sorry to disappoint him.'

Lady Mary smiled. She, too, understood.

CHAPTER VII

Christmas

It was the afternoon the tenth day of Christmas. It had not yet snowed, but a grey cloud prevailed, and a cold damp mist hung everywhere. 'If the wind gets up, it will snow,' remarked the young Sir Ranulf to his faithful servant, Henri. They were safely home from their excursion to England, and Ranulf was enjoying the comfort of his father's manor house, and his favourite sport, falconry. Chérie, perched on his wrist, was waiting for his command to go and kill. As they rode over the rough open land, his mare stumbled and almost lost her footing. Looking down, Ranulf saw that she was losing a shoe. The rough stony ground must have dislodged some clenches, and the shoe was hanging by just one nail. He dismounted at once and led her.

'We must make for the village, and Frédérique le Forge*' he decided. 'I'm sorry to make him work on a Christmas feast day, but I can't ride the mare back in this condition.'

'Will you take my mare, and I'll walk yours to the smithy?' offered Henri.

'No, I must speak to Frédérique myself,' said Sir Ranulf, and they walked on.

As usual, Frédérique had kept a small fire smouldering in the smithy, which he soon fanned into a larger one, and he had some strips of iron ready to shape to a horse's foot. 'Let's look at you, my beauty,' he said. 'Oh, you will do well enough. Your master noticed the trouble before you had gone far enough to hurt yourself.'

'While you're doing that,' said Ranulf, 'I'll take Henri's mare, and go to see the folk at the farm. I'll be back in good time, Henri.' He galloped off, his falcon still on his wrist, not noticing the wink which passed between the two men.

---

* 'the blacksmith'

Frédérique hammered the iron into shape, held up the horse's hoof and tried it for size. A sizzling sound and a pungent smell of burning hair and horn came out, as the hot iron met the insensitive part of the hoof. A few more blows, and it fitted. Frédérique plunged it into a tub of cold water. 'Who's the young master's fancy, then?' he asked with a broad grin. 'Don't pretend you don't know.'

'I love Sir Ranulf too well to notice what he does,' answered Henri wisely. 'There is only one young girl at the farm at Maisse, isn't there?'

'What does his mother say about it?' went on Frédérique.

'That I've never heard,' replied Henry cautiously. He knew quite well exactly what the Lady Ethelburga thought.

Meanwhile, a few snowflakes were falling as Ranulf galloped along. He tied up the horse in the farmyard, and, with Chérie still on his wrist, knocked hard at the door. Pierre, who was feeding the oxen and hens in the barn, heard the knock, and looked out. His heart sank. If there was much more of this, they might lose their farm.

Anne and Mairie were sitting in the firelight waiting for the Christmas singers to arrive. Mairie, who was wearing her new green dress in anticipation of their visit, jumped up to open the door. Delight showed in her face.

'Hullo!' Ranulf greeted her. 'My horse has thrown a shoe, so I'm going to sit by your fireside until it's ready to collect from Frédérique. How have you been getting on?'

Anne stood up and curtsied, before offering him the best chair. 'It is good to see you back from your travels, sire,' she said. 'I hope you enjoyed your visit to England?'

'England? England? What a place,' exclaimed Ranulf. 'Don't ever think of going there. Their fogs are unhealthy, their ale is undrinkable, their speech unintelligible, their houses draughty, and their romps insufferable.'

'What are romps?' asked Mairie.

'They are barbarous games by the fire,' Ranulf told her. 'They blindfold you, and therefore you are in danger of falling in, if you don't fall over the hounds first.' And he described the evening at Lord Harold's manor. 'But what was worse,' he went on, 'was the way we were treated when we landed at the port called Pole.' And he told them about the incident of 'Gardez loo'. By now they were all laughing merrily in the enjoyment of his company.

'I met something rather like that when Matthieu, my priest-uncle, took me on a visit to my cousins in Paris,' ventured Mairie.

'Paris? You have been to Paris?' Ranulf was intrigued. He gave her another look. Certainly the dress was beautiful. 'Let me light your candles for you,' he offered, forgetting that the poor did without them whenever they could for the sake of economy. 'Yes, I see you have been to Paris,' he commented, as he held a candle above her head.

At this point, Pierre entered with Philippe. 'We are both very hungry,' he called to Anne, pretending not to notice Ranulf.

'Good evening, sire,' said Philippe, more politely.

'My horse will be ready and Henri will be waiting. How late it is,' cried Ranulf, carrying the headed Chérie on his shoulder to the door. 'Good night, all.'

'Why, Sir Ranulf has dropped his brooch,' cried Mairie a little while after, as they moved towards the supper table. 'He will need it to fasten his cloak on a night like this. I must take it to him.'

'No, lass, you won't,' called Pierre. 'He can either do without it, or come back.'

'I can't let him do that. I'll catch up with him,' cried Mairie, as she flung her cloak over her dress and made for the door. It was now snowing fast. 'Come back, Mairie, do not be so foolish,' called her mother. But she was gone.

Mairie intercepted Ranulf and Henri where the grassy slope from the farm crossed the path from the smithy. It was now snowing hard, but she did not notice the cold as she ran towards them, holding out the brooch. Ranulf bent down from the saddle to see what she was holding. 'Why, yes,' he cried, putting out his hand for the silver circle surrounding a cross. 'It is mine. It is the crusading cross which King Louis gave to my father. It would have been a dreadful shame to have lost it.' He looked down at her lithe figure, with its beautiful green dress showing through the snow beneath the well-worn cloak. 'You are catching cold!' he exclaimed. With that, he passed Chérie onto his shoulder, and, reaching down, cried, 'Spring!' and caught her into the saddle in front of him.

Touching his horse lightly, he sped towards the Manor House, followed by Henri. Another servant appeared to take the reins and the falcon while he carried Mairie into the Great Hall. As he set her down before the fire, he noticed a figure at the window which looked into the Great Hall from the solar above. His mother!

A moment later, she had descended the stairs, and was with them. 'What has happened to have kept you out so long, Ranulf?' she asked. 'I will call for hot water for you: it is almost time for supper. And who is this?' she asked, as an afterthought.

'This lady has returned to me the brooch which I dropped,' replied Ranulf. 'She must not be out on such a cold night. I insist that she keeps warm and dry here. She must be our guest for supper.'

Lady Ethelburga looked very displeased. An awkward situation, indeed. 'Of course she must sup with us,' she said, 'and Henri will take her home, if home is in this village, afterwards.'

'It is a league away, my lady, as you must know,' returned Ranulf. 'She cannot undertake the journey on a night like this.'

'Then she must sleep with the serving maids, behind the screen,' decided Lady Ethelburga, privately resolving that she should sup at their table, too.

And that is what happened. In the morning, a chastened and dishevelled Mairie was getting ready to go home when Ranulf appeared in the kitchen. 'Come, I will take you myself,' he said. 'You must have suffered enough already. Perhaps it was not very wise of you to return my brooch in the way you did. I should have come back for it, you know.'

The snow had drifted overnight, and some paths were swept clean by the wind as they rode together on one stout horse over the rough ground. Ranulf and Mairie were both worrying in silence about the kind of reception Mairie would receive.

Pierre was feeding the hens in the barn. He came out to stand in the doorway, but said nothing as Ranulf set Mairie down gently on her feet. He, too, was worrying. Would he be turned out of the farm? 'Your daughter's home again, unharmed,' explained Ranulf. 'She has spent the night at the Manor, under my mother's protection.' Pierre nodded and bowed. He was beginning to feel a little proud. But Anne was not. When Mairie entered the farm house, some hard words awaited her.

Even harder ones awaited Ranulf. The Lady Ethelburga was sitting in the solar, where her daughter Eleanor was embroidering a tapestry ready for her own house after her marriage. Lord Ranulf stood by the window. 'Did you not realise that it was a serious thing to do, to bring a woman from the village in here as your guest?' he asked. 'What did her family say on her return?'

Young Sir Ranulf drew a deep breath. He knew his own mind. 'I wish to marry Mairie,' he said, adding, 'with your permission, my lord.'

Lord Ranulf was furiously angry. As he struggled with his speech, his wife interrupted. 'Have you any idea what you are saying?' she asked, also very angry. 'Can you seriously see that woman as mistress here one day? Look at her family. Her brother will marry Catherine le Court! Do you want her children to be the cousins of yours? Your position in life is very different. Have you forgotten your vows as a knight?'

'No, I have not,' exclaimed Ranulf, now equally angry. 'Because I wish to remain always honest and true, I wish to marry the lady I truly love, and not one provided for me as suitable!'

'Lady, which lady?' asked his father scornfully. 'Your wife will take her title from you! I shall never consent.' And furiously, he left the solar. Young Ranulf stood, defiant and stubborn, then he too left, to visit his falcons and find a horse.

Striding past Henri, he went up to Chérie, hooded on her perch. He found his glove, and placed her on it, stroking her back. 'Wonderful bird,' he said. 'We'll go out. It will be easy for you to spot voles and rats against this white background.'

'Take care, sire,' cautioned Henri. 'Will you take the heavier mare this time? She is firmer on slippery ground.'

'As you like. Just saddle her for me, and find yourself a mount quickly,' replied Ranulf. He was still hurt and angry from the scene in the solar. He strode into the courtyard, where Henri shortly followed him, leading two horses.

As they were about to mount, galloping hooves called their attention. A riderless horse dashed in, snorting and distressed, his saddle awry and stirrups jangling. Ranulf's heart turned to stone, and an indescribable pain seized him. 'My lord!' cried Henri in haste and alarm, not realising the prophetic nature of the title he was giving his young master.

'Quickly! Call all the men you can find to come with us and search!' called Ranulf.

A little later, they found Lord Ranulf. He had attempted to jump the stile which led onto the path through the woods, and his gelding had slipped at the take-off and thrown him. His head had struck a large boulder partly concealed in the snow, and death had come instantly.

CHAPTER VIII

The Aftermath

The wintry sun gleamed on the windowseat in Lady Ethelburga's solar, a few days after Lord Ranulf's funeral. Eleanor sat there, sewing her wedding gown. The pale pink silk contrasted with the mourning gowns worn by herself and her mother, as it flowed from her lap onto her mother's knees. The cloth had been spun from the finest silk thread of Lyons, and woven there, before being dyed with mulberry juice.

Eleanor, who was usually very quiet, found a few words to say to Lady Ethelburga. 'Mother, you are so very brave,' she said. 'I hope that when my turn comes I shall behave with equal courage.'

'I have your wedding to look forward to,' replied her mother. 'I am determined that nothing shall spoil that. It will be easier for us, because we are all going to Lord Augustus' castle at Thierry.'

'I shall have a great deal to learn in managing such a large household,' said Eleanor thoughtfully. 'But then, you have taught me much already. And it was fortunate that Ranulf rode with Father so often over this estate. He knows all the tenants, and understands husbandry so very well, doesn't he?'

'I wish he could manage his personal affairs rather better,' sighed Lady Ethelburga. 'Yes, he is good with the estate. But I think I must persuade him to engage another bailiff. Since old Mark the Controller died a few years ago, your father and brother have managed splendidly between them, but now Ranulf is on his own, he must find someone in whose charge he can leave the Manor when he is away. I will ask Lord Augustus if he can help us. It would also help me to have a Chaplain living here again, and then we could use our own chapel more often. I dislike the delay of having to send to the village whenever I wish to talk to Père Jean-Baptiste, and he does not exercise a firm enough influence over Ranulf.'

'You mean with regard to his marriage?' asked Eleanor.

'Indeed, yes,' was the reply. 'He refuses to give up the idea of marrying this peasant girl.'

As if in answer to this, there was a knock at the door of the solar, and Père Jean-Baptiste entered, wearing a heavy black cloak over his cassock. Lady Ethelburga looked with displeasure at the snow which had fallen from his boots, and was melting into black, muddy pools on her carpet. After a few polite remarks, the priest explained the reason for his visit. 'I have been talking to Lord Ranulf,' he began. 'As you are aware, my lady, it is important that he should marry soon. There must be an heir to these estates. He is very firm in his determination to marry Mairie, the daughter of Pierre le Laboureur.'

Lady Ethelburga regarded him with great annoyance. 'Think again, my lady,' the priest went on courageously. 'He is now the Lord of the Manor, and his wishes cannot be refused. Think of yourself and your influence here, which is good and great. You have done so much for all of us on this estate. The tenants are deeply grateful for all your practical help in having their homes kept in good repair. You will wish to continue this work. We all wish it to continue. You must remain the most important lady here, so that your work may continue. Suppose my Lord marries a noble woman who is lively and extravagant and not interested in the manor, and who will not be pleased if you continue your good works? Suppose on the other hand, that my Lord marries a person of no importance. Then your work and influence will remain unchanged.'

Lady Ethelburga had not thought of that. She smiled. The priest talked a little longer. 'Of course,' the lady sighed, 'we could not have a grand wedding, not so soon after the death of my dear Lord. We should have a quiet one, in the chapel here rather than in the parish church. There would not be room for all the villagers, naturally. Eleanor, you would miss the ceremony because you will soon be married, living far away. Just the nearest relations could come. Her gown would, of course, be very plain, and I think only one bridesmaid, don't you?' She began to make plans, and look happier. Père Jean-Baptiste smiled at Eleanor, and left.

A few weeks later, on one beautifully warm afternoon at the end of March, Gertrude set out from the Manor at Maisse towards the farm. She carried two parcels. The de Villaincourt family were all away attending Eleanor's wedding at Thierry. Before leaving, Lady Ethelburga had given Gertrude two bundles, wrapped in coarse cloth, to take to the farm of Pierre le Laboureur.

Gertrude was English, but, as she had joined her mistress soon after her marriage, her understanding of the French tongue was quite good. The winter shutters from the windows of the farm's kitchen living room had been taken down, and angry voices came from them. A young one, which she recognised as Mairie's, was shouting, 'No, no. I cannot wear it. It has a long splash of grease all down the front. Whatever did you do to get your wedding dress in this condition?' As Gertrude drew nearer, she saw that the girl was holding up a beautiful green dress, covered with tiny coloured beads attached by gold thread.

Gertrude knocked cautiously, and waited. Mairie tossed back her long fair hair, and advanced towards her. Gertrude curtsied and held out the larger bundle. 'It is for you, Madamoiselle, for your wedding dress. Lady Ethelburga wishes you to have a plain dress of pale colour. Can you make it, with your mother's help?' Mairie nodded. At least it was new. 'And this bundle,' went on Gertrude, 'contains six beeswax candles. They will give a much better light then tallow ones, so that you can sew in the evenings. You have only two months to complete your dress.' Then she noticed the spinning wheel. 'I see you have a spinning wheel. Can you spin? That is good. I shall be your own maid, and will help you dress, and teach you what you should do all day.'

'Well, I hope you won't teach me to weave,' said Mairie, rather crossly. 'I should hate that.'

'Lady Ethelburga does not weave. Most noble ladies do not, or, if they do, it is only in silk,' explained the maid. 'But all ladies spin. My lady told me that her old friend, Queen Margaret of France, was buried with a silver distaff in her coffin. The Queens of France always are. But I shall teach you much more. In the kitchens you must learn how to make conserves from fruit for the winter, and sweetmeats like marchpains, and pleasant perfumes from scented rose petals in boiled water, and medicines from herbs.'

'My daughter knows much about that already,' interrupted Anne. 'Mairie, you will show your maid how to make that delicious syllabub from strawberry juice.' Mairie curtsied to her mother to show Gertrude that she had some good manners, too, and Gertrude departed, realising that she had a self-willed pupil.

At the end of May, Père Matthieu arrived for the wedding, bringing Claudette with him to be Mairie's bridesmaid. 'Show me all the things you have collected for your home,' commanded Claudette, a few days before the ceremony.

'Mairie does not need any of the ordinary things for a house,' explained her mother. 'All she needs is in the Manor house already.'

215

'Oh, I shouldn't like that,' said Claudette. 'It is such fun collecting things.'

'Let's see your wedding dress,' suggested her uncle, noticing Mairie's crestfallen look. 'It is new, isn't it? And is this yours, Claudette?' he asked, pointing to one of white silk, which had been sent over from the Manor. The bridesmaid's dress was not new, and they had to work hard to make it fit Claudette in time for the service.

The chapel adjoining the Manor House was so small that the number of guests was limited. Père Jean-Baptiste stood there, waiting for Mairie with Lord Ranulf, and the little page who had come back with the de Villaincourts after Eleanor's wedding. He was the son of a friend of Lord Augustus, a Breton, with dark hair and eyes, and a round, study figure. He was still missing his parents after eight weeks with Ranulf, who hoped that the wedding would cheer him up.

Claudette came in, followed by Mairie and her family. The altar boy holding the book before Ranulf balanced it uncertainly, and the pile of golden coins he had placed there for the poor spilt over the stone floor. The little boy gave a merry wink at the page, and they both collapsed in giggles.

Mairie gave a burst of laughter, and then took hold of herself. Lady Ethelburga was very annoyed, and decided that Mairie had much to learn. She looked at her closely. The girl was certainly very beautiful, with long limbs. Her hair, arranged beneath her veil, was fair and lovely, and her blue-grey eyes matched her dress. It was said that she came of Viking descent. Ranulf was equally handsome, with his inheritance of mixed English and French blood. She listened while they made their vows, and the priest pronounced them man and wife.

Everyone moved through the narrow passage from the Chapel into the Great Hall, where the wedding feast was spread out. This was rather a sorry sight. Because they were in mourning, the Lady Ethelburga had decreed that it should not be too sumptuous. So the cook had restricted it to meat pies, custards and a few little sweetmeats. The villagers and servants assembled, and sat at the trestle tables, at right angles to the main refectory table, where the bride and groom and their families were placed. It did not take long to eat the 'feast'. Afterwards, they folded away the tables and began to dance to the music of a pipe. But, almost before the dancers had got used to the rhythm, Lady Ethelburga gave a sign to Ranulf, and he seized his bride in his arms and made towards the stairway into the solar. Although it was not yet dark, the serving men took the hint, and seized torches which they lit in the fire, and ran to form an escort for their Lord. All the rest began clapping and singing, as Ranulf, only pausing for the priest's blessing, mounted the stairs, and entered the solar. Below, the merriment continued.

* * * * * * * * * *

Next morning, Gertrude entered the solar after Ranulf had left to go hawking, and helped Mairie to dress. 'You must not take too long,' she cautioned, as Mairie combed her long hair, before turning it into braids. 'Lady Ethelburga does not approve of ladies who spend too much time over their appearance.'

'Bother Lady Ethelburga,' thought Mairie. Aloud, she said 'Neither does my mother.'

When she came down into the Great Hall, a servant brought a message that her mother-in-law had gone out already to take a potion of herbs to some sick villagers, and that she wished Mairie to explore the herb garden. Mairie did so joyfully.

It was a beautiful sunny morning, and she loved being out-of-doors. They went into the walled garden, where rosemary and lavender were beginning to blossom in the shelter of the wall. 'We covered them with branches from the fir trees during the frosty weather,' explained Gertrude. 'Just look at them now. I expect you are used to growing thyme. There are two kinds here. This one, which looks like a bush, is used for flavouring stews. But it grows too tall, unless the flowers are cut back as soon as they turn to seed. In a week or two will you bring out a pruning knife, and cut them back? The other is the sprawling variety, and will have a pretty mauve flower later. It is best to leave it to cover the stones.'

'That's rue, isn't it?' asked Mairie, pointing to a pretty green plant, just in bud. 'It will have yellow flowers, won't it?'

'Yes, it is,' replied Gertrude. 'Lady Ethelburga has taken the potion she made from it to bathe old Margaret's eyes. She is nearly blind. The other yellow plant is tansy, which we also use to flavour the stews. That plant which is showing shoots over there is dill. One of your tasks will be to cut the seed heads when they are ready, and hang them in the kitchen to dry. They are used for stews, too.'

'What is that?' asked Mairie, pointing to another clump with yellow buds.

'A long name: elecampane, I think,' said Gertrude, looking rather puzzled. 'I think my lady pulls out the root, and grinds it up. Yes, I'm sure that's what she took to old Jacques, last winter, when he could hardly breathe. She put it on his chest under a piece of woollen cloth, and it cured him.'

A bee buzzed straight at Mairie. She jumped to avoid it. Gertrude warned her. 'You must not be frightened. We have several hives here and you must watch Thomas when he comes to take the honey and make sure it all goes into the kitchen.'

'I think I'd rather cut thyme,' thought Mairie.

'Are you good at conserving fruit in candy?' asked Gertrude. 'It is made from honey, you know. You see the lovage, over there? You must cut the stems and conserve them in candy to place over puddings and custards for feasts in the winter.'

'I shall enjoy learning how to make it,' replied Mairie. 'I'm going to enjoy both being inside and outside the Manor.'

All the same, she hoped that she would sometimes be outsides with Ranulf. He had told her that he would have to leave her often, to ride over his estates and visit his tenants, and inspect the common land. If only she could ride.

She thought about this for several weeks, but before she could suggest it, she discovered that she was going to have a child. Lady Ethelburga was delighted, as were Ranulf and her own mother. She became so busy with the preparations that she forgot her desire to ride, at least for the time being.

CHAPTER IX

Knighthood

Ranulf William was born in the spring of 1292, and it was decided that he should be known as William, in order to avoid confusion with his father, as had happened so often in the de Villaincourt family. Lady Ethelburga discovered a very good nurse, and, when he became old enough, Mairie began to teach him his letters, and the rudiments of reading, as Père Jean-Baptiste had taught her.

'Don't spend too much time and trouble over those things,' her husband said one day, as William struggled over easy words. 'It is enough that he can write his name and read the manorial accounts. Reading and writing is mainly the work of servants, like the bailiff or the monks.' Mairie was enjoying the lessons as much as her son, but, as she always tried to please her husband, she obeyed his wishes, and did not press their son too strongly.

When it was not possible to be with Lord Ranulf, which was all too often, she took great comfort in attending the herb garden. She also found great satisfaction in superintending the cooks in the kitchen. She was a good cook herself, and soon learned how to provide for a large household. This won her the approval and respect of her mother-in-law and the servants. As she often said to herself, she had settled down very happily to married life, and to a higher position in society.

By the time he was seven, Ranulf William could ride well, and showed great interest in his father's falcons. It was arranged that he should become a page in the household of Lord Augustus de Thierry, and his wife Eleanor, Ranulf's sister. Ranulf rode to Thierry with him, spending two nights at court in Paris on the way.

Mairie wept bitter tears at losing him, to the scorn of her mother-in-law, who pointed out that this was the normal education for a member of the nobility. It

219

was all the sadder for her, as she could not ride over to see her son, as Lord Ranulf did twice a year. He reported good progress. William was settling down very happily with the other two little pages, who liked his sense of humour and mischievous ways. Lord Augustus was very tolerant of these, and told his father that William was becoming very skilled in the use of the sword and battle-axe, and was naturally good with falcons.

'He rides well,' he said, with a twinkle, 'when he remembers not to stand on the left side of his horse and put his right foot into the stirrup.' They all laughed at this, including William, who recognised the joke. By the time he was fourteen, he had become Lord Augustus' squire, and bore his banner depicting his coat-of-arms before him when he rode to court.

Mairie and Ranulf followed the strange tradition of the house of de Villaincourt. There were no more male heirs, and, in fact, no further children at all, after the birth of Ranulf William.

On a mild October day in the year 1310, Ranulf William rode before Lord Augustus along the road through the oak forests from Thierry to Paris. He bore his lord's coat-of-arms on his shield, depicting a rose, with shafts radiating from it. He wondered how long he would remain a squire. Some young men remained squires for ever, and never became knights. He was already eighteen years old.

'King Philip IV is called Philip the Fair, because he is considered so handsome,' explained Lord Augustus to him. 'You must show him that you can ride and handle a sword as well as his own squires. And do not forget to polish your horse's harness tonight. Good appearances are very important to the King.'

William was just going to say, 'Surely, sire,' when a group of three horsemen appeared on the horizon. They were galloping fast, their horses were badly equipped, one stirrup was hanging unoccupied, their clothes and hair were filthy, and, as they drew nearer, the sun glittered on their drawn knives.

William didn't hesitate. Passing over the shield to his lord, he drew his own short sword from his belt and advanced. Approaching the middle rider, he wielded the sword over his head, narrowly missing him. He then turned on one of the outer riders and lunged into his arm, drawing blood. Lord Augustus, meanwhile, had attacked the third, and all three turned and fled.

'Well done, well done, Squire William,' called Lord Augustus, as they drew together again. 'You did not hesitate to protect me, instead of considering your own safety. You shall have your reward.' William glowed with pride and happiness.

KNIGHTHOOD

That night at dinner in the Palace in Paris, the story was told to King Philip IV. 'You must knight him,' said the King.

* * * * * * * * * *

It took some weeks to announce the news, and to make arrangements for the ceremony of knighthood at Lord Augustus' manor. By early December all was ready. Lady Ethelburga, who was now too lame to ride, travelled in a covered wagon with her daughter-in-law, Mairie, and their maids. It was a difficult journey, with much jolting over the frozen ruts along the mud roads, and, although they paused to spend several nights at the King's court in Paris on the way, they arrived very bruised and shaken. Lord Ranulf came by horseback, with his faithful servant, Henri, who was now rather old for this kind of journey, and was cheered only by the reason for it.

Meanwhile, Lord Augustus had been helping William to make preparations. His armour was forged and fitted at the village smithy, where the smith also made his helmet, sword, belt, and spurs. The latter three pieces were sent to Paris to be gilded, and were only just returned in time.

Lord Augustus' chaplain talked with William often and at length, explaining that he must spend a night of vigil in the chapel before the ceremony. 'It is unfortunate that you are to be knighted in winter,' he said, 'when the nights are long and cold. But do not worry. You will survive. You will go into chapel alone, fasting, and remain there until first light. That is for about nine hours in all. I shall place a candle beside you marked off in nine sections, and you will pray during each of these to be given one of the Nine Virtues of Chivalry. At the end of each hour, you may rise from your knees, and walk about for a few moments. Your helmet, spurs, belt, sword and shield bearing the de Villaincourt coat-of-arms will be placed on the altar before you, to encourage you.

'Now, we will talk about the Nine Virtues in turn. You must memorise them, and then you will be able to contemplate each one. First, you must be merciful to all. Remember that, only if you forgive, can you be forgiven, and that in your position, you are much stronger than those about you. Secondly, do no harm to the poor. You will inherit great estates. Do not drive your tenants from their homes, and give succour to them if they cannot produce enough food for themselves, or if they fall ill. Show hospitality to strangers. Give them shelter, bed and board, as your father and grandfather have done before you. Protect the widows of your friends, and those on your estates, from being robbed, or ill-treated in any way. This rule, too, applies to girls who have not yet married.

221

Take care of them, and choose a lady for your wife who is not only beautiful, but will help you to carry out your duties, especially among the tenants on your estates.' And so he continued, until he had taught William all the virtues.

Lord Augustus also advised him, 'Do not worry if you feel alone in the chapel. You will not be alone. We shall be thinking of you. Your father, the chaplain and I will take a watch of three hours each, and pray for you until dawn.'

It was a frosty, clear evening in December when William entered the church to begin his vigil. He had gone through the ritual of the cleansing bath, and he knelt on the stone floor before the altar, scorning a cushion. Beside him was a stool, where he could rest if he felt very weary. As the pages left him, taking their torches with them, he gazed at the shaft of moonlight which penetrated the stained glass window, and fell on his accoutrements on the altar. He tried to forget that he had had no supper as he concentrated on the virtues of a knight, spending rather longer on his duties to widows and virgins than the others. He had began too reflect on his choice of a wife when he realised that this was not the time and place to do so. He went on to remember his duty to keep his word to both his enemies and his friends, and to promise never to slay a prisoner in cold blood. At times, sleep almost overcame him and he fell forward, and raised himself to rest his head on his stool for a time. After his ninth promise, he had hardly placed his head on the stool when the chaplain's hand shook his shoulder gently, and raised him up. He stood rather shakily for a moment, until a blue, silken cushion was placed before him and he fell again onto his knees. He became aware of further movement. People were coming in. The tapping of a stick on the flagstones told him that his grandmother was entering. The scent of rose water suggested that his mother and his aunt Eleanor were there. Rustling of skirts announced the arrival of their attendants. On the other side stood Lord Ranulf, and some men servants, and men-at-arms. Before him, beside the chaplain, stood a tall knight in bright clothes. Lord Augustus loved an excuse to look a fine figure. From his own belt, he drew his sword. He laid the flat side of it on the back of William's neck with such a mighty whack that it almost knocked him sideways. He barely managed to prevent a cry from leaving him. He felt weak and tired and defenceless. Lord Augustus' voice, with its mixture of humour and authority, announced, 'Arise, Sir Knight.'

Sir William rose to his feet. Two pages fetched his gilded belt, spurs and sword from the altar, and Lord Augustus buckled them on him. Then he embraced him, as did his father. William turned to his mother and grandmother for an embrace, and then, stiffly and with difficulty, walked to the porch, a page following with his shield and helmet. Outside, a groom had his horse. He mounted a little unsteadily. Someone handed him his gauntlets. One he threw down as a challenge, and rode round and round the courtyard. No one responded to his challenge to fight by picking up the glove. The sun rose above the bare trees in the bright sky, tinted with pink, his hair flowed free in the breeze, his limbs regained their vigour, and he realised that he was a knight, with all the honour, glamour and responsibility which knighthood brought him. He remembered a line of a prayer – or was it a wish? – given to him in childhood, perhaps by his nurse: 'Confirm the will of eager lives, to quit themselves like men!'

As he reined in his horse, the cheerful voice of Lord Augustus said, 'Well, Sir Ranulf William, thank goodness you remembered to place your left foot in the stirrup. I was worried for a moment as to which way you were going to face. Come, let us all break our fast, before we break our bones.' And everyone moved towards the Great Hall of the Manor House for the feast.

CHAPTER X

Epilogue

The sun shone brightly on those frosty December days of 1310, in Paris as well as at Thierry. Jeanne sat on an oak settle before the fire in the shop living room in the shoemaker's street. Her husband, Robert le Boeuf, and their son, Ralph, were busy sewing boots and shoes in the sunlight. Outside, the sign of Ralph le Boeuf, Robert's late father, swung in the gentle breeze. The sound of singing reached them from the street.

Robert opened the top part of the shop's door and looked out. A company of wandering minstrels were dancing down the street, in costume, while some of them played pipes and one a stringed instrument. Several wore hideous headpieces, made from dark brown cloth, with horns and large ears, and a forked tail hung down behind them. Others had animal heads. The most striking was that of a real boar, which had been hollowed out. Its owner could not see, and put his hand into that of his neighbour. They were thinking of Christmas already, and singing, 'Il est né, le divin enfant' to a melodious tune on the pipes, over and over again. They skipped to and fro across the street, leaping over the gutter in the centre.

'Go and join in the fun, Ralph,' called Robert to his son, as the rising cries from the street showed that their number was increasing.

As Ralph joined his neighbour's children, a voice from the far end of the street called out, 'A knight is coming, a knight is coming,' and the company divided into two to let the party on horseback, through.

Young Sir Ranulf William de Villaincourt rode down the street, avoiding the gutter. He wore his father's surcote, with the family coat-of-arms showing three ravens and a white owl, over his coat of chain mail. Beside him, his page carried his shield, while he himself carried his sword, drawn and held upright.

His father, Lord Ranulf, followed with an escort of four men-at-arms. They were going home to Maisse, to celebrate young William Ranulf's knighthood at the feast of Christmas. As they rode through the crowd, neither of them noticed the sign of the shoemaker Ralph le Boeuf, nor did they realise that they were passing the shop which had been the home of William's great-grandfather.

The minstrels cheered and waved to the noble party, but their songs and dance had been interrupted. Young Ralph le Boeuf felt rather cross at this. So did his father. He did not realise that the young knight who had just ridden past in such splendour was his great-nephew. 'These knights in armour always remind me of war,' grumbled Robert to his wife. 'It is all very well for knights to ride bravely in their armour. Fighting for them is an opportunity to show their valour and win fame. For ordinary folk like us, war means destruction, armies marching through the streets, pillaging and stealing, the wounding and killing of fine young men.'

'There is no war in France at present, my husband,' replied Jeanne. 'The English have not invaded us, and we hear that the fighting in Scotland has ceased. Do not be so gloomy.'

'But it will start again,' said Robert, 'and maybe the English will come to France again, as they did in the time of their soldier-King Richard, called the Lion Heart.'

'We cannot look too far into the future,' counselled Jeanne. 'And we could not change it, in any case. Come, sit by the fire with me. Let us enjoy what we have.'